Booty Call

Black Print Publishing
289 Livingston St
Brooklyn, NY

D1444842

Black Print Publishing
289 Livingston St
Brooklyn, NY 11217

ISBN 09722771-8-8

Printed in Canada

Acknowledgements

First of all, I got to give praises to the Lord, for giving me the talent, the strength, the patience and the mind to create and bring together these stories, blessing me with a gift that can take me somewhere further in life. I know he's always watching over his children. And I also got to thank him for blessing me with a strong, supportive family. First with my moms, a wonderful and supporting woman, who's always been there for me and everyone she cares for. And my father, the hustler that he is, being there for his children. And my brothers and sisters that keep a family strong and motivated. I also like to give love to my crew 148 and Rockaway, Gregg, Jamel, Sean, David, my brother Corey, DJ K.T., Ryan, Mel, Rome, Ebony, Gale, Ervin and the hood, South Side Queens. I also got to give love to my baby girl, Emari, the bad li'l angel that she is, and her mother, Lauren, for being the lovable, strong, motivated woman that she is. Carl Weber, for looking out for a brotha, by helping open doors for me and giving me that chance. And also, to those who picked up and purchased this book. I hope that you'll enjoy it. But love to everyone out there who's doing their thing and ain't trying to let nothing stop them from doing what they got to do, and reaching where they're trying to reach. Determination, once you got that, then there isn't a soul that can steer you wrong.

SHANA
1

Damn, I wish this mutha-fucka' would hurry the fuck up and be done wit' it already. I shoulda never let his sorry ass eat my pussy. He is whack! He done talked all that shit in the club about, how he got this, and he got that, and how he could do this. Shit, he really had me feeling him for a minute. But now I'm at the point where I need to get the fuck outta here and go home. Ain't nothing worse than a niggah that lies on his dick and tongue. I mean damn, I know not every mutha-fucka' can eat pussy but he ain't got but three inches of dick. His shit looked smaller than my six year old brothers. No wonder his boys was calling him Peewee Herman. He ain't no real playa. I'm starting to wonder if his ass is really in the music business. He couldn't even afford to fill his tank up at the gas station. Who the fuck puts ten dollars worth of gas in a Lincoln Navigator? I bet that shit ain't even his. It's probably rented or borrowed from one of his boys.

I could smack myself for falling for this stupid mutha-fucka'. I really shoulda known something was wrong when he couldn't even afford a hotel. He got me downstairs in his man's basement apartment—talking about he don't like hotels, they ain't his thing. Niggah, if you really were a baller, then you would put up for a hotel. When I asked him about his crib, he said it's under renovation. He probably still lives at home with his mama or some white girl with a dick that small.

And why the fuck does he keep looking up at me? What's he looking for my approval or something? Well he ain't getting it. Him and his goofy ass smile. I laid my head back down on the bed and decide to give him a few more minutes. After that, I'm out. I know he's gonna want to fuck, but it ain't happening, not tonight and definitely not with that thimble he's working with.

After a while he finally hit the right spot and I moaned a few times. That should have been the signal for him to keep going but for some reason he stopped. When I sat up to see what was going on his jeans were already off, and he had a condom in his hand. That's when I quickly got up and pulled my dress down. He gave me this baffled look, as I reached for my purse.

"What...we're not gonna do this?" He asked.

"No, we're not gonna do this."

"I'm saying though...I done went down on you."

"Oh...you want some ass 'cause you ate my pussy?"

"Yeah, I mean you got yours can't a brotha get his? I thought you was feeling me?"

"Please niggah, you whack! You didn't even eat my pussy right. So what makes you think I wanna fuck you?"

He balled up the condom and stared at me. I know what he was thinking. He was thinking he should slap me. But I wish he would try to come over here and hit me. My older cousins taught me karate. So if he decided to act stupid he was in for a big surprise. 'Cause I was gonna fuck his ass up, like I was Ike and he was Tina.

"This is fucked up," he cursed. "Get the fuck outta here, you stupid bitch, your pussy smells like shit anyway!"

"Yeah, well you must like eating shit cause it's all over your face." I smirked as I collected my things and left.

My name is Shana and I'm tired of these whack brothas who claim to be all that. People say I'm promiscuous, conceited and rude. I just like to keep it real and be straight up with people. If I think you're ugly, then I'm gonna tell you. If you're cute then I'm gonna tell you that too. I don't keep secrets. I'm honest with others and myself.

I know what I want, and that's a sexy, wealthy and well equipped brotha in my life.

I like to have fun. Shit, I'm only nineteen, so I'm gonna live like a nineteen year old, partying, meeting guys, having sex, dissin' ugly brothers, admiring the cute ones, roaming the streets and being cool. I've graduated high school and don't plan on going to college. Whatever I have, I get it from guys who willingly buy it for me. They offer, I accept. It's just that simple.

I live with my mother and Aunt, who are just as promiscuous and conceited as me—they say that's where I get it. My mother's only thirty-five and my Aunt is twenty-eight. They're still young women and doing their thing. When we hang out together, men think we're all the same age. When I tell them that one of them is my mom and the other one is my Aunt, they freak out. *"For real?"* They ask.

I don't have any sisters or brothers, but I have a shit load of cousins. My grandmother gave birth to seven children. My Aunt Tina is the youngest, she's the one that lives with us. The oldest is Uncle Tommy, who's forty-nine. He lives out in Seattle, Washington. I haven't seen him in years.

My mother always told me that I was born to be a model. I don't argue. I get compliments wherever I go. I got guys wanting to take me away on vacations, to places like Jamaica, Bermuda, Barbados, you name it. I turn them down because you know if they're paying to take you to some tropical island, they're going to want some pussy in return. And I'm not all for fucking a niggah just because he paid for my plane ticket so I can lie on a beach in the sun. Don't get me wrong, I do like to fuck, but I just don't give my pussy up to any niggah with fat pockets and a cute face. I can be a bitch, but I'm no *Hoe* or *Slut*—don't get it twisted!

When I arrive home I jumped in the shower pissed off. That niggah wasn't worth my precious time. My friends tell me that I'm very picky, but I have the right to be. I just don't go for anything. I feel that my body is my temple. You must be about something, be honest, funny, smart and most important—look good. They say, that it's what's inside that counts. Bullshit! I know I don't want to be waking up every morning and looking over at some butt ugly man for the rest of my life. Worrying about when I give birth, what my kids are going to look like. The first thing that attracts you to someone is their appearance, the way they look, dress and talk. Then you get to know there personality.

My mother, Denise, knocked on my door and entered my room to tell me that *Jakim* was on the phone. I look at the time and it's eight-o clock in the morning.

"What he want?" I asked.

"He wants to talk to you."

Jakim's my ex-boyfriend. We broke up about a month ago. After being together like we were Barbie and Ken for the past two years, he recently started to act like a jerk. I guess he thought he was a mack or something cause a few bitches wanted to give him some ass. What really made me mad was that he was paying more attention to them bitches than he was me. I'm sorry but I'm not the type to be playing second. So if I can't be first I won't be anything. Now he's calling, trying to seduce and romance me over the phone. A week after we broke up, four of his friends tried to talk to me. Out of the four, I'm only feeling one of them, Tyrone. He's definitely a cutie and he drives a BMW.

"Hello."

"Shana, did I wake you?" He was trying to sound all concerned.

"Yeah, what do you want?"

"I want to talk to you, baby."

"Jakim, it's eight in the morning. I ain't get in the house until five…"

"What? Where were you?" He shouted.

"That's none of your business, were not together. Remember, you wanted to fuck with them other bitches."

"But I'm saying though..."

"You're saying what, Jakim? Just do you and I'll do me. 'Look, I'm going back to sleep.' I hung up the phone.

A few seconds later the phone rang again. I shouted out the door, "I'm not here." I knew it was Jakim calling again. He doesn't like to be hung up on. Not that I cared. As far as I was concerned he could kiss my ass.

I didn't get out of bed until one that afternoon. Besides Jakim calling me so fuckin' early in the morning, I had a good sleep. Like the rest of the women in this house, I get money from men, so I don't stress employment. You'd be surprised how much cash brothers like Jakim, Tyrone and a few others will hand over when they think they gonna get some ass.

My mother is on section 8 and sometimes works different jobs here and there, but her boyfriend Danny supports her, just like every other man that has come and gone over the years. Men swim around my moms, wanting a piece of the action. My mom, like me, has gorgeous silky black hair that reaches down her back. She's red-boned and full figured. I look just like her in the face, only I'm taller, slimmer and I have light brown eyes. My Aunt Tina, she ain't nuthin' but a fuckin' gold-digger. I ain't hating, because she be doing her thing out there.

I walk into the living room and see Danny sitting on the living room couch. He's five years younger than my mom and got it going on. He has neatly cared for long dreads, muscular arms, and a strong looking chest something a female could definitely work with. He's tall, handsome, and has a nicely trimmed beard. He goes to the barber to get his shit shaped up like once a week. He's also got money! He drives around in a green Range Rover. Rumors around the way say that he's a big time drug dealer, but he owns his own barbershop and a nice little bar on Merrick. I'm not gonna lie, I envy my mother. She's got the kind of man that I dream of every night. I know he be doing her right in the bedroom too. Shit, I hear her through the walls. Danny makes my pussy wet every time I see him. And no I ain't fucked him. I keep my affection to myself. After all, he is my mother's man.

I walk past him as he sits there flipping through the TV. I have my robe covering me, with nothing on underneath. A part of me just wants to jump on his lap and fuck the shit outta him, but I just smile.

"Good morning."

"What up, Shana?" He smiles.

He watches me as I pass by to enter the kitchen. My mom is cooking up a late breakfast, scrambled eggs and sausages. I go into the fridge and pour a cup of orange juice.

"Late night, huh? Have a good time?" She asked

"Please, my night sucked." I leaned against the sink, as I sipped my orange juice.

She's in her robe too, I know she just finished getting her groove on with Danny.

"Aunt Tina left already?"

"No, that bitch got a date with Michael tonight." She informed me.

"Michael? What the hell she's doing going out with that faggot, what happen to T.J?"

"He got locked up last week."

"Oh! I know she's mad."

My mother nodded her agreement. "So, what's up with you and Jakim, y'all getting back together again?"

"Hell, no. He had his chance and fucked up. I'm over that mutha-fucka' now." Yeah, I curse in front of my mother.

"You know, y'all do look good together."

"We used to, but I've moved on. I just wish he would."

She fixed Danny's plate and placed it in front of him. Then she sat next to him and started to feed him as he watched TV. Damn, that dick must have been real good earlier.

I grab two pieces of sausages off the stove and head back to my room. I sit in my room and contemplate on where to go, or who to call? I'm not about to stay in the house. Soon after, the phone rings. My mother picks up and hollers that it's for me. I pick up and it's my girl, Sasha.

"What's up, bitch?" Sasha hollers through the phone.

"Nuthin'. What's up with you?"

"Yo, Shana, you know there's a party tonight over at that new club on Merrick?"

"Word? Who's popping there tonight?"

"Everybody, you ain't heard. There's going to be mad cuties rolling through. Are you rolling or what?"

"Yeah, I'm rolling. Come pick me up now though. I ain't got shit to do for the rest of the day."

"Aw'ight then, I'll be through there in a half, be ready bitch."

"I was born ready. Just hurry your ass over here...oh, and Danny's here." I let her know; she has a crush on him too.

"Word, what his fine ass up to?"

"You know, chilling with my mom."

"Damn, your mom is one lucky bitch."

"Ain't she though?"

I hung up and slowly walked over to my closet to find something to wear. I knew there was no reason to rush. Sasha wasn't gonna be here in no half-hour. Shit, I'll be lucky if she showed in an hour. So, I take my time getting ready. I jumped into the shower and fantasized about having Danny in there with me. About how big his dick was. And about what he could probably do with it. Shit, I got so carried away daydreaming about him that I slip my fingers into my pussy, and begin to play with myself. And once I got started there was no reason to stop. After my shower, and a good nut I walked into the room, leaving the door cracked, just in case Danny walked by. That idea is a bust 'cause he was in the bedroom with my mother. Probably about to fuck the shit outta her.

I throw on my tight fitted Guess jeans, my gray Guess sweater and a gray baseball cap. All I was going to do today was hang out with my girls, then tonight, go partying again.

It's going on three and this bitch Sasha still hasn't showed. She got me sitting around on the couch watching afternoon talk shows. My mother is still holed up in the bedroom with Danny, which is making me more impatient.

"Shit, I wish this bitch would hurry up." I think out loud. The doorbell rang, and I knew it was her. I rushed to the door and to my surprise it isn't Sasha, it's Jakim who decided to stop by unannounced.

"What's up, Shana?" He said, standing there smiling.

"What the fuck do you want, Jakim?"

"What, I can't stop by no more?"

"No, you can't be just stopping by. Why are you here?"

"C'mon, Shana, I just came to see how you was you know holding up."

"What the fuck you mean by that? Niggah, I'm doing fine. I know what you want, and it ain't happening. Go get your dick wet by one of your trifling hoes down the street."

"Shana, it ain't even like that..."

"Niggah, didn't I hang up on you just this morning. Didn't you get the fucking hint? Bye!" I hollered, trying to slam the door in his face. He blocked it with his foot.

"Shana, c'mon, I've been thinking about you all week. I missed you baby." He was pleading with his foot jammed in between the door.

"Move your foot, Jakim!"

He was still standing there, pleading. Damn, is my shit that good? He didn't budge and I yelled at him again.

"Move your foot, Jakim!"

I couldn't really get that mad with him. I still loved him. He's my heart. He just needed to know, that I come first in his life, and will always be first. He thought that we were going to break up, and he'd be able to fuck other bitches, then when he's done, come running back to me, begging for forgiveness. Well, it doesn't work that way. I got too much respect for myself. I'm not one of these stupid bitches in the streets that he can game and always get his way with. After being together for two years, he should have known better. He should known me and exactly how I get down. Unfortunately, he wasn't taking notes.

"Jakim, I ain't playing with you, please move your fucking foot!" I repeated for third time with a little attitude.

"What's going on out here?" My mother walked out her bedroom tying her robe together.

"Fucking Jakim won't leave." I explained.

"Jakim, I like you but you gonna have to respect my daughter's wishes and leave." My mother calmly said to him.

"But I just want to talk to her, Ms. Banks."

"I understand that but it's obvious that she doesn't want to talk to you. Now do yourself a favor and come by another day. Don't get her more upset than she already is."

Jakim backed off. He apologized to my mother for the noise and disturbances, then stares at me and leaves. I stand in the doorway and watch him drive off in his black Nissan Maxima. I close the door. I could still feel my mother standing there watching me, watching Jakim leave.

"You still love him," she said, "I can see it in your eyes."

"Yeah, right."

"It's Okay, Shana, we all go through the same problems with men. You just have to know how to deal with them." She then went into her bedroom to attend to her man.

My mother always saw right through me. She knew that I was still in love with Jakim, but he fucked up and needed to be taught a lesson.

As I was about to give up on that bitch Sasha showing up, the doorbell rings, again. I go answer it, and there she is standing at the door smiling.

"Bitch, you know what time it is?" I shout out.

"Yeah." She responded smartly.

"Fuck you!"

"Yeah, I love you too, c'mon lets go." She grabbed me by my sweater and pulled me out the door.

As we're driving, listening to music and checking out cuties, sasha shouts, "Yo, I saw Jakim turn off your block, what's the deal with dat shit? I thought y'all broke up?"

"Yeah, we did. But he's still sweating me."

"Word? I don't know why? I saw him with that bitch, Theresa the other day. He was all hugged up on her in the park like they was getting' married!"

"Well thank you for that useful bit of information." Shit, she could have kept that kind of news to herself. What the fuck? I thought we were supposed to chill today, not bring up my ex and some bitch he was with. Sasha's my girl and all, but sometimes she talks too fucking much.

We pulled up into Mickey D's. I haven't had anything to eat since those sausages I had for breakfast. Sasha wants to go through the drive thru, but I prefer to go inside. The drive thru always fucks up my order. So I persuade her to park and eat inside, since we weren't in a rush to go anywhere. As soon as we enter the restaurant, I had three niggahs clocking me. I just turn my head and ignore them, only one of them was cute, but his shoes were jacked up. Sasha pays them no attention, just stands on line with me and looks up at the menu. I turn around to see if they're still gawking, and yes all three are still looking. I sigh, and continue to stand on line. When we approach the counter, I can feel the bitches working there hating on me with stares and smirks. I place my order to the female cashier who has a bit of an acne problem.

"Yo, do they still got that game where you connect the dots?" Sasha yelled loud enough for everyone to hear.

"You're wrong bitch." I say, while laughing.

The cashier looks up at us in disgust, and continues to take our orders. She looks like she doesn't want to be there. Me personally, I could never take a job working at McDonald's, getting paid minimum wage—it isn't up to my standards.

"I don't wanna see any foreign skin floating in my Pepsi." Sasha continues to clown, as I continue to laugh. We were so wrong. The cashier never said anything back, just kept on being polite and filling our orders. A few of the people on line with us thought we were funny, while some looked on in disgust and shame.

We received our food and went to look for a table. As I walked, I heard someone saying, "Yo, shorti'!" I knew who was trying to call me out, but I wasn't answering. I just sat down at my table and looked the other way.

"Yo, Shana, look at them three sorry ass niggahs over there clocking us hard."

"Yeah, I already seen them."

As we ate we joked around and made fun of the three guys. They'd finished their meals, but still sat at their table, probably trying to cough up enough courage to come over and approach us.

"It's a damn shame how some men can be so soft when seeing pussy. A scared man can never get any." I said.

Sasha laughed choking the whole time on her drink. She gulfed down her last bit of fries and we were ready to leave. I got up and headed out the door, still ignoring the three. They followed us into the parking lot. One of them had enough courage to shout out, "Yo, shorti', come here, I wanna chat with you for a minute?" It wasn't the cute one either. He was some black, monkey looking mutha-fucka!

I didn't even turn around, I just kept walking to the car. He should've figured it out, but he kept coming toward us, thinking he was going to get some play. As I was about to step into the car, he grabbed a hold of the passenger door, preventing me from closing it.

"Excuse me!" I shouted.

"I'm saying though, a brotha can't get no love from y'all?"

Seeing him up close was even worse. His lips were dry and cracked. His skin was so black that it looked purple, his clothes were whack and dirty and his hair was nappy. In disgust, I looked up at him, and asked, "Niggah do I look interested?"

"Blacky, please don't touch my car." Sasha says to him.

He looked over at her for a sec, then focused his attention back to me. I didn't want him near me. Now he was trying to talk to me as his two friends stood by and watched.

"I'm saying though, you look too good, boo. I can't get your number and call you sometime?"

"Hell no, now please get away from me."

"Oh, it's like that, boo?"

"Yeah, it's like that, ugly...leave." Sasha interrupted.

I saw his two boys laughing and watching their friend get dissed. I guess he was trying to impress them or something. He tried to play it off and shout back at us. "Fuck y'all bitches!"

"You wish you could!" I shouted back.

He felt so stupid. We drove off, laughing. Me with him? Not in this lifetime.

Sasha looked over at me and said, "Next time, we're going though the drive thru." I couldn't argue.

The rest of the day, we went shopping on Jamaica Avenue. I picked up a few outfits, including something to wear for tonight. Sasha picked up a pair of these fly Donna Karan shoes, broke her pockets by $300. By then it was time to leave and get dressed for the party. Personally, the only reason I was really going was to get my mind off of Jakim. I wasn't stressing him like that, but I still had feelings for the man. Sasha dropped me off at my front door, and promised me that she'll pick me up around nine, nine-thirty.

I didn't rush to get dressed. I spoke to a few people on the phone, took a shower and did my nails. I'm home alone, so I walk around the house butt naked. It feels good to just let your body breathe once in a while. I admire myself in the mirror. "Damn, this bitch got the perfect body." I said, posing in front of the mirror. Noticing the time, I run into the room to get dressed. I already know what outfit to sport for tonight, my black leather mini skirt, slate blue stretch silk shirt, and my black open toe heels. I let my hair fall down past my shoulders, combing it out a few times. I put on just the right amount of make-up and sprayed on some Michael KORS fragrance.

It's twenty past nine when Sasha comes to pick me up. She has Latish and Naja in the car with her. Naja is already riding shotgun, so I climb into the backseat. We laugh and greet each other. I've only known Latish for two-years, and Naja and I go way back since the sixth grade. She's one of my closest friends. Latish and me had our little feuds, because she always tried to talk to Jakim, when she knew he was my man. She said that they just talked, it wasn't physical between them, but deep down, I knew she fucked him. Both of them just ain't telling. But I keeps it cool with her, no beef.

We arrive at the club and there's a line already formed outside. Sasha parks the car two blocks down. Everyone steps out and straightens their outfits, checking their make-up and hair. I know I look good, so I don't stress myself. We head for the front of the club.

"Fuck this!" Sasha blurts out.

"What's wrong, girl?" I asked.

"This fucking line, that what's wrong." She steps out of her place in line and heads for the front entrance. "I'll be right back."

Ten minutes later, Sasha makes her way back to us, smiling, "C'mon, Y'all, we're getting in."

We all look at each other, thinking what is this bitch talking about? We follow her, passing many standing on line, hating, smirking and bitching. Damn, I hope this bitch don't embarrass us and we get turned around by security and sent back to the end of the line. We get to the entrance, and to my surprise, we are easily escorted in. We pay the $10 admission and head to where the party is.

I look at Sasha, amazed, "What did you do? Who hooked you up?"

"I gave the main bouncer my phone number and promised to suck his dick before I leave tonight."

"You serious?"

"Hells yeah, we got in, didn't we."

I had no words for her, I would rather wait on line for two-hours. It was all good when we stepped into the party. The music, the crowd, the scenery was bumping. The DJ had the crowd hyped. I was feeling the music. I glanced around the place checking out the cuties, and who was up in here that we knew.

"I'll be back." Latish said. She went straight to the bar. It figured. She always got her drink on before she got her party on.

I'm still standing there, and this chubby niggah walks by me and is just staring me down from head to toe. I hope he doesn't come my way. The only thing he had going for him, was the piece around his neck. I knew it was real,

Cuban links, with the phat diamond cross. But he just stares, which was just fine with me.

After an hour, the place is so packed and tight; you have to dance with your arms close to your sides. Drinks are being spilled on people. A fight breaks out, because one guy bumped into another and they were both thrown out. I danced with this cutie with hazel eyes and a fade. He bought me two drinks and asked for my number, but I refused. I told him that I already had a man. He didn't care. He still continued to chill with me.

Latish is a little tipsy, as she holds her sixth drink in her hand, and is being accompanied by some fine chocolate looking brotha. Sasha is doing it up on the dance floor, grinding and hugging up on a few men as Naja stands with me at the bar. I needed a little break. Every passing second, I got some guy, grabbing me, touching me, either wanting to dance or talk. I told Naja that I was going to the bathroom, and she came along with me.

I'd barely got to the bathroom when I felt someone tugging on my arm. Fed up, I angrily turn around, to curse out who ever it was but to my surprised it was Tyrone, Jakim's main man.

"What up, Baby girl?"

"Oh, what's up, Tyrone."

He was chilling with three of his friends, all of them looking thugged out with hoodies, jewelry, Tims and attitudes. He smiled and gave me a hug. "Damn, you look good."

"You're not looking bad yourself." He was standing there in a blue and gray Georgetown sweatshirt, Sean John jeans, and some black Tims. His braids were freshly done and his diamond earring sparkled. Damn, he was too fine!

"So, can I get a dance with you?" He asked.

"Sure." I said, forgetting about the bathroom and my girl, Naja.

We strolled over to the dance floor. He grabbed me and grinded his pelvis against mine. His moves were so smooth and coordinated and he had so much rhythm and energy, it was hard for me to keep up with him. I noticed other ladies on the floor checking him out as he moved and grooved. I started feeling guilty because I was getting wet and aroused whenever he touched me.

Eventually, we stopped dancing and he asked if I wanted a drink. I said yes, and he escorted me over to the bar. We were talking and laughing when Sasha interrupted us. She said, "hi" to Tyrone then gave me this weird look.

She pulled me, a few feet away, and said, "You know you wrong, that's your ex's best friend."

"So!" I responded.

"What do you mean so...Jakim will kill you if he finds out you're playing touchy feely with his best friend.

"Did you forget Jakim and I are no longer to-gether? That I can do whatever the fuck I want! Damn, I'm just trying to get my itch scratched tonight. And Tyrone sure seems like the right one to scratch it."

"You are so wrong, Shana." Sasha said, finally leaving me to my business. She didn't understand. Shit the last time I had sex was two-weeks before Jakim and I broke up. That was a while ago. Tyrone would understand. It would be just a sex thing, no feelings involved. He gets what he wants, and I get what I want. I knew he would do me right tonight. Shit, I heard stories about him from my girls.

I went back over to the bar, and told Tyrone that I wanted to leave with him. He gave his boys dap and left with me under his arms. Sasha stared as I left with him. I didn't give a fuck what she thought. That bitch wasn't an angel, she did her dirt too.

Riding in his BMW, he had a slow jam mix tape playing and his hand deep between my thighs. He was fingering my pussy. His fingers felt so good. I spread my legs apart more, so he could get a better feel.

He smiled and said, "You're bugging, but I'm feeling you, boo."

We were heading to his crib for the night, not his mama's, but his shit, which he shared with a roommate. I've been there once, with Jakim its cool. They've got a phat entertainment center. We stopped at a light and begin to kiss, tonguing each other down. The light turned green and we drive off. I was horny as hell. My panties were so soaked, that I ended up pulling them off in the car.

Fifteen minutes later, we were at his crib. His roommate was still at the party and he wasn't coming home any time soon. So we began to do our thing—leaving my panties in his car. He pulled up my leather mini skirt, and had me lay down on the carpet. He spread my legs wide apart, sticking his tongue so far into me that he had me moaning with pleasure. It had to be about a good ten to twelve minutes before he lifted his head up for air and a rest. I was done with the oral action. It was time for us to move on to the next stage. I got naked. He did the same, standing there with a hard, eight and a half-risen dick, a chest like Tyson, and a washboard stomach. I pushed him down to the floor, mounted him, and started riding the hell out of him. It felt like he was reaching into my stomach. He palmed my ass with a tight grip, and thrust it into me harder and harder, absorbing my juices and filling my needs. Then he turned me over on my stomach, and rammed it in me from the back. I bit down on my tongue. It was so fast, hard and oh so good. I clawed the carpet. He spoke not one word to me as he fucked me vigorously. Position after position, the dick was feeling so good, that I had tears in my eyes. This mutha fucka' Tyrone had strength, stamina, and endurance. Thank God for him!

After we were done, I didn't feel any regret. My itch had definitely been scratched. I got up and dressed. I zipped up my skirt, as he buckled his jeans. We didn't leave right away. Tyrone had other treats in store for me. He went into his bedroom, and came out with a phat L. We smoked and talked as we continued to get high and fondle each other. I was definitely feeling this niggah groove.

A few hours later, Tyrone dropped me off at my front door. He kissed me goodnight, smiled and said, "Whenever you need that favor again, you know who to call."

I nodded my head, and headed inside. I turned around and watched him drive off the block. As I was watching him leave, I started to feel guilty. Damn, Jakim would trip right now, watching his man dropping me off and kissing me goodnight in front of my door. I started looking around to see if his car was parked anywhere on the block. Luckily for me, it wasn't. Not that it made a difference, we weren't together anymore, I tried to convince myself.

I went inside and saw my Aunt all over some man on the living room couch. His pants were down, and her blouse fully opened. She smiled, and asked if I had a good night. I smiled back, and told her definitely. She felt where I was coming from, and continued to do her thing.

The one thing about us females in this houses, we aren't shy when it comes to getting our groove on in front of each other. I remember one time, when I came home early from school and caught my moms' ass naked on the floor, with some red-bone niggah in between her knees. It didn't take a rocket scientist to know what was going on. She looked up at me, smiled, asked why was I home from school so early, then went right back to her business—not giving a fuck that I caught or interrupted them. Shit, there were a few times when my mother caught me and Jakim doing our thing. She would always ask if I was using protection, that's the only thing she was concerned about.

I got ready for bed with my mind on Tyrone. I didn't know what it was, maybe it was just good dick, and smoking a joint afterwards. I hoped I wasn't catching feelings. That would cause problems. No matter how hard I tried to rid my thoughts of him, he kept creeping back into my head. I threw the sheets over my head, and tried to get a good night's sleep—without Jakim, Danny, or Tyrone in my thoughts.

SPANKY
2

I sat watching her feast on lobster. Damn, taking a girl to Red Lobster on our first date is pretty much over doing it, but what was I supposed to do, she insisted. I didn't fuss or argue, I just went along trying to please her. I'm hoping that I was gonna get some at the end of the night. My date's name is Vanessa and she's beautiful. I've known her, or should I say I've had a crush on her since we were in the 10th grade. That was four years ago. She recently broke up with her man a few months ago, and is probably just using me, but I've always dreamed of getting between her legs. So here I am. Word on the street is, even when she had a niggah, brothers were running up in her like it was all right. I figure why not me? My boy, Tommy told me, he went out with her once, and fucked her on the first night. And I believe him too. One thing about Tommy he's a pain in the ass at times but he don't lie on his dick.

"Everything alright?" I politely ask.

"Yeah, everything's cool, Spanky."

"How's the lobster?"

"It's good," She replied.

I sit there, staring at her. I'm nervous, my heart's pounding. I don't want to fuck it up with her, so I try to be cool and say the right things. We just came from the movies, and being with her in that dark theater was hell. My hormones were speeding. I wanted to put my arm around her, but didn't have the nerve to do so. Shit, everywhere I looked around, niggahs were hugged up on their girls, some of them snug on each other so tight, they could share a seat. I was jealous. I wondered if I should make a move, too. I didn't and I regretted it.

After the meal, Vanessa orders desert. Damn, lobster, now desert, she's trying to break my pockets tonight. I'm scared to receive the bill. Our conversation is at a minimum--small talk here and there as we dine. That can't be good. Either we have nothing to talk about or she doesn't find me interesting enough to start a real conversation with. I can't fuck this up, I keep telling myself. I try to compliment her, by saying, "That's a nice outfit you have on."

"Thank you." She says back, not even giving me eye contact. At least smile bitch, I wanted to say to her. But that would have been rude, and I definitely would have ruined my chances on getting some ass tonight. During this whole night together, she probably said only eight complete sentences to me. I looked at my watch. It was twenty past ten. The night was still young.

"What do you want to do after this?" I asked her.

"Don't know...what is there to do?" She stupidly asked.

I knew what I wanted to do—fuck the shit out of her right now! Other than doing that, my mind was a complete blank. All I could think about was having some hot, sweaty and nasty sex with her. The waiter came with the bill and handed it straight to me. I was getting kind of frustrated. We've known each other since the 10th grade, and here she was acting like I was some damn stranger, refusing to speak to me. She was letting other niggahs fuck her, so why not let me? I thought to myself. I mean, I haven't had a piece of pussy in two-years, and that's when I lost my virginity. I'm 21, and only tasted one piece of pussy in my whole life. I wasn't ugly, no elephant man looking mutha-fucka', but for some reason, the ladies always see me as being a good friend. It was driving me crazy.

Now here I was, having dinner with this beautiful looking girl and everything was going wrong for me. There wasn't any physical contact between us the whole night, no touching, hugging, or kissing. We were just having dinner. What boiled my nerves even more was her eyeing other brothas in the restaurant and while we were out on our *"Supposed to be "* date.

"You ready to go?" I abruptly asked.

"Yeah, I guess." She said.

I tipped the waiter a dollar, which was all I could afford after the bill which came to a total of $48.45. I also paid for the movies which was a total of $17.00 and snacks that came to $9.00. Tonight, so far, I spent a grand total of nearly $75 on her. I thought, it better be some sex involved later on tonight.

What to do next still roamed through my head. It was a Friday night. There had to be something to do, a party happening, a place to chill and hang out. Vanessa wasn't helping with any suggestions.

"It's getting late." She said, looking at me, trying to see my reaction.

What the fuck did she mean by it was getting late? It wasn't even near eleven. I knew this bitch hangs out until six or seven in the morning, partying, drinking, and getting her freak on. Here it was a Friday night and she's talking about it's getting fucking late. Ooooooooh, I could pimp slap this bitch.

"So, what, you're ready to go home?" I asked.

"Yeah. I'm kind of getting tired."

Oh. I wanted to cry—this night was a bust. I reluctantly walked her to the car, and drove her back home. It was going on 11:10. The ride was silent. So silent you could hear the crickets chirping outside. I pulled up in front of her crib, and walked her to her front door, thinking maybe I can salvage the night by receiving a kiss and feeling her up a little. She walked three steps ahead of me the whole time. When I reached her door, she already had her keys out.

She turned, looked at me and said, "You know, you're a cool friend, Spanky." I needed this, thanks." Then went inside. I got not even a hug or kiss, just a lousy thanks.

My heart ached and my feelings were crushed. My night was a bust. I kept myself from ripping this bitch's front door down. All this money I spent on her tonight, and no kiss on the lips, no hug around the neck, there wasn't even a give me a call sometime.

I moped all the way back to my car, and took the long drive home. I really liked this girl. She only saw me as a cool friend. I made it home ten minutes before midnight. I saw my stepfather was home tonight. Usually he works late. The only time he comes home early is to get some from my mother. Shit, at least he was getting some play. As I enter the house, I can hear them in their room. It was disturbing to the mind, hearing my mother and stepfather getting their groove on, while I was horny as hell. I went into my room, cranked up my stereo, and put in one of my stepfather's porno movies. He has over three hundred different pornographic movies in the basement-some dating back to the seventies. He threw none of them away. He also had hundreds of dirty magazines to add to this collection, Playboy, Hustler, Black tail, Pictorial, you name it, and he had it. My mother didn't mind, she could be just as perverted sometimes. My stepfather, he's a cool guy, but is a bit of an undercover freak—if you know what I mean. At least he don't cheat on my moms.

My mom was cool though, always down to earth, and hip to things. She is in her early forties and a factory worker. She's been married to my stepfather, Leroy, for five years. Leroy is a security officer. Him and me are cool. My biological father lives in Canada. I don't see or hear from him much. He comes by whenever he feels like coming by. I haven't heard from him in two years.

My mother thinks I'm having sex on a regular basis, so she supplies me with condoms, telling me to always have safe sex.

I'm watching this porno, "**Big Black Ass 2**" and I'm thinking about Vanessa. I get the Johnson's baby oil, and get to work, whacking my meat off. This is a regular thing for me. After I'm done, I turn the tape off and go to bed.

The next morning, I'm waking up to the same thing I came home to-my mother and stepfather in the bedroom. Damn, don't they ever take a rest? I get up frustrated and go into the bathroom to wash-up. It's Saturday morning.

I don't work on weekends, that's cool. I work for a private company in Queens, filing paperwork, sweeping floors, getting coffee, answering phones. I'm like a receptionist/ janitor. But I get paid decent; working for eight hours, with a forty-five minute lunch break. My stepfather, who knew the manager, hooked me up with this job. After I graduated high school, I immediately started working. College was not an option. I just barely made it out of high school with a C average. I ain't ready for college yet, maybe in a few years. My mother doesn't stress it. She says if I'm not going to school, then I'm going to have to work, which I do.

It was Saturday morning. The one thing I do on every nice Saturday before the cold season comes around, is head out to the park to meet up and play ball with the fellas. I throw on my basketball shorts, a Knicks Jersey, my black Nike Air Force Ones and head out. I'm just six blocks from Baisley Pond Park. I meet up with Clarke-he's the clown, the loud mouth, and the jokester who's always got something to say.

"Spanky!" He shouts out.

"What's up, Clarke?" I greet. He 5'8", a little chubby, dark skinned, with a caesar hair cut. He's in a gray sweat suit. We give each other dap, and he snatches the ball from my hands and drives to the hoops.

"Niggah, your fat ass can't do no lay ups." I say to him.

"What? I be laying it up in your moms every night." He jokes.

"What, I just came from your mom's crib, she cooked me breakfast and shit." I weakly respond back.

"Niggah, come at me with some better shit than that." Clarke said.

We begin to get in a little one on one before the others arrive. He takes possession first, shooting it straight into the basket-nothing but net. I recheck him the ball, and he tries to drive, blowing by me, but misses the lay up, giving me the rebound. I take it back and shoot, nothing but net. We played for another ten minutes before the others started to arrive Limp, Peter, Mark, Tommy and Abney. They all come laughing and clowning around with each other. They see Clarke and I already on the court, and come rushing towards us. Limp snatches the ball, interrupting our little game. Peter comes and grabs on to the rim, swinging like a monkey. Abney grabs me in a headlock, and we begin to play fight.

"Yo, lets get this little game started." Mark shouts out.

There are seven of us, so one of us will have to sit this first one out. While the other six start a three on three. We choose teams. The first team is Mark, Abney and Clarke. The second team consists of Peter, Limp and I. Tommy sits the first game out. We get our game underway, Mark's team has possession of the ball. They score the first three points of the game; then we come back and score four points. I'm sticking Abney, and we go at it, pulling at each other's jerseys, and driving by each other to lay the ball up. The first team to score 16 points wins. The score is 10-8. Mark's team is in the lead. I come up and shoot two straight jumpers, making them both and, tying the game at 10. The other team scores three straight baskets, giving them the lead by three. After twenty-five minutes of play, we all take a quick water break, drinking from the fountain. We then resume play. We score three more points. The score is now tied at 13. After that, we score again, making it 14-13. But Mark becomes Air Jordan; hogging the ball, and scoring two consecutive baskets, having it become point game for them. Mark then tries to shoot the winning shot, but it's blocked by Limp, smacking his shit across the court. They still have possession of the ball, when Abney drives to the hoop, and lays up the winning basket.

"Damn, Spanky, you can't stick your man?" Limp shouts out.

"Yo, fuck you, your man Mark scored half the points, don't come to me wit' that bullshit." I say to him.

We all sit around on the bench to take a breather and drink some more water. I'm sweating and tired from that one game. "Yo, didn't you go out with Vanessa last night." Mark blurted out.

"Did you fuck her?" Clarke wanted to know..

Now here I was, getting put on the spot in front of everybody. What was I suppose to tell them? Do I tell them that last night was a bust. I ain't get no pussy. I smiled and looked around at everyone as they stared at me, waiting for an answer.

"Why y'all wanna know?" I say back.

"Ah, man, you ain't fuck her." Clarke declares.

"How you know?" I asked.

"Niggah, your dick ain't even scrape against the pussy." Clarke says back.

The crew started laughing. "Yo, that's the easiest bitch to get into around the way." Mark informs.

"How you know?" I asked.

"Because, I fucked her."

"Same here, Spanky." Tommy added.

"So, what y'all do last night?" Limp asked.

"Chill." I respond.

"Niggah, I know you didn't let a good piece of ass like that go wasted and untouched." Limp said.

"Nah...we went to the movies, then afterwards, we ate at Red Lobster..."

"Red Lobster!" Everyone shouted out.

"Spanky, I know you didn't take that bitch to eat at no Red Lobster..." Tommy said.

"I'm saying though..."

"Yo, put him on, Clarke." Tommy said.

Clarke looked at me and seriously said, "Spanky, you don't treat a five dollar hoe to no ten dollar meal. It's the way of the game. Shit, you might as well pay that bitch's way through college if your gonna treat her to dinner like that."

"And you didn't even fuck." Abney interrupted.

"Yo, I'm telling you Spanky, you missed out, her pussy is good as a mutha-fucka'. That bitch sucks dick, fucks in the ass and all. Vanessa is a true mutha-fucking freak." Tommy said.

I was envious that some of the guys got to hit it, and she only saw me as being a friend. They bragged and bragged, and talked enough dirty and nasty shit that she'd done to them, where it went on and how. They sat on that bench and discussed how big her titties were, how deep her pussy was and how she gave head.

After ten minutes of talking about bitches and pussy, we got another game started. I sat this one out. I was feeling kind of down. Mark's team won the second and the third game. They were on a roll today.

Afterwards everyone was tired, sweaty and hungry. We decided to go home and wash-up. I walked home with Clarke and Peter, who lived two blocks down from me. Clarke told me that tonight, the fellas had plans. There was this underground place that they were going to check out. It was on the down low. I agreed to tag along.

I walked into my home to see my mom's cooking breakfast and Leroy watching an Old Western movie on cable. I went upstairs to take a shower and come back down to eat. My stepfather was glued to the TV.

"So, how was your date last night?" My mother asked.

"It was cool." I lied to her.

"So is she a potential girlfriend, or what?"

"I don't know mom, it's too soon to tell."

"Well, she would be crazy not to call you. You're such a handsome young man."

Blushing and feeling embarrassed, I retreated to the bedroom with my plate. I closed the door, turned on the stereo, and popped in the porno *"Crazy Ass 4"*. I masturbated and fell asleep for the next three hours.

I lost my virginity when I was sixteen, and that was luck. The girl I lost my virginity to was a high school freshman who wanted to fit in with the crowd. She was invited to a cut party and she came along with some of her friends. There were about twenty-five people in attendance, including my homies and myself. The guy who was giving the party's parents were away for a week. Some of the guys had the idea to get a train started on one of the females, and Angela was the perfect target. She was young, cute, gullible, with a nice body, and a freshman. She seemed willing to do anything just to fit in with the crowd. Limp served her a few drinks. He then escorted her to one of the back rooms, where he began kissing and touching on her. He took his time with her, made sure it went straight. There were six of us waiting outside the door.

After Limp came out, he signaled for one of us to go in next. Tommy went in. I stood there, contemplating should I go along with the train too. I was a horny virgin, and felt that this was my one big break. Seeing Tommy coming out of that room, zipping up his pants and smiling, I decided that

I'd go next. I couldn't have my boys thinking that I was scared of pussy. After Tommy came out, I stepped in.

I entered the room, and see Angela lying on the bed, with her pants and panties on the floor. She looked at me as I came towards her. Her legs parted a little. She didn't seem nervous, just anxious, looking like she wanted me to hurry up and leave. I couldn't front, I was nervous as shit. I didn't know what I was doing, or where to put it. I heard stories in the locker rooms, but none of my boys knew that I was still a virgin. They thought I lost my virginity a while ago. She just layed there, waiting. I slowly took off my jeans, then climbed on top of her. She spread her legs, and waited for me to enter her. Damn no condoms! I thought. My mother always preached **safe sex** into my head. "Never lie down with a woman unless you have protection." She would say to me.

I looked around the room, searching for a condom lying anywhere, but I saw not one. Angela looked up at me and asked, "You gonna do this or what?"

"Yeah, give me a minute." I said.

She rested back on the bed, as I debated whether I should go raw. I mean Tommy and Limp probably did. I didn't see a used wrapper anywhere in the room. My manhood was talking, my hormones magnifying the situation even more. So I went against my mother's preaching and stuck it in her raw. My first time with a girl, and I was fucking bareback. My mother would have had a heart attack right about now. As I did my thing, she just laid there. It was quick for me. Real quick-almost a minute. As soon as I was in, I was out. I looked down at my dick, and was amazed by the powerful nutt I'd just busted. Angela just sat up, and asked if I was done. I was in shock. I'd just lost my virginity. I finally knew what it felt like to fuck some pussy. I pulled up my pants and left the room, Binzo went in after me. I was on a special high that whole night. Too bad I wasn't going to feel that high again for a few more years.

When I finally woke up, I went downstairs, to find my step-pop cutting the grass, and my mother sitting out back reading a book. Their lives seemed so simple, going to work, relaxing on the weekends, and having each other. My life felt like I was horny twenty-four seven. I wasn't getting any, and right now, I needed plenty. Watching porno's and constantly jerking off is how I was getting mine—shit, I've been watching x-rated movies since I was ten. Hell, if I wasn't getting any pussy, I can at least see it.

I left, and went over to Clarke's crib. We get to smoke weed, watch movies, and crack jokes on each other. His mother was cool; she was passive when it came to her son. He was her only child.

When I arrived, Peter, Tommy, and Limp were already there. They had a joint rolled up, and were in the basement watching old Rambo movies. I joined 0n the fun.

"Yo, your mom's got a sign on her pussy, saying "Warning, may cause drowsiness, and irritation, proceed with caution." Limp said to Clarke.

"What, niggah your moms ain't got no fingers, talking about she gonna point me in the right direction." Clarke responded back.

I was laughing so hard I almost fell out my seat. Limp came back with a good one, saying, "Niggah, your moms ain't got no legs, talking about she stepping up in the world." He did the handicap motion and all.

"This big lip niggah is trying to diss." Clarke said. "Yo, his lips are so big, white boys be hang gliding off his shit. Limp be making good money renting out his lips on the holidays."

Yo, I was in tears. The fellas continued to smoke and crack jokes on each other. I was so high that I thought every little thing was funny. I would just look at someone and start laughing. We all were bugging out.

Eventually the crew decided it was time to go home. Some said that they were going to get ready for tonight.

"Yo, we about to roll up to this club, where the action be happening." Limp mentioned.

I thought he meant madd bitches. Clarke turned to me and asked, "Yo, Spanky, would it be cool if some of us roll in your whip tonight?" referring to my old 84 two-door Toyota. It was a graduation gift from my mother and stepfather.

"Yeah. No problem, just tell me what time y'all heading out." I said.

On the way to my crib, I ran into Adina. She was the last person I wanted to see right now. Adina lived up the block from me, and was always trying to hang with the fellas and me. She wore these thick eyeglasses, with grandma frames. She always dressed like a boy, wearing baggy jeans, sweaters, and Timberlands. She sported no make-up or jewelry. Adina was brown skinned, with black hair and acted goofy most of the time. She wasn't ugly, she just didn't apply herself. The way she looked or dressed seemed to be the furthest thing from her mind. We attended Junior High together. Afterwards she went off to attend St. John's College, on a full scholarship to study law. She was smart, graduated with a 4.0 average and was just one student away from becoming our class valedictorian. Adina was a female version of Steve Urkel from the sitcom Family Matters. At leasts that's my opinion.

"How you doing, Spanky?" She hollered out and waved.

I wanted to ignore her, but she came running up to me, walking by my side.

I looked at her and asked, "What is it, Adina?"

"You're high, aren't you?" She asked.

"Yeah. And what does me being high got to do with you?"

"What do you guys get from smoking an illegal drug?"

"It feels good, Adina...keeps my mind off of stupid shit that bothers me while I'm captive on this planet. You know, you should try it one time. I guarantee it will boost that intelligence of yours even more."

"No. That's quite all right. I'm smart enough as is. I don't need to take drugs to make me feel smart."

"Well, it will definitely make you feel good." I said, while stopping in front of my crib. She had me discussing nonsense. She stood before me in this long gray overcoat and a ski hat. It wasn't that cold outside. Why was she here anyway? I thought to myself.

"Look, Adina. I'll see you later.... Peter's chilling over at Clarke's crib, go stop by, they'll love to see you." She had a crush on Peter. He's been dodging her since the eighth grade. I'm just glad that it wasn't me she had a crush on. I couldn't take having her follow me around, ruining what little reputation I had.

She left, strolling up the block towards Clarke's crib. Too bad I had to rat them out in order for her to leave me alone. But it was either them or me. I walked in the house with my eyes red and all. As I entered the house I heard the two of them upstairs going at it again. They were like fucking rabbits. By now, I'm surprised that I'm still the only child in this house. Either that birth control really works or Leroy is sterile. I couldn't blame Leroy for always wanting to be physical with my mother though-she's a beautiful woman. She still had her figure, acted young inside, dressed nice, and was sexy. She doesn't look to be in her forties.

After hearing those two in the bedroom, I went into my room and performed my regular routine. Turned on the stereo and popped in the porno "**Coochies Under Fire.**"

It was a quarter to ten when Clarke, Limp and Abney came knocking on my door. I wasn't fully dressed yet, so I let them into the crib, and went back upstairs to throw on some clothes for the night. I head back downstairs and ask, "Y'all ready?"

"No niggah, we came by to clean your crib." Clarke smartly answers back.

"Fuck you! C'mon, my cars in the yard."

We piled into my car, with Limp riding shotgun. I asked what happened to the rest of the fellas, and Clarke said that they had other plans for the night. So that just left us four. He gave me the address. The whole ride there was nothing but jokes in the car.

"Yo Spanky, when you gonna trade this piece of shit in and get you a nice ride, you know something, where everything works?" Limp said.

"You know! Shit, turn on the heat and the fucking air-conditioner comes on. Niggah rolls down the window and the fucking radio changes stations." Clarke added.

Abney is dying laughing.

"Fuck Y'all!" I shout out. "But y'all niggahs ain't got no problems riding in my shit."

"We gonna be like the Flintstones soon when this mutha-fuckin' floor collapses-be jogging in this mutha-fucka'." Limp stated.

"Yo I bet you he don't even need a key to start this shit." Clarke added, "Just kick the shit to cut it on and off!"

I had to admit that was funny. I couldn't argue, because it was a piece of shit. My mother bought it for me so I was able to travel back and forth to work with no hassle. But it was better than walking and using public transportation.

By ten thirty we arrived at the place. It was located near Mother Gaston Ave. in Brooklyn. I parked the car, put the club on my steering wheel, got out and pressed the alarm.

"Niggah, you put an alarm on this piece of shit?" Clarke asked. "Shit the alarm is probably the one thing worth stealing."

It may be a piece of shit, but it was my piece of shit, and I treated it like gold. It was a gift from my moms and was worth protecting and securing. We all walked over to the place, where there was one guy watching the door.

"Fellas, how y'all doing?" He asked in a loud voice.

We all nodded. He stared at each and every one of us as we stood in front of him. I was nervous. This didn't look like any ordinary club.

"Yo, It's ten to get in and you must see the bar." The man said.

When we entered, there was another man standing behind the door, who collected the fee. He patted us down, then told us to proceed down the stairs. One by one, we entered. The bar was to the right as I walked in.

"Yo, you must buy a drink." A chubby, black man said.

There were a few guys just standing around and a pool table dead center in the room. Two old couches lined the wall near the entrance and there was another door that everyone kept walking in and out of. They had a large screen TV in the room, playing the Porno movie. **"Sugarwalls"**. I should know. Leroy has it in his collection.

"What'cha having, Youngblood?" An old bearded man asked, with this one shinny gold tooth.

"Give me a Heineken." I said.

I noticed two ladies in the room; both of them had on jeans, sneakers, and thin jackets. The fellas and I received our drinks and just stood against the wall wondering is this it?

"Yo, what'cha doing?" The same chubby black man that told us we had to buy drinks asked. "Don't be standing out here, go inside where all the excitement's at." He pointed to the door, where I had seen people exiting and entering since I arrived.

We all slowly walked through the door, where you heard music bumping and a lot of people's voices. Once we enter the room, my eyes got wide, oh My God! I thought. I was in Heaven. I looked around and saw about twenty bitches, stripping, dancing, grinding and lap dancing. They had a stage set up, on which there were two females completely naked, spreading their legs apart and showing their pussies. Niggahs were touching all over them--sticking their fingers into their pussies and playing with their breasts. The ladies were grabbing back, too. Some of them were feeling up on dicks, chests and butts. It was one freak fest in that room. Limp, Abney, Clarke, and I didn't know where to start or what the fuck to do. We all were dumbfounded. One lady came up to Limp; she had nothing but high heels on.

"You want a lap dance, sugar?" She asked.

"Damn you got some big titties." Limp blurted out.

She laughed, then took his hand and placed it on her breast. He squeezed, rubbed and smiled.

"Follow me, sugar." She said, taking him by the arm, and leading him into a dark corner. She began to grind up on him, allowing for him to touch anywhere he wanted. I was getting jealous and so were the others. I wanted to touch and feel too.

Soon, Abney grabbed himself a girl; then Clarke and I did the same. We were all in our private little parts of the room, groping on the girls. I had this pretty, red-bone honey, with blond hair. Her titties weren't big, but her ass was. She pushed and grinded up on me so hard, that my dick had swelled to the max. It was ten dollars for a two-song lap or wall dance.

Spending about two hours in the room, I must have rubbed and fondled every girl in that room. I felt like I was ready to explode. Limp was at the bar buying some girl a drink. Clarke and Abney were by the stage tipping these butt naked bitches that were letting every niggah up in there finger and play with their pussies.

I was chilling with this chick named Honey. She had thin black braids with a few blond strands. She was slim with pretty eyes and naked. She hadn't bothered to get dressed. I bought her a drink from the bar and we began chitchatting. I'd spent $60 up in this place already. I had $80 left. It was going on one in the morning, but I still wasn't ready to go yet. I was horny and ready to fuck.

Honey hit me up with the bomb question, asking, "Do you want a VIP?"

"VIP, what's that?" I curiously asked.

"It's forty for a fuck, twenty for a blowjob." She informed.

My eyes bubbled up. Did she just say what I thought she said? I couldn't believe it. She wanted me to pay to have sex with her.

"You want me to pay?" I asked her.

"Yeah. My shit doesn't come for free. C'mon, I promise you'll have a good time. I do everything."

I had my doubts, I never paid for pussy before. I stared at her, and she stared back, waiting for my answer. She was looking fine, standing in front of me naked, drinking her beer. Around the way, niggahs who paid for pussy were considered bums. It was kind of embarrassing if one or all of your boys found out you paid for ass. That meant you were so shameless, lonely or homely, that you needed to pay for a bitch to get you off. I wanted to say yes so bad, it was killing me. My dick was taking control over the conversation.

She pushed up on me stronger, placing her hand on the bulge in my jeans. "C'mon, let me make the both of y'all happy tonight." She seductively said.

I smiled, getting very excited. She was very convincing. I turned my head to see where Limp was. It seemed he went back into the room with his female friend. Abney and Clarke were still inside. If I'm going to do this, here is my chance, I thought. My heart raced and my palms were sweating. I looked at her and said, "C'mon, lets do this."

She grabbed me by my arm and led me towards the back, past the entrance into this very narrow, dimly lit hallway. There were three brown doors on both sides of the corridor, and a black door at the end. There was this guy standing in between both doors. He wasn't big, stocky or intimidating. He was the exact opposite, no taller than 5'5, with a pot- belly and wearing a T-shirt that barely fit him.

"He's paying for the house special." She said to him.

"It's twenty dollars for the room." The little guy told me.

"I gotta pay for the room too?"

He nodded.

That was fifty I was paying. I looked over at Honey again, as she stood there stark naked in some pumps, and agreed to pay. I went into my pockets and gave him two tens. He opened the door to my right, and let us in.

"You got twenty minutes to do your thing,." He informed me as he closed the door.

It was a dull gray room, with an old wooden floor. There was a mattress placed in the corner near the back, and an old wooden chair. Besides the two pieces of furniture, the room was completely bare. Damn, I'm supposed to have sex in here, I thought. The mattress had some stains on it. The ceiling was peeling with asbestos and there were a few holes in the wall. I couldn't help but feel a little uncomfortable.

"That's forty." Honey reminded me.

She wanted her money up front, before anything else went on. I reached into my pocket and pulled out two twenties and passed it over to her. She examined it like it was fake or something; she laid the money down on the floor next to her.

"So how do you wanna do this?" She asked, staring at me.

"I don't know." I said shyly to her. I really didn't know how to start this. I was feeling uneasy as it was.

Honey takes a hold of my arms, and leads me toward the mattress. She lies down on the mattress, pulling me down on top of her. She then rolls me over on my back, and starts to unfasten my jeans. I feel her take me into her mouth, giving me my very first blowjob. I try to relax and act like I had done it before. She sucks me down to my balls, then rises back up. Shit, she had my eyes rolling to the back of my head. She continues for another three minutes, and then wants to move on to stage two.

"Damn. I forgot the condoms." She curses. "I'll be right back. Have them jeans off before I step back into this room."

She storms out the room for a quick minute, leaving me lying on the mattress with my jeans pulled down to my knees.

I got up and pulled my jeans completely off and sat back down on the mattress waiting for her return. My dick was completely erect, the most it ever been. I waited five minutes. I was wondering what was taking her so long or if she was going to come back. She came back with a pack of condoms. "Sorry. I had to discuss something very important with someone." She explained.

"I see you're ready." She said, staring at my dick.

She opened the pack of condoms, dropped the package on the floor and walked over to me. The closer she got, the more excited I became. It was definitely going to happen tonight. I paid for it and it was here.

"Lay down on your back." She instructed.

I willingly did so, as she strapped on the condom and climbed on, inserting my shit slowly into her. My lips tightened as she came softly down on it. She started to ride me, pressing her hands against my chest. Damn it was feeling good, too good, too fucking good, and then it was over—I came.

"Damn, that was quick, too quick." She said, climbing off of me.

I just lay there, embarrassed and ashamed of myself. I wasn't up in it no longer than fifteen maybe twenty seconds. I knew she wanted to laugh. Shit, if I were her, I would laugh too. I didn't want to leave out that door yet. It wasn't even a fucking minute. I'd paid fifty dollars just for fifteen seconds of pleasure.

I put on my jeans, and left the room. Damn, I hope she doesn't go telling her friends how quick and fast I was. I looked over and saw Limp and the rest of the fellas standing by the bar. They all looked at me. "You alright, damn niggah, where you been?" Limp asked.

I lied. "Getting a private lap dance."

"Word. It was cool?"

"Yeah. Y'all ready?"

"Yeah, soon, let me just get this bitch's number real quick, then we can bounce." Limp said.

I wasn't enjoying the environment any longer. That quick sexual escapade fucked up my mood for the rest of the night. Only fifteen seconds, I kept running it through my head. Even a minuteman had more stamina than me.

The drive home was ridiculous. It was more jokes from the crew about stupid shit. Limp bragged about the number he had gotten from some cutie. Abney talked about how shorti' massaged his dick in the club, giving him a hand job while he stood leaning against the wall. I kept quiet about my little experience. I asked Limp how he knew about the underground place, and he said, his cousin told him about it.

I dropped the fellas' home, parked the car, and walked into the house to once again, hear them going at it again. I went upstairs and as usual, turned on my stereo and popped in another porno to watch. This time it was, ***"Chocolate Covered Cherry Poppers."*** I got into the bed and cursed my dick for that too soon ejaculation. I then made a conscious decision to get over it because tomorrow would be another day.

SHANA
3

I lay naked on Tyrone's bed. He's getting dressed and is letting me stay the night in his apartment. It's two o'clock in the morning, and he just got a page from one of his homies. Now he's headed out the door to take care of some business. This is the sixth time we've been together physically. The dick is just too irresistible and too fucking good. For hours, we were going at it. Non-stop fucking until he received that page. Now it's business first, then sex. I'm growing feelings for him, and I know he's feeling the same. I start to think about Jakim and what we had. I still love Jakim, which is why being with Tyrone is hard for me.

I know Tyrone is feeling guilty too. He keeps telling me to tell Jakim about us. "Y'all not together, so tell him what the deal is between us." I refuse, thinking that maybe someday we will rekindle our relationship. I always thought that someday Jakim and I would get married and have kids. He could be the husband type.

Tyrone is a straight up street thug, a roughneck brother, who did a few years in prison for a gun charge, and assault. But there is something about him that just drives me crazy.

I watch Tyrone walk out the door. He leaves me a hundred dollars and says if I get hungry just order something. I throw on a robe, flip on the television, and relax for the rest of the night. I was kind of upset that Tyrone didn't finish his business with me, but I blew it off. I figured he was coming back soon to finish fucking me, but he didn't. I went to sleep, horny and frustrated.

I arrived home the next afternoon to see Jakim parked in front of my crib. It was a good thing I took the bus home.

"Shana, what up?" He hollered through the driver's window.

"Nothing. What up with you?"

"I'm saying though, I came through twice last night looking for you and you weren't home…. you fucking some other niggah?"

"That's none of your fucking business…I'm gonna fuck who I wanna fuck. This ain't your property. I don't see your name on it." I yelled out.

"Why you always gotta catch an attitude with me when I ask you a question?"

"Because, you be asking stupid questions."

He stared at me. I didn't want to argue with him today. I wondered if he waited out here for me all night. He's either really stupid or he's really in love with me.

"Let me take you out to get something to eat." He said.

"I already ate." I said back.

"So, lets go for a ride."

"I'm too tired."

"Damn, so what the fuck do you wanna do?" He sputtered out.

"Right now, get the fuck away from you." I rudely responded. I walked away from him, leaving him staring at my back, as I went into the house, slamming the door behind me. Seeing him right now was not an option for me. I peeped out the window and saw him still standing there, sulking—looking miserable. I remembered back in the day when we were together, if I would have played him like that, he would've cursed me out and tried to slap the shit out of me. Now, he was acting like a straight pussy. Damn, was his heart really that broken from our break up? He was the one that felt we should be separated for a while, because he wanted to fuck with bitches.

My moms came into the living room. "Jakim came by for you last night." She said.

"I know."

She saw me staring at him through the window and gave me a foul look.

My Aunt Tina came out in her robe. "Jakim came looking for you last night." .

"I know!" I yelled.

"Well, damn...you need to give the niggah some pussy, you can't be letting your man starve out there. He'll go eat somewhere else." She warned.

"He's not my man. He's my Ex, get it straight!"

"You get it straight bitch, you keep teasing his head like that...he'll bite you and go find comfort somewhere else." She warned.

What the fuck did she know? Aunt Tina couldn't hold down a man her damn self. My Aunt couldn't keep her legs closed long enough to be in my business. She got dumped three times this year.

I went into my room, stripped, and then took a long hot shower. Before nightfall, Tyrone gave me a call. He wanted to see me. Damn, I just came from his crib earlier. He apologized for skipping out on me earlier. He said he had to take care of some business.

I told him that I would see him tomorrow. I was tired and wasn't leaving the house any time soon. I needed some rest. He was pretty upset. He wanted to finish what we started. It was tempting but I told him no, and that was that.

Around ten, Sasha gave me a call. She informed me about a party tonight. She'd just found out about it and wanted me to come along, so she wouldn't have to roll alone with Cell and his friend. I told her no, I don't go out with mutha-fuckas' that I've never seen or met. Next thing you know, you're going out with a big, black, nasty, toothless mutha-fucka' who thinks he's all that, and want to stay trying to get up in your draws. She begged and pleaded, bragging that his friend was real cute. But if a bitch is that desperate, she'll say anything about the next guy just to have you tag along.

Cell is the bouncer that helped us get in the club a few weeks ago. Sasha went out to his jeep in the parking lot, and she sucked him off real good. She said for a big dude, his dick didn't match with the rest of his body. He was feeling her so much afterwards, that he passed her his home and cell number, and begged her to call. She also gave him her number and she actually gave him a call.

"Why?" I asked.

Her response was, "That niggah may got a small dick, but his tongue is wicked!" That was her. Personally, I like a man to come with the full package.

After hearing her beg, plead and say that she would owe me, I gave in. She said, she would be at my crib in an hour. She's lucky she's my girl.

I went to my closet to look for something to wear. A closet filled with clothes, and I couldn't decide what to wear tonight. I threw on my animal print mini skirt, black stockings, a black deep keyhole neck top with flare sleeves, and my black ankle strap pumps. As usual, I applied just the right make-up and perfume' cause you never know what kind of cutie you might meet at the club. I stared at myself in the mirror and was pleased with what I saw. I was looking too fine.

An hour later, I heard a horn blow outside. It had to be Sasha. She was fifteen minutes early. I walked to the door, opened it, and saw her standing outside a blue Pathfinder jeep. There were two silhouettes in the jeep.

"You ready?" She asked.

"I see you came early this time." I said, staring at her outfit. She had on a very tight, blue, strapless stretch ottoman dress, with blue pumps.

I pulled her into the house, and asked, "Where did you get that stink, tight, hoochie mama dress? Goddamn girl, you look like a fucking tramp."

"Yeah, but Cell thinks it's cool. Girl, he got money. He took me out to his crib in Long Island. That mutha-fucka' got a four bedroom house. With a swimming pool in the back."

"You fucked him already, didn't you?"

"Yeah, he got a little piece of it." She said.

"Damn…."I started.

Before I got to say anything else, she hit me with, "You can't say shit, Shana. I'm not the one fucking my ex's best friend. You wrong, bitch!"

"I'm wrong? I'm looking out for you tonight, don't forget that." I added. "I don't know why?"

"His friend was asking about you. He wanted to meet you and shit." She said.

"What? I don't even know his friend. Sasha, you run your mouth too fucking much." I loudly said to her.

"I ain't said shit about you to him. Cell was bragging his mouth off about you to him. Then he put me on the spot, asking me to hook his friend up with you."

"Is he cute?" I worriedly asked.

"He's cool." She said, sounding not so reassuring.

"I got a fucking pit bull waiting for me outside, right?"

"No! Go chat with him. Homeboy pushing a Lexus." She added.

I wanted to turn away from this so-called blind date Sasha had planned for me. I knew he was ugly, just by the tone of her voice. She didn't seem too excited about the guy. But I'm a female of my word, and I'd promised to come with her so I did.

We both walked out together towards the Jeep. I tried hard to peer into the jeep's window, trying to get a better glance at my doomed blind date. "Promise to be nice to him, Shana." Sasha pleaded. But that was a promise I knew I couldn't keep. If he didn't attract me, why be nice? Get it out fast, let him know the situation between him and I, "I'm not interested!" plain and simple.

As we came closer to the jeep, Cell stepped out from the driver's side and came up to us. He looked different from the other night. I didn't realize he was so ugly up close. His face looked fat and swollen, his lips protruded, especially his bottom lip. He had a weak fade, and his gear was off balance. He had on a tight yellow muscle shirt, some black slacks, and brown alligator shoes.

Muscle shirts are not sexy!

His arms were large, but so was his gut. I thought to myself, Sasha actually fucked him and gave him some head.

"How you doing?" He asked, his voice loud, raspy and retarded sounding. He stared at me, making me feel uncomfortable.

A few seconds later, his friend steps out from the back seat of the jeep. He was even worse. His eyes were big, like a fucking bug. He had an unattractive goatee, his lips were chapped, and his hair was braided into tiny twists which made his head look deformed and weird. He had this one shiny gold tooth in the right corner of his mouth. A thick gold rope chain hung from around his neck. They were so played out, like in the late eighties. He wore a bright orange collar shirt, with the collar flipped up, like he was Elvis, and cream khakis.

I wanted to throw up!

He introduced himself as, Jimmy. He stuck out his hand. I stood there and just stared into his face. I wasn't shaking his hand. I didn't want to touch him. I looked over at Sasha. I wanted to strangle her for hooking me up with some horrendous looking shit like him. I didn't want to be seen anywhere in public with any of them.

I pulled her over to the side, and whispered in her ear, "What the fuck is that?"

"Jimmy…"

"I'm not going out. Shit, I don't wanna even be seen with him in public. That niggah is so ugly I'm about to throw up." I warned.

"C'mon, Shana, just chill…you ain't gotta fuck him. Just keep him company. He's a nice guy."

Now she knew better. As much as we be hanging out together and dissin' ugly mutha-fuckas' like him, was her mind warped? Cell and his friend looked like something out of Swamp Thing.

She pleaded and begged, but I refused. Fuck a promise. He made me shiver every time I turned around and looked at him, he was so ugly. They both stood next to the jeep, talking, and waiting. Sasha went as far as giving me fifty dollars. Then she offered a hundred. I agreed to the hundred, and she slipped it to me on the low.

I took a deep breath, exhaled and went back over to the jeep.

"Y'all ready?" Cell asked.

"Yeah, we're cool." Sasha said.

Jimmy, Mr. Too Ugly, tried to be a gentleman and open the passenger door for me. I gave him a nasty smirk, walked around to the other door, and let myself in. Cell looked back at me, and then glanced over at Sasha. Jimmy entered the Jeep last and gave me a smile.

I sat up against the door.

Cell suggested that we go out to this nightclub in Brooklyn, called *The Jackpot*. It was becoming one of the more popular nightspots. He knew people inside that would let us in for free, no long lines, no waiting. I refused. The Jackpot was a well-known spot for everyone. I do mean everyone. My plea of no, was overruled with yes. I was out voted 3 to 1.

While in the jeep, Mr. Too Ugly tried to make conversation with me. He kept glancing over at me and smiling.

"You go to school?" He doofily asked.

I ignored him, staring out the window. Even his voice was ugly. Sasha looked back at me. I gave her a phony smile, and thought, Yeah bitch, you're gonna get yours.

"You got a man?" He asked.

I ignored him, asking Cell to turn up the radio a little. Mr. Too Ugly was still smiling and being friendly.

I continued to stare out of the passenger side window. I could feel his eyes trying to undress me. The shit gave me goose bumps just thinking about him seeing me naked.

"You're so beautiful." He said.

I gave him no response. He tried to place his hand on my knee. I turned, looked at him like he was crazy, and quickly smacked it off my leg. "Don't touch me." I said in a harsh tone.

Sasha and Cell were making conversation up front, while I was in the back seat trying to tame a wild animal.

"You don't speak?" He asked.

"Only if interested." I said back.

I already said three words too many to him. I sighed, and thought, why me? Jimmy A.K.A Mr. Too Ugly started making conversation with his boy up front. I guess he was starting to get the picture. I crossed my legs and tried to isolate myself from everyone in the jeep as much as I could. I thought, as soon as we get to the club, I'm ditching Sasha, Cell, and *the creature from the black lagoon*.

We pulled up to the front of the club. There were so many people outside it looked like the Grammy awards. I was embarrassed. I couldn't be seen with him, not in this fucking lifetime. Cell parked the car. Everyone got out accept for me. I just remained seated in the car.

"C'mon, Shana." Sasha said.

Cell and Jimmy just looked at me. I took one look at them and caught a serious attitude.

"What's up with your girl?" Cell asked.

"Shana, what's the matter, you coming or what?" Sasha asked

"What the fuck do you mean, what's the matter? You know what the deal is, bitch." I angrily replied.

Her face tightened, her eyes beaded towards me. Cell and Jimmy looked at each other, then glanced back my way.

"I think y'all two ladies need to sort this dispute out. Jimmy and I will be standing at the corner." Cell told us.

They walked slowly towards the corner, while Sasha focused her attention on me.

"Get the fuck out the car, bitch." She snapped.

"I know you not about to trip." I said to her.

"No, I'm not gonna trip. Why the fuck you gotta be embarrassing me like that. All I'm asking is for you to just keep him company. You act like I want you to give him the world. Bitch, you can keep your stank pussy to yourself."

I didn't say anything, I just stared at her, and slowly stepped out of the jeep. She looked at me, and walked away. I followed behind her. Cell and Jimmy were at the corner waiting for us. Sasha walked off with Cell, while Jimmy waited for me. He stood there smiling. He was getting on my damn nerves with all his smiling. I just wanted to smack that fucking disgusting grin off his face. He waited for me so that we could walk side by side into the club. I hurried by him and caught up with Cell and Sasha. We got in with no problems. I turned around and there was Mr. Too ugly already breathing down the back of my neck.

Inside was wall-to-wall jam-packed. The DJ was playing my song, "*It's a Groove Thang.*" by Zhane. This was my jam. I had started dancing and grooving; when I felt this figure pushing up behind me, dancing. I turned around and it was Mr. Too ugly. I quickly stopped dancing and walked away. He followed behind me, and asked, "Can I buy you a drink?"

"No!" I shouted.

I wanted to get the fuck away from him. I couldn't be seen with him up in here. There were too many cuties around. He tried to follow, but I evaded him by sneaking into the women's bathroom. I was getting frustrated. I couldn't get my party on with this ugly mutha-fucka' following me around all night. Shit, no matter how nasty or rude I was to him, he still didn't get the picture. Maybe he was slow or retarded?

I laid low in the women's bathroom for about five minutes. Then went back out into the party. I wasn't feeling it. I knew once that ugly mutha-fucka' saw me, he was going to start hounding me again. If he did, I decided I was going to curse him out so dirty and nasty and embarrass him so much in front of everyone in the club, that he would finally get the picture. He didn't know whom he was fucking with. But the club was so crowded you seldom ran into the same person twice.

I went to the bar to order myself a drink. Maybe I should've let him buy me a drink; at least he would have been good for something. It wouldn't have been worth it. He would have probably thought that I'd started liking him.

The DJ was definitely doing his thing. One nice jam after the other. He was playing Wu Tang Clan, *"Cream."* Them my niggahs right there. The cutest one to me, and also the illest is, my niggah Method Man. I felt somebody's hand grab my arm from behind. I thought it was him, so I was about to turn around and smack that fool, but it wasn't. It was some light skinned cutie with baby brown eyes and braids.

"How you're doing love?" He asked.

"Fine."

He was more flamboyant than rough. But he was still cute. Worth a conversation and a dance. We made our way to the dance floor, where he pulled me in front of him and started grinding up on me. I could feel his dick becoming hard. It poked me repeatedly in my butt. That was starting to get annoying. But I continued to dance with him. Then he started to get fresh and squatted down so he could put his hand up my skirt. That's when I had to put him in check. I grabbed his nutts tightly into my fist, squeezing the living shit out of them.

"Niggah, don't you ever disrespect my wonderful body like that ever again. You don't fucking know me to be trying to feel me up. I should rip your fucking balls off right now."

A few people took notice, and watched. Some laughed and pointed, some just stared. Homeboy's eyes started to water as I continued to squeeze his nutts. I finally let them go and he fell to his knees, clutching both his hands in between his legs. That sent the message to every male in the club, I'm nothing to "play" with.

I returned to the bar, and ordered a Long Island Ice Tea. A few men glanced over at me as I placed myself by the bar and sipped on my drink. I knew they wanted to approach me, but after that little incident on the dance floor, they were probably feeling hesitant. It was cool. I wasn't in the mood for any more negative male attention. After dealing with Mr. Too Ugly and Mr. Touchy Feely, they made my need for any male company disappear.

I continued to drink and chill at the bar. I saw Sasha with Cell on the dance floor. She was feeling all over him. She had no shame in her game. The bartender kept smiling at me as he served me my drink (three of them were on the house from him), but I wasn't interested. He was too beefy for me. I like em' slim and cut up. I like a nice long dick, smooth skin, good hair and a nice butt. He also has to have a good job—or at least holding down some kind of an account and have some integrity. The man has got to respect himself and he definitely has to respect me. He must know that I'm just not a sex toy to stick his dick in. If a good man treats me with respect and dignity, then I'll treat him like he's my world. I'll do anything in my power to satisfy him and take care of him, as long as he is willing to do the same for me. My pussy would always be open and willing to accept him with its softness and pleasurable sensation.

I looked at the time. I was getting restless and bored, even though I was receiving free drinks. The club was over crowded, and the cuties were becoming less interesting to me. I was feeling a little tipsy and not in the mood for stupidity. The DJ threw on *"Don't Stop, Shake That Bootie."* by Luke, and the whole club went crazy. Everyone started to grind and rub on each other. They were sweating, bumping and skirts were being hiked up. I couldn't front. Every time I hear this jam, I wanted to get my grind and feel up on a niggah too, especially a really cute one.

One niggah just grabs me by my arms and ask me to follow him into the crowd. I told him no you just don't be pulling on me like I'm some rope. I gave him a nasty glare. He got the hint. Then I felt some other niggah just squeeze up behind me, pushing his pelvis into me, his dick was already hard. I turned around, and it was Mr. Too Ugly. Oh my god! No he didn't, I thought to myself. I got so mad, that I just shoved him off me, pushing him into another girl, and having her fall into some guy. He looked embarrassed. I didn't give a fuck how he felt about me. You just don't be pushing your nasty self up against me like that. God, he was so fucking ugly and nasty.

Bitches started staring at me. I stared back. I'll scratch every last one of these bitches' eyes out up in this club. I made my way back to the ladies bathroom. Sasha came in behind me, pulling down her stink hoochie dress.

"What's the matter, Shana?" She asked me, like she didn't know.

"Nothing!" I told her while fixing my hair. I had no words to say to her for the rest of the night.

Other bitches started to walk into the bathroom, whispering among each other and staring hard at me. I knew they were talking about me. I looked back at them, and shouted, "If y'all bitches got anything to say about me, come say it to my fucking face. I'll bring it to any one of y'all fake bitches up in here!"

They all stared, but none of them had the courage to say anything. I just threw up the middle finger at them and went on with my business. Sasha just gave me a smirk and walked back out to attend to her dilly ass man. If she wanted to act up, she could get it too.

After straightening myself up in the bathroom, I went back to the club scene. My temper and attitude was on high volume. I looked nasty and hard at every niggah and bitch that passed by me. It was definitely time to leave. But Cell was my only ride. And I wasn't trying to hitch hike with some perverted, no pussy getting niggah, who thinks just because I'm riding in his car, it gives him the opportunity to put his hands all over me.

At 2am I decided that it was time to go. I approached Sasha while she was hugging and dancing up on Cell.

"I'm ready to go." I told her.

"Don't be pulling on me." She said.

We were getting on each other's nerves tonight. I could see it in her face that she wanted to fuck me up for being such a bitch. But she knew better.

"I'll see if Cell's ready, Bitch!"

I just stood there, fuck her too. Mr. Too ugly came around. He couldn't even look at me he felt so embarrassed. I laughed and walked away from them. I went back to the bar, where the bartender slipped me another free drink for the night, but this time he also slipped his number to me on a napkin. I gave him a little smile, then crumbled it up and dropped it to the floor when he turned away. There was no way in hell I was giving him a call.

We finally left the club at 2:30am. They wanted to stop and get something to eat. I wanted to go straight home.

On the way out Cell must have stopped and gave everyone he knew five and chatted for a few seconds. He thought that he was the fucking man because he was able to get us into the club for free. I had to laugh. When it was all said and done, we piled into his jeep and left. Mr. Too Ugly finally got the hint and didn't say a word to me the whole time we were in the car. He didn't even look at me.

Finally unable to take it anymore, I looked at him and asked, "Why are you so ugly?"

Sasha didn't even look back at me.

"Yo, why you trying to play my man out like that?" Cell asked.

"Ain't nobody trying to play your man out, he played himself out thinking he could get with me." I responded.

It was on now I was about to rank on the both of them. They ruined my night, so now I was about to ruin theirs. I laughed and said, "Look at your man, he would never see my pussy, no matter how hard he tries."

"You think you're all that! You ain't nothing but a stuck up stink ass bitch!" Cell said in his man's defense.

"Niggah don't get jealous because you're not whiffing it either. I don't even know why Sasha is with your ugly ass."

"Shana, chill." Sasha begged.

"Chill… bitch you need to wake up. I've seen you mess with much better looking guys than him. That niggah look like a fucking spider monkey, trying to be sexy in his tight banana looking muscle shirt. How you gonna wear a muscle shirt with a big ass gut?"

"Fuck you, bitch!" He shouted.

"Yeah, you wish. Don't get mad when you know I speak the truth."

He quickly made a short stop at the light. I jerked forward as so did the others in his jeep. Mr. Too Ugly just sat there in silence. Shit, not only was he ugly, but he sat there and let me diss him in front of his man. If you're gonna be ugly, have heart, be a man and stand up for yourself.

"Yo, Sasha, I'm about to throw that fake bitch out of my car." Cell warned.

"Fake bitch! Niggah you need not to talk with your tight little dick." I said, throwing up my small pinky and wiggling it for him to see.

"What?" He said, sounding stunned.

"All that gut and a dick lost somewhere under it." I added to the insult.

He looked over at Sasha, and then shouted, "Fuck y'all bitches!"

I looked over at Mr. Too Ugly and peeped him crying, willing himself to stare out the window. Pitiful, I thought.

"Take me home, you fat, small dick, no pussy, stink ass niggah!" I said to him.

Sasha tried to put her two cents in, but Cell cursed her out too. That led to another argument. It was just the three of us arguing amongst each other. Jimmy just kept quiet in the corner.

The entire ride was nothing but insults. Then Sasha and I started arguing with each other. This shit got—so crazy, that this punk niggah kicked me out of his ride, telling my ass to walk home. Sasha didn't even stand up for a sista. She continued to sit in the front seat, and let this niggah have me walk home—but I didn't stress it—fuck her, too.

Two days later, Sasha and I had it out in front of my crib. She came banging on my door early in the afternoon talking some nonsense. She had the nerve to say that I'd disrespected her. I'd disrespected her? She was the one who disrespected me. She knew my standards. She knew the type of guys I preferred. So how the fuck she gonna get mad after hooking me up with some wildebeast? Everyday we made fun of guys like him, trashing them, dissin' them.

Now she had the nerve to bring one to my front door, talking about he's cool. Then she said I'd embarrassed her in front of Cell. Bitch! Who was Cell in the first place? He was nobody. Just some fool whose dick she sucked outside of a club.

Next thing you know, she was up in my face, screaming and yelling, arms moving around like she wanted to swing on me. So, I went up in her face, and that set the shit off right. We wrestled with each other, falling down to the ground, scratching and tearing at each other's hair and clothes. It seemed like the whole neighborhood came out and started to crowd around us to watch.

"Yo, ain't they best friends?" I heard someone in the crowd ask.

I had on my black Sean John jeans, and a blue Gap T-shirt, with my black Nike's. My hair was wrapped up in a ponytail, so it was hard for her to get at it. But her hair was out, and freely spread down to her shoulders, so I just kept yanking at it and snapping her neck back. Her nose started to bleed. I had her pinned to the ground and I kept hitting her. "Stupid bitch!" I yelled out. She was smaller and I was stronger, wilder and faster. No one attempted to break it up until they saw blood. Somebody came and grabbed me from behind, pulling me off of her. I felt a few niggahs cop a feel on me as they broke us up, but I didn't think anything of it. A few people held us apart as we threatened and cursed at each other.

"You gonna get yours, bitch!" Sasha kept shouting.

"Fuck you!" I replied.

"Get the fuck off me!" She yelled, "I'm gonna kill that stupid bitch!"

People continued to hold us back, keeping us from tearing into one another. I struggled fiercely trying to free myself.

"Take her home!" I heard a woman shout out.

I saw one male carry her off my lawn and into the streets. He continued to drag her down my block as she cursed and hollered at me. Her car was still parked in front of my home. I wished they would leave it there. I guarantee that shit would be demolished by tomorrow morning. But someone got a hold of her keys and drove her car down the block to where she was being detained.

"Stupid bitch!" I shouted out one last time and stomped into my house, mad, heated, slamming my door shut.

I looked in the mirror and noticed she had scratched me over my right eye. I looked out my front window and saw a crowd still standing out front excited about what just happened. Some were imitating how it went down. I closed my blinds and went upstairs. Damn, she was my home girl, I thought, one of my best friends. Now we were tearing at each other's throat over some silliness. I cried myself to sleep that night.

SPANKY
4

We all sat around in Clarke's basement smoking on a freshly rolled joint, and watching a porno that I bought over, **"Soul Feast."** It was a Sunday night, and everyone was chilling down in the basement watching some light skinned shorti get it from the rear. We had no plans for tonight, so it was an in house thing. I was laid back on his couch, sitting next to Limp and Tommy.

"Damn, that bitch would catch it." Limp said, staring at the TV screen.

I was high, bored, hungry and horny. It's been a week since I had some, and that was with the hoe I fucked for forty dollars. I was tempted to go back this weekend, but I didn't want to roll out there alone. No one mentioned anything about the place since we left. Limp passed the L my way, and I took two long pulls and passed it to Tommy.

"Yo, that bitch got a phat ass." Limp said, referring to the porno star on the screen.

"Not as phat as your mamma's." Clarke joked.

"Niggah what? I just finished dusting the ass off from your mama's. She at my crib right now cooking me up some corn bread and grits butt naked." Limp said back.

"Niggah, get off my moms, because I just got off of yours, and lets talk about your pops." Clarke said. "Niggah your pops is like concrete, it takes him two days to get hard!"

Limp was stunned for minute. That was a good one Clarke hit him with. He had to laugh himself.

"See now, you wanna get on niggahs fathers and shit." Limp said. "Niggah, your father...fuck you! You fat bastard." Limp replied back. He was lost for words.

Clarke sat there smiling, he won the battle between him and Limp, but the war wasn't soon to be over. I couldn't snap as good as them. Once in a while I would come up with some good and funny material, but Limp, Clarke, Mark, and Abney could come up with funny shit out of the blue. They were born for snapping and dissin' on mutha-fuckas.

After the tape stopped, I popped in another one, "***Creamy Sides 3***." The tape started off with some really fat bitch riding some really slim niggah. She had to weight at least 300 pounds. He couldn't have been no more than 150lbs. But she was riding him, and he seemed to be enjoying it.

"Yo, Clarke, I didn't know your moms did porno's." Limps said. "That bitch almost weighs as much as you."

"Shut the fuck up, you big lip niggah." Clarke replied.

The jokes started up again. This time everybody started snapping on everybody. It was nothing but jokes for the rest of the night.

During the middle of the tape, things settled down a little, this really dimed out bitch was catching it doggystyle. Her body was blazing. The guy laid her down on the bed and started to eat her out.

"See, now money is wilding out right there." Tommy said. "How he gonna be fucking her, then take a time out to eat her pussy after his dick done been all up in it already?"

"It's his dick, he can do whatever he want." Mark said.

"Nah, shit like that's unsanitary."

"You don't eat pussy?" Peter asked.

"Hells no!" Tommy answered back. "Eating pussy is like a sin. I'm telling you, that's shit's in the Bible."

"Get the fuck out of here with that silly shit, Tommy." Limp said. "Where does it say in the Bible that eating pussy is a sin to man?"

"So what about if a girl gives you head, is that a sin too?" Peter asked.

"See that's different, giving a guy oral sex is easy and not as nasty. Our organ is already out. It gives the woman easy access to it. But when you're eating pussy, it's all deep in her, you got to lick, suck, stick your tongue into her..."

"Niggah how you know unless you already done it?" Mark said.

"I've seen it done plenty of times." He said.

"That niggah's frontin." Limp shouted.

I just sat there listening to this nonsense. Tommy was a dick head. Shit, if I had the chance I would eat a girl out, the right girl though, not just any stink bitch. This niggah had the nerve to say that eating out pussy was a sin. I wonder what Bible he was reading? Limp, Mark, and Peter snapped on him the whole night about that shit. Limp and Mark admitted that they eat pussy. The others were frontin like they never did it before.

At about a quarter to one I left and went home. I had to work in the morning. The house was quiet. My parents went out to some function that evening, so there were no pleasure screams coming from the other end of the hallway.

My alarm went off at 7:30. I didn't want to get out of bed. It was Monday morning, the first day of a long week. I usually grabbed breakfast on my way to work. Why couldn't weekends be every day, I thought. No bosses, co-workers or busy traffic. The reality is I need a check to live And I need some new Timberlands, my old ones were becoming worn out.

I gave my car time to warm up before I drive off. It is a piece of shit, but it gets me back and forth.

I run out the door in some white khakis, a cream dress shirt and tie. Sometimes I wonder why I even wear a tie to work. I'm not a businessman, just some young niggah who's stepfather hooked him up with a job. Every night when I come home, I got some kind of stain on my clothes. I'm the only person in that office who doesn't hold a position or a title. I take orders from everyone, even the lowest guy with the lowest salary--not as low as mine's of course.

I can't complain. I get paid a decent amount for being twenty-one. I don't have any kids or pay any bills, axcept for my Visa credit card, on which I have a $2,000 credit limit.

I arrive to work at 8:50 am. Mr. Price, the manager hates tardiness. He can be a cool guy at times, but can also get on peoples fucking nerves. When I arrive, the first thing I do is ask him what he has for me to do. Others, they already know their jobs, but me, I have to ask. It can be embarrassing sometimes. The first thing he usually has me do, is get him another cup of coffee.

"Day, get me another cup of coffee." He calls me by my last name, Day. My full name is Jamal Sean Day.

Like a plantation worker, I go ahead and do it. Mr. Price is a black man, like the majority of the workers in this little business, a real estate company. Some of the people who work here, my own people, act like their shit don't stink. It pisses me off.

"Yo, Spanky." Michael hollers out. He's an intern who always dresses in loose slacks, a sports jacket and matching ties. He's a handsome guy with dark thick eyebrows and a trimmed mustache.

He approaches me with a cup of coffee in his hand. He's only twenty-two and calls himself a playa. He flirts with every female in the office, he gets love, but not that much. He drives around in a souped up 93 Mazda FD3S RX-7. He has one of the illest performance cars I've seen around here in Queens. He had a custom paint job done and has a Sony stereo system. I can't front. I get jealous when I see him in that car. Pussy comes knocking on your front door with a car like that.

"Old man Price ragging down on you today?" He asks, sipping his cup of coffee and looking up at me.

"Nah, you know the routine. First thing in the morning, go get his stupid cup of coffee." I say to him.

"Good morning, fellas." Patrice says as she passes us by.

"Good morning." I holler back.

"I fucked her." Michael blurts out.

I think this niggah's lying. She seems too sweet and too nice a girl to be messing around with him. He looks back at her as she sits down at her desk. He smiles at her and she smiles back.

"When?" I asked.

"Last week, niggah. She dropped them draws for me after I took her out to see some movie. Yo, it felt like she was a virgin, she was so tight. But you know, I opened it up a little to make it easier for the next time I run up in it." He brags.

"Day, where's my coffee?" Mr. Price shouts out from his office door.

"It's coming, Mr. Price." I respond back feeling embarrassed.

"Yo, holla at me later." Michael says as he walks back to his desk.

I, like a fool, go running around the office trying to get Mr. Price his second, maybe third, cup of coffee for the day.

"And Day after that, I want you to file these forms for me." He orders.

"Not a problem."

A few people look my way, including Michael, who shakes his head and turns back to his work for the day.

By noon, he had me mopping the hallway floors. The regular janitor had called in sick for the day.

It was during lunch when I saw her. She was beautiful, cute and sexy. I never saw her around before, so I figured that she must be new. My heart was pounding as I gawked at her. Her skin was coffee brown, her eyes onyx black, and her light brown hair hung down to her shoulders. Her skin was flawless and her figure had me speechless. It was love at first sight.

Who is she? I thought.

She had on a three- piece pinstriped suit, with a double-breasted jacket and a straight skirt, with sheer black stockings and black high heels. Her legs were nicely shaped. It seemed like all the men in the office took notice. I was in love.

She took a sip from the water bottle she carried. I watched the way her lips wrapped around the top of the bottle. I wanted to introduce myself, but I was too scared. When she smiled, it was radiant and warm.

She was perfect.

She walked off with Ann, and I wanted to follow, but I stayed behind. I knew I was going to think of her all day long. She was the one. She didn't look like a bitch or a chicken-head.

On my way back to the office I ran into Michael. He tapped me on my shoulders and said, "Check out brown skin…she is too fine."

I agreed.

"Yo, I bet you within a month's time, I'll be fucking her." He said, sounding so sure of himself.

Hearing that made me angry. Here it was, her first day of her job, and this niggah was already talking about dropping her draws. I prayed that he wouldn't be successful, because just by looking at her, I knew she was different.

Johnny came up to us and said, "Yo, did you check out the new receptionist."

"She's a receptionist!" Michael replied back.

"Yeah. It's about time old man Price got rid of that old bag Mandy and bought in something decent to look at." Johnny said.

"I feel you with that one." Michael said.

"God she is hot!" Johnny said. He's a white boy from Minnesota.

"What is she, like the third one this year?" Michael asked.

"No. She would be the fourth one. This place goes through receptionists like a prostitute goes through condoms." Johnny answered.

"What's her name?" I asked.

"Carla. I think." Johnny said.

I wanted to know everything about her. What did she like? How old was she? What kind of men she dated? As they talked, I stood there and gazed at Carla as she sat there trying to get use to her first day on the job.

"Yo. I'm going for that." Johnny said.

I quickly turned my head and looked at him. How dare he suggest making a move on her. She don't want an uppity white boy. She needs a brother in her life, not no fuck them and do them wrong, playa like Michael. She needed someone like me.

"Please, Johnny. She don't want no white, no rhythm, off beat, square head fool like you." Michael insulted.

"What? Michael you know I got game. I hooked up with Lisa, right."

"Yeah, but did you fuck her yet?"

"I'm working on it…"

"It don't count then."

"I'll bet you $100 that I'll get to them draws before you do." Johnny wagers.

"C'mon, Johnny, the bets in my favor, you don't stand a chance...I already saw her looking at me earlier." Michael said.

"$100 then. Let's say within two months."

"This is going to be like taking candy from a baby. The easiest money I'll ever make in this place." Michael bragged.

They shook on it and the bet was on. The first person able to fuck her had to capture her panties as a souvenir.

I didn't take part in it because I knew I didn't stand a chance. I didn't have the game or the skill and I wasn't full of myself.

I also wasn't eager to see who would win. I wanted both of them to fail, get dissed, and fall flat on their faces.

Towards the end of the day, Johnny went over to her and introduced himself. They shook hands, chitchatted for a few minutes and that was it. He looked over at Michael and gave him a nasty smirk.

Michael caught up with her after work. He asked if she needed a ride home, but she refused. He was trying to be smooth and told her he'd wait with her for the bus. They talked while they waited. She looked at him like she was kind of interested. She laughed at his jokes and looked into his eyes. I was glad no numbers were exchanged. I left, thinking I should've made my move too. It was to late now.

I went home thinking about the new girl at work named Carla.

SHANA
5

It's been a week since my fight with Sasha. The day after it happened, everyone around the way knew about it. Word spreads quick in the hood. Jakim came by the next day and asked if I was all right. Like I was the one who got fucked up. I didn't flip on him. It was kind of cool to see him. Ten minutes later, Tyrone pulled up. Jakim and I were sitting on the porch. My heart skipped a beat. I knew they were boys, but I didn't know how Jakim would react seeing his man coming to check me. I just sat there next to Jakim, while Tyrone walked up.

"What up, dawg?" Jakim greeted. He got up and gave his man five and a hug.

I smiled and stared up at Tyrone. I played it cool. I knew he would. Tyrone asked if everything was cool. He asked what happened. I explained. He laughed.

"Yo, Shana, you be trippin'." Tyrone said.

I sat there staring at the both of them. They both were looking good. Fine and sexy. Jakim, he was my sweetheart, but Tyrone was my freak thing. He could put a hurting on some pussy. I couldn't help but to clock him even more.

We sat around for the next half-hour, smoking and talking. Tyrone had a bag of weed on him and we went through that within minutes. My uncomfortable feeling was relieved once we got high. I forgot all of my worries and chilled out. Jakim tried to push up on me with Tyrone still there chilling with us. He said, "You know I still love you."

Tyrone gave me an unpleasant look, but he didn't say anything. He knew the situation between Jakim and I. It was getting late and Tyrone decided to leave, but I knew he wanted to say a quick little something to me before he left. It was this look in his eyes. But I didn't want to have any little private conversations with Jakim still around. He wasn't stupid.

"Yo, Ty', jet me to my crib real quick so I can pick up my whip." Jakim said. His man dropped him off earlier.

"C'mon, niggah. I should charge you for gas." Tyrone joked.

They both walked toward his car, I followed behind. Jakim went around to the passenger side. Tyrone gave me a quick look, and whispered in my ear while Jakim was getting in the car, "I'll be back around tonight, be here."

He was smooth with his.

My mother came in later on that evening with Danny. They had just come from Kentucky Fried Chicken. I swiped a leg, two thighs and some biscuits and ran my ass to my room. Naja gave me a call, she wanted to know the deal between Sasha and I. Latish called too wanting to know the same thing.

Tyrone as promised, came back around eleven that night. I bought him into my room where we talked for an hour, then fucked. He wanted to know if it was really over between Jakim and I. I told him yes. I wondered if he was catching feelings for me. He knew what it was between us, just sex. We even had a quick talk about it. We agreed that if our feelings got involved that would fuck everything up. Tyrone continued to see other people and I did the same. We just both got what we wanted from each other.

There was a rumor spreading around the neighborhood that Sasha was planning to retaliate and jump me with a few girls. But that was a rumor I heard a week ago and still hadn't seen any action. I haven't even seen her since our little incident. I went on with my life.

Naja and Latish called and were planning to go out to Manhattan to check out a club. I decided to roll out with them and get my party on too. My plans changed when

Jakim pulled up. He insisted that I go out with him tonight. He said he wanted to talk to me about something serious. I told him yeah, although I really wasn't in the mood to travel out to Manhattan anyway.

I forgot how sweet he could be as he opened the passenger door for me and carefully let me in. I informed him that this wasn't a date; we're just hanging out together. It didn't mean we're getting back together. He agreed.

We stopped at a Burger King. He then drives out to Coney Island in Brooklyn where everything is closed for the winter. He parks the car, and we get out to walk across the boardwalk.

We strolled and discuss old times.

"I'm surprised you're not cursing me out." He says.

"No reason to right now."

"You always had a wicked tongue." Jakim says.

I look at him and say, "That's because I keeps it real. You should know better, my man or not. You played yourself when you hurt my feelings, Jakim."

"I didn't play you out."

"Two years together and you want to fuck that stink hoe down the block from me."

"Well, I was wrong about that, Shana. You know how us men get. Sometimes we think more with our dicks, than with our feelings. I know I fucked up with you."

"Yes, you did."

He stopped walking, looked over at me, and asked, "But me and you, we're still cool, right?"

I smiled. "Yeah, We're still cool."

"That's all I needed to hear." He responded.

We continued to walk. I gazed out into the ocean, seeing the moonlight gleaming across it. I started to reminisce on the days when he and I would do this frequently. Jakim was always romantic and smooth. He knew all the hot spots to take a girl. He knew the right words to say. If we got into an argument, the very next day he would show up to my door front with flowers and candy like it was Valentines Day. I would forgive him and we would have the most wonderful sex. Whenever he used to run the streets with Tyrone and his peeps, he would take time out to give me a call. One of the things I liked the most about him, was he never showed off in front of his boys while I was with him. He would always show me affection even with his friends watching.

They would watch us and hate. They would say he was pussy whipped, but he didn't care. He even said, "I love you." to me in front of his friends a few times. Sometimes I even wondered whether it was even necessary to break up, but like he said himself, men think more with their dicks than their hearts. I still thought that was just an excuse.

Jakim takes my hand into his, holding my hand softly. I don't resist. It felt like we were a couple again. I had to erase that feeling from my head and get back to reality. He cheated on me, hurt me and now we were separated. I still needed time apart from him.

We stayed on the boardwalk for another fifteen minutes then headed back to his car. I knew Jakim wanted this night to turn out to be something more. It was obvious he wanted to be out here as lovers instead of friends.

"You ever think about us?" He asked, after we got in the car.

"Yeah. Sometimes."

"I miss you, Shana."

I remained quiet, staring out of the passenger window.

"Do you ever see us getting back together?"

I kept quiet. I had mixed feelings about the situation. I still loved him, but us getting back together wasn't an option. I was still having my fun being young and living my life. I explained this to him. He listened and nodded his head.

It was a quarter past ten when he finally dropped me off at my front door. As I got out, he said, "Shana, just think about us. I love you."

I gazed at him for a few seconds, then headed inside. He sat in his car and watched me enter the house. I knew that I was his one and only true love. Many females have tried, but they couldn't conquer what he was still feeling for me. They wanted him so bad, but it wasn't happening with me still around. Even though we were separated, we were still in love with each other. His love for me showed on his face, while I kept mines on a more discrete level.

I walked into the living room, flicked on the lights and saw my mother getting her pussy eaten out by Danny on the living room couch. If any other normal teenage girl would have walked in on her mother while she was getting her shit eaten out, it probably would have freaked them out. I was use to it. This damn sure wasn't the first time I caught them and it probably won't be the last. She didn't get up and cover herself and he didn't miss a beat.

I couldn't move. I just stood there, watching Danny go down on my mother. It turned me on to him even more. I looked at his body, his tattoos and his scars. He had two gunshot wounds on his back and a knife wound on the side. I was frozen in that spot. Why not me? I thought to myself. He was so fucking fine, too fine for my mother.

"Shana, you gonna stand there and watch us all night?" My mother asked.

"No!" I quickly said. I turned and rushed from the room. I could hear my mother's passionate moans throughout the hallway and in my bedroom. I shut the door; it was becoming too much for me.

Danny, he could definitely hit this, I thought as I laid down on my back on my bed with my legs spread wide open. I fingered my pussy. I was horny. In fact, I was so horny, that I went into the fridge and pulled out a cucumber. I used it as a sexual toy, putting it inside me.

That would be my passion for the night.

Early the next morning, I went out shopping with Aunt Tina. We hit the Avenues and the Malls. I told her about my seeing Danny and my mom. She fantasizes about Danny too. I mean what female didn't—his nice brown skinned ass. We laughed and hit up all the stores. It was fun shopping with my Aunt; she had very good taste in clothing. Too bad I can't say the same thing about her choice in men. As we walked around, almost every guy that passed by us tried to hit on us. I took a few guys numbers because I wasn't giving out mines.

We got free cab rides each way because we flirted with the cab drivers. We gave them phony numbers and gassed their heads up. Tina would ride up front with the man, giving the cabby a hand massage while he was driving. I would sit in the back and laugh. My Aunt was a slut.

My day was going great until I ran into Sasha. She was with three other girls. I tried not to pay her any attention. My Aunt took notice. She knew what went down between us and asked do you wanna beat the bitch down. I thought she was kidding. The three girls kept staring and giving lip. I acted like I was looking through some skirts, paying them no mind at all. Aunt Tina glared back at them, cursing them under her breath. If anything went down in this store. I knew she had my back. My Aunt could throw down worse than me.

One of the girls came toward us. She acted like she was browsing through some stuff as she came closer to my Aunt. I knew they were going to try and start something with us, so I took off my earrings discretely and stuffed them into my purse. Sasha stood a short distance away and stared at me. The first girl acted like she bumped into my Aunt accidentally.

"Watch where the fuck you're going, bitch." The girl yelled out.

That was all she said. My Aunt lashed out at her something serious. She pulled her by the hair and knocked her down to the floor. It was so quick and intense, no one saw it coming,--not even the girl she was beating down. The rest tried to come to their friend's aid. That's when I stepped in and punched one in her jaw. We had a wild catfight right in the middle of the store.

My Aunt was holding two of them down, while the other one and Sasha tried to jump on me. I knocked Sasha across her head with my purse. Her friend, some chubby bitch, tried to bum rush me to the ground. She knocked me into a pile of clothes. She had the advantage for a quick second, holding me down and hitting me across my face, but that changed when I knocked her across the head with a belt buckle. Sasha came swinging at me. She caught me with a few good hits, making me stumble over a rack of clothes. I yanked her by her shirt and tossed her hard against the wall, hitting her with some serious blows to the head. My Aunt was more than handling the other two. She was fucking them bitches up.

The employees in the store didn't know what to do. Some just stood out the way and watched in horror, while others scrambled to get security or the police. Some of the customers even ran out the store. No one attempted to break it up. There were too many people involved.

By now, a mass crowd had gathered outside of the store, curious to see what all the commotion was about. I now was fighting the fat bitch. I ripped open her shirt and had one of her titties hanging out. She didn't care. Enrage she came at me full force and knocked me down to the ground.

"Ooohhh that had to hurt!" I heard someone from the crowd yell out.

I was in pain. She was strong and fat. She grabbed a handful of my hair and tried to pull it out. I grabbed her by her wrist and tried to get her off me. Suddenly, I looked up and saw Sasha standing over me. She had a razor in her hand. I wanted to cry out. Please God! Don't let her cut me, I prayed.

My prayers were answered when about four police officers came and restrained Sasha, throwing her to the ground. Then they pulled chubby off of me and restrained her fat ass too. Within minutes, six to eight additional officers were on the scene taking control. They had Sasha and her friends in handcuffs and were questioning me. My Aunt was coll although, she was bleeding from a scratch by her right ear.

The cops questioned the store manager asking what happened and who started it? She pointed to one of Sasha friends and explained that she had bumped into my Aunt and cursed her out. Other witnesses said the same thing. I felt relieved. I guess they felt that it wasn't fair for four girls to jump on two girls. Then Sasha pulling out that razor, made it even worse for them.

They hauled Sasha and her friends off to jail and asked if my Aunt and I would like to press charges. The store manager wanted to press charges. They ruined her store with their nonsense. My aunt and I refused. Where I come from, we don't press charges against each other, we settle our disputes in the streets. Your hood is your judge, jury and executioner.

My hair was looking horrendous, my lip was bleeding and my eye was swollen. I was so mad. Whatever friendship Sasha and I had left, dissolved after she pulled out that razor. She just declared war. There was no way I was gonna let this shit slide.

Some of my shopping bags were lost, probably stolen, and my new shirt was ruined. Aunt Tina lost her shit too. She was more upset than I.

We called ourselves a cab and took our asses home. When my mother heard what had happened, she was ready to go knock down Sasha's front door. I convinced her not to. The rest of the day I just stayed in the house. In fact, I stayed indoors for the next three days until my face and bruises healed. Of course Jakim heard what had happened and he stopped by. He spent a few hours with me. We talked and laughed.—He cursed Sasha out, telling me that he never liked the bitch anyway. Tyrone was a no show. I was surprised. Maybe he didn't hear what happened, I thought. I didn't stress it.

SPANKY
6

Another day at the office and I find myself staring uncontrollably at Carla. She had on this wicked leather skirt and a button down white-collar shirt. I was doing some filing across the room from her. She was at her desk doing her usual routine, working on the computer and answering the phone. It's been a week since her arrival and I still haven't introduced myself. Almost every male in the office approached her this week, introducing himself and complimenting her on how beautiful she was. She'd have short conversations with each of them and continue with her job. I still hadn't approached her.

Michael and Johnny were still working hard on their little bet. Michael asked to take her out three times this week, but she rejected him. Johnny bought her a small bouquet of roses and set them on her desk. All he got was a kiss on his right cheek. The women in the office were getting jealous. Even Mr. Price tried to get in the game, he offered to take Carla out to afternoon brunch, but she declined. All the offers she was rejecting was making my confidence in approaching and asking her out dwindle even more.

Shit, it was so bad that during the weekends when I was chilling with the fellas, I would think about what she'd wear Monday morning. I would pray that she didn't have a man. Then again, it would make perfect sense on why she was turning everyone down at work. Maybe she was a lesbian...NO! I had to block that idea out, she looked too good to be starting bush fires with other women.

I'd decided I wanted to marry Carla.

It was around one when Nadine, a real estate agent, came into the office ecstatic. She sold a house that was on the market for one year. It sold for $800,000, and she would receive a 6% commission from the sale. Everyone was happy for her.

Nadine was so happy, that she planned to throw a party next weekend and everyone was invited. I'd probably bring my peeps along, too.

That afternoon I went home feeling so good about myself, I didn't know why, I just did. My parents were in the backyard raking up leaves that had fallen off an old oak tree. I smiled on the inside because autumn was my favorite time of the year, the way the leaves turned colors during the change of season. It was the season when you were able to break out your leather jackets, sweatshirts, hoodies, ski caps, even baseball caps. And if the day was warm enough you could still rock a T-shirt or short sleeve shirt. My most favorite thing about Fall is that it is the beginning of a new basketball season. My favorite NBA team is the New York Knicks.

"How was your day at work?" My mother asked, when she saw me standing there.

"It was cool." I told her as I picked up the extra rake. My mother and I began to rake the leaves while Leroy stuffed them into big black garbage bags. It took us two hours to finish the job.

When we were done my mother went inside to take a shower and of course, my stepfather joined her. They made me sick with all that smooching around the house. I understood that it was their home, but Goddamn!

I went to my room, rolled up a joint and popped in a porno flick, this time, *"Afro Whores!"* I couldn't concentrate on it because my mind was on Carla.

The night of the party, I invited Clarke, Limp and Mark. We were all squeezed in Mark's white Acura Integra Coupe.

I especially wanted Mark to come along. I wanted Carla to see me riding in something nice tonight, even though it wasn't mine.

I had on an espresso lambskin jacket, a camel colored mock turtleneck sweater, black slacks, and a pair of black alligator shoes.

The guys nagged me all night, asking if there were going to be any fine bitches there. I told them yes, and warned them not to refer to the ladies as bitches. Some of my co-workers were going to be present at this party and I didn't want them embarrassing me. I was the only one in the car really dressed for the occasion. The others had on baggy jeans and Timberland boots. I wanted Carla to notice me tonight.

I fantasized about us finally getting to meet each other, and she confessing that she had a crush on me since the day she started. We'd talk, our eyes would meet and deep in our minds, we both wanted the same thing, for us to be all over one another, naked. She'd suggest we go somewhere private and I agreed. We would leave the party and head to a room located in the basement where there is a love seat.

We entered the room and she held my hand.

"I want you, Spanky, take me here, fuck me now!" She'd demand.

My mind fast-forwards and we're butt naked on the couch. She's taking me into her mouth. She stops, smiles and says, "Damn Spanky, you got a big dick…after this, will you marry me?"

I tell her yes and get ready to enter her. She accepts all of my size into her, as I start to stroke and work it. She yells out my name, scratches my back, nibbles on my ear. I'm loving it. It feels so good, her pussy is so warm and inviting. I'm in it for about an hour! The harder I stroke, the bigger it gets. Carla is screaming out my name, "Spanky! Spanky! Spanky!"

"Yo, Spanky!" I heard a loud voice shout, interrupting my fantasy. "Spanky, where do I go from here?" Mark asks.

"What?" I say.

"Niggah, where were you a few minutes ago?" Limp asked.

"Yo, this niggah got a hard on." Mark blurts out.

I look down, and yes I do, it's bulging out. I'm embarrassed. I cup my hands over it.

"What the fuck was on your mind just now?" Clarke wants to know.

"It's gotta be some pussy at that party you're dying to dig into." Limp says.

"Yo, don't be getting no hard--ons in my car. I don't wanna be seeing that shit while I'm driving." Mark says.

"Niggah why you're looking at his dick in the first place?" Clarke asked.

"Shut the fuck up, Clarke. Ain't nobody staring at his dick!"

"Let me find out, Mark…you're a meat watcher." Limp joked.

"Yo, I ain't no meat watcher. The only meat I be watching is your mother's titties falling over when I be fucking her from the back." Mark says.

Clarke is in tears in the backseat. I try to bring my hard on down by thinking about something negative. I give Mark the directions to the place.

We arrived a little past ten. It is a huge brick-catering hall located in Hempstead, Long Island. There are a few cars parked out front and the parking lot is almost full. I see a few of my co-workers standing outside as we try to find a parking space. I get excited. We approach the building with our young cool attitudes. There is a man in a black suit checking for invitations at the front door. We all step up and he looks at us.

"Y'all young lads know that this is a formal gig?" The man asked.

"And, so." Clarke answers back.

"So, y'all can't be coming up in here with jeans and boots." The man says, giving all of my friends the stare down.

"Look, my friend is throwing the party, she invited us and said you can come as you are." I tell him. I didn't come all this way to be turned around.

A group of people pass by us, and he lets them through with no harassment at all. They all had on slacks, skirts, blouses and shoes.

"See, now that's how you're supposed to look. I can't allow no hoodlum looking young boys up in here." He says.

"Yo fuck this Bougie place." Limp angrily says.

"You, I can let in." He says, pointing to me, "Your boys, they're a no, no."

"Yo, Spanky, lets go, this faggot, uptight, bouncer ain't gonna let us in your friend's party." Clarke says, as he walking down the steps.

"Nah, I need to go in." I say, standing my position.

Soon after, I see Michael coming toward us, he's alone. He's dressed sharp in a black blazer, some crisp slacks, and a black silk shirt. "Spanky, what's up?"

"This bouncer won't allow my friends into the party." I say to him.

"What, nah, we're going to have to see about that." He says. "I'll go look for Nadine, just hang tight."

I do, trying to keep my patience while the fellas crack jokes about the bouncer, who doesn't say a word.

He just gives them angry stares as his nostrils flare and his fists clinch and unclench.

"Y'all a bunch of comedians, hah?" The bouncer finally said.

Before anything else was said or done, Michael comes back with Nadine by his side. She smiles at me, gives me a hug and kiss on the cheeks, and asks, "What's the problem out here?"

"He won't let me and my friends in." I informed her. "I thought you said we could come dressed anyway we like?"

"This place has a dress code." The guy tells her.

"Well, I personally know the owner of this place, and he told me my guests can come dressed any way they choose. Now, would you please let him and the rest of his friends pass through or do I have to take this matter up with your boss."

"Go on through." He quietly mumbles.

"Yeah, finally you fat bastard, keep yourself occupied and eat a cheese steak." Clarke said to the man, as he slowly walks by him.

"I'll bring you the buffet, so you can have a little late night snack on the job." Limp mocks.

Nadine stops and says to the bouncer, "Oh, and if any more of my guests come through, you let them in with no fucking problem at all, I don't want any more complaints about you!".

"Damn, Nadine, I didn't know you had it in you." I said.

"Baby, that's how I work my way to the top, not taking shit from no one."

Nadine was cool, she was in her late thirties, beautiful, married with three kids, and ambitious. She was well liked and respected around the office.

We followed her down a brightly lit corridor with fancy chairs lined up against the wall. She had on a sexy, knee length dress, with open toe heels. Her hair was wrapped up in a bun and the aroma of her perfume clogged my nostrils.

We entered a grand hall. The room was already crowded with people. The DJ was playing the old school jam, *"To Be Real."* by Sherryl Lynn. The room was dimly lit a twenty-foot buffet table filled with food was lined up against a back wall. There were quite a few young ladies present.

Everyone seemed to be having a good time, dancing, drinking, talking, and flirting.

"Jamal, I'd like to introduce you to my husband, David. David this is Jamal and his friends." She introduced.

We shook hands, said hello--nice to meet you, and never said another word to each other after that.

"Jamal, mingle, go and have a good time." She said, taking her husband by his hand as she began to dance with him.

The fellas and I looked around the room. While they were looking at the fine honeys present, I was searching for Carla. A few ladies passed by me, giving me very welcome stares. That boosted my ego a little.

Clarke and Limp glanced at every booty that passed by them. Mark wasted no time trying to meet people. He was already snuggled up on some red hair bimbo with a very short skirt and tight shirt.

I stood next to Michael, as we both kept quiet staring into the room.

I was wondering what was he thinking about? Was it Carla? It had to be her. No wonder why he wasn't out flirting or mingling with the rest of the crowd. He was doing the same thing I was, waiting patiently for Carla. He thought he was slick. I knew what he was up to. He was a persistent fuck. He wanted to hog the girl for himself all night, giving no one else the opportunity.

I looked at my watch and it was close to eleven. Clarke, Mark, and Limp were in the midst of the dance floor getting their party on. I was still holding up the wall. She had to be coming soon, I thought.

The DJ was rocking the joint with his funkadelic old school music. The crowd was over thirty-five. It was a party up in this mutha'.

Nadine was all over her husband on the dance floor. She could dance her ass off. She went from one old school dance to the next. She danced so well that a crowd had gathered around her and her husband to watch them get their dance on. Her feet would shift back and forth to the rhythm, her arms swinging in the air, her butt swaying from the left to the right.

I was still holding up the wall, but this time with a drink in my hand. I was in my little two-step mode, bobbing my shoulders back and forth to the music. Michael was jamming next to some cute honey in a tight dress.

"Alright, for y'all ladies out there on the floor, I'm about to slow it up just a little for those romantic gents." The DJ announced over his microphone. Everybody was with a partner, well almost everybody.

By a quarter to twelve, I turned my head and finally saw her by the door. She looked beautiful. I had butterflies in my stomach. My heart felt like it was about to jump out of my chest. Michael noticed her too. He glanced over at her, smiled and headed towards her. I followed right behind, we quickstepped over in her direction. We were just a few feet away, when an unknown male came and stood by her side. Oh shit, she bought her man. She did have a man, I thought. I stopped in my tracks and so did Michael. He tried to play it off and grabbed a female to dance with that was standing next to him. I felt stupid. But the guy that she was with looked so familiar to me, I knew him from somewhere. He had on black loose fitting slacks, a nicely fitted Armani sweater and Gucci shoes. He had a gleaming, cleanly shaved head, a nicely trimmed mustache and thick eyebrows. I thought, damn, I can't compete with him.

He walked into the room and automatically all the females gawked at him. Some of them got into small huddles and whispered among each other while staring at the guy that was with Carla. They couldn't take their eyes off the dude.

"Damn, he is gorgeous." A female standing next to me said to her friend.

My night was a bust. There was no way that I was going to approach her now.

Nadine went over to Carla to say hi. They spoke briefly. I stood my distance, getting jealous. I couldn't stop wondering where I knew this guy?. Some of the ladies went over to Carla, but it wasn't because they wanted to say hello, it was because they wanted to get a better look at Mr. Handsome, Mr. Perfect and Mr. Too Fine.

Yeah, I was hating. Hard!

He shook their hands and continued to smile and keep company with Carla. The girls strutted off looking back over their shoulders at him. I continued to watch everything from a distance.

"Yo, Spanky, what's the deal, why you ain't dancing?" Limp asked, sweating something serious.

"I'm just chilling right now." I said.

"Yo, there are too many bitches up in here." Clarke said. "Where's Mark?"

"Lost with some hoe in this crowd." Limp said.

"So, yo Spanky, where's that bitch that was raising your mountain up in the car?" Clarke asked.

"She's in here somewhere." I replied softly.

"Where? I wanna give you a rating on her, let you know if she's a dog or not." Clarke added.

"Yeah, son, she better not be ugly!" Limp said.

I was in no mood for their silliness tonight. The girl of my dreams came in with another guy. I felt heartbroken,keeping my emotions in check.

"Yo, ain't that Kaleem?" Clarke asked Limp.

"Hells Yeah. What the fuck is his pretty ass doing up in here...he about to cramp my style." Limp says.

That's who he was! I knew I'd recognized him from somewhere. He was a year younger than we were. The girls in our school used to go crazy over him. They probably still do. He'd come to school dressed in the finest gear. The ladies hounded him all the time. Some of the fellas' envied and hated on him big time. Limp and Clarke was cool with him, they all hung out together. I just knew him through those two knuckleheads.

"Damn, his date is fine like old wine. That bitch could get it." Limp said, referring to Carla.

I gave him a quick unpleasant look and focused my attention back over to Kaleem and Carla. It was just like him to bag the fine ones.

"C'mon, let's surprise him and go holler." Clarke suggested.

They walked off. There was no need for me to go over and make my emotional situation even worse. He was with the woman I desired. He was with my future wife and baby's mother.

Limp tapped Kaleem on his shoulders, he turned around and was in shock to see the both of them standing there. They greeted each other with bro' handshakes and hugs. I couldn't look on any longer. I needed some air. On the way out, I bumped into Johnny. He was wearing a gray three-piece suit and some nice white and black shoes. He wore a black derby and wire-rimmed glasses.

"Jamal, you're out already, party's that whack?" He asked.

"Nah, I just needed some air."

"So what's the situation with the booty up in there? It is popping or what? Cause you know, I'm about to mack some of these hoes tonight."

He was worse than Limp and Clarke. He eyed himself in the giant hallway mirror. Then rubbed his hand repeatedly over his goatee. He straightened out his glasses and smiled, thinking he was a too pretty white boy.

"Yo, is Carla up in there yet? Cause you know once she sees me, I'm gonna be smacking the dust off that chocolate pussy tonight."

"Bitch, don't play yourself." I quietly mumble under my breath, barely having him hear me.

"What you say?" He asked.

"I said go ahead with yourself."

"Word dog. Once the honeys in here git a whiff of me, I'm gonna need some pussy repellant to drive them back. I can't fuck it all in one night."

He proceeds to stride into the room with his fake ass pimp walk. It looked more like his leg was injured than a pimp walk. As for me, I needed some air and a break from some of the clowns up in that place. I took a seat down on the stone steps and pulled out a Newport.

I was the only one out. Everyone else was still inside having a good time. My mind was still on Carla. All my dreams and fantasies about her burst like a bubble when I saw her walk in with Kaleem. It was hopeless, I thought. I was a dateless mutha-fucka'. Pussy wouldn't creep my way if I was born again. I thought, the only way I would probably get to see it again is if I would pay for it. Bitches wasn't feeling me, I was just a cool friend to them. Always a friend. This sucks.

I sat there and continued to mope, feeling sorry for myself. I was and had only been with two ladies in my life. The second time, I'd paid for it. I was completely pitiful. I wasn't an ugly mutha-fucka'. I just didn't have that playa's game, that sharp tongue, the gift of gab to get the ladies into bed with me. Maybe I should become a monk or something. They don't have sex in their lives. I was already living one of the traditions.

I continued to sit alone. I could hear the music from the hall and the noise of the crowd inside. I wanted to go home, but I couldn't let my lousy night spoil it for everyone else that was having a good time. It's been ten minutes since I've stepped out and a cold wind started to pick up. I was giving myself five more minutes to sit out here until I went back in and became miserable again.

"You got a cigarette?" I heard a voice from behind asked. It was a female.

"Yeah." I responded, reaching into my pants pocket and pulling out my pack of Newport's.

I turned around and nearly choked. It was Carla.

"Here you go." I said, giving her a cigarette.

"May I have a light?"

I pulled out my lighter and proudly lit up her cigarette.

"Thank You. You know smoking is bad for you." She said while standing.

I chuckled; she had a sense of humor, that's a good thing.

But I'm not a heavy smoker, I smoke weed more than I do cigarettes. I usually smoke cigarettes really when I'm nervous, and yeah, I'm trying to cut back on both of my nasty habits.

She stood there looking up at the sky. We both remained quiet. I wanted to say something, but was afraid I'd say something stupid. We were finally alone together. I felt that God had sent me a chance and I was desperately trying to think of something brilliant to say. She spoke first.

"You work with me, right?" She asked, blowing smoke from her mouth.

"Yeah, I do." I responded shyly. My eyes kept averting hers. I was too shy to even look her straight in her eyes.

"What's your name?"

"Spanky, I mean, Jamal."

"So which one is it, Jamal or Spanky?"

"Well its Jamal, but my friends call me Spanky." I said.

"Spanky, that's a cute name. Hi Spanky, my name is Carla." She said pleasantly, extending out her hand. "I hope you don't mind if I call you Spanky?"

"No, I don't. In fact I would love if you continued to." We shook hands. She was even more beautiful up close and personal. My dick rose nearly an inch touching her smooth and warm skin. I didn't want to let go of her hand. It was the first physical contact that I'd had with her and it felt so damn good. She could call me her man if she wants or her husband, she could call me anything she wished as long as it wasn't a good friend.

"So, Spanky, why are you out here alone on this chilly night?" She asked.

"I just needed to get away from the party scene for a few minutes."

"I hear that. I needed a break myself."

"But aren't you worried about leaving your man alone in there with all them ladies. I mean you had to see how they were clocking him earlier?"

She laughed. "My man. He's not my man. That's my cousin."

"Your cousin?"

"Yeah. I didn't want to come here alone and be harassed by every raised dick I pass."

I discreetly looked down at my erect dick. It was a good thing that she didn't notice. I had to stare away from her, because that would make my problem even worse. Watching her in the tight black dress she wore just turned me on.

I was elated to hear that Kaleem was her cousin. My confidence level rose just a little. I wanted to keep the conversation moving by asking smart and meaningful questions.

"So, who did you come with?" She asked.

"Oh, just some friends of mine. So Kaleem is your cousin?"

"Yeah, and how did you know that his name was Kaleem?"

"We went to high school together." I said.

"For real?"

"Yup." I said.

"I don't know what these females be seeing in my cousin. He ain't all that to me."

"Because he's family to you. Believe me, if he wasn't family, you would be jocking him too."

"I think not. I don't like pretty boys." She boldly said.

I wanted to ask what was her type, but I was too scared to go there with her. "So, um, Carla, how do you like the job so far?"

"It's cool, you know, I've had worse jobs. The workers are friendly, you know some of them can be a little too friendly. Like Johnny and Michael, them two are something else. What? Is there some competition between those two?"

I wanted to blow up their spot, but I kept a cool head. It was getting colder, but I didn't want to go back inside. I was having too much fun standing out here talking to her. I wanted to get to know her, see what she was about, and now that I had the opportunity, I just couldn't let it go. There was no one around to disturb us.

"So Carla, how old are you?"

"23." She answered, as she took one last pull from the cigarette and tossed it out in front of her. "What about you, how old would you be?"

"Me, I'm 21." I wanted to say that I was older, like 26, but you know haters in the office would have blown up my spot to her once they found out. Besides, females hate when you lie to them, they think if you did it once, then you'll do it again.

"Damn, you're still a young buck." She said.

"Yeah, but age ain't nothing but a number."
A cold wind picked up, making the both of us clutch ourselves as we stood outside.

"Damn, it's getting really cold out here, I'm about to go back inside." She said, shivering. "You coming?"

"Yeah, in a few more minutes." I replied.

Like a true female, she grabs me by my hand and pulls me into the building. "You've been outside long enough, Spanky. I don't want you catching a cold and not being able to report to work Monday...C'mon."

I didn't resist or talk back. I just went along with the force. I let out an enormous smile as we entered back into the building. We walked down the hall together, still talking. I wanted to ask her to dance when we got back to the party, but I hesitated. I was still too scared to try and make a move on her. Michael was standing outside the doors. I gave him a broad smile, feeling like I was the man.

"Carla." He blurted out. "Can I have this dance?"

"Of course Michael." She answered.

She left my side and went into the party with Michael arm in arm. She didn't even look back at me. It was ok, we finally got to meet each other. She finally knew who I was. Even though I was upset about her dancing with Michael. I couldn't stress it. The process had just begun.

Carla and Michael seemed to be hitting it off real strong on the dance floor. Almost every gorgeous and pretty young girl at the party surrounded Kaleem. He danced with a few and received a couple of numbers. It was just like when I was in high school with him. The fellas gave him a secret nickname; *the panty dropper*.

Limp was drunk and making a fool out of himself. Clarke was trying to hang around with Kaleem and Mark was still on the dance floor. I was holding the wall again. The only female that I wanted to dance with was being occupied with Michael or Johnny. They hogged her almost the entire night.

By 4am everyone began to leave. Clarke and I had to carry Limp out. Mark was already outside with some big booty blond and Carla was near the exit chatting with Michael and having Johnny trying to cock block him.

As I passed Carla, I looked over at her and said, "See you Monday, it was nice talking to you."

She smiled, and continued chatting with Michael and Johnny. Nadine, was outside saying goodbye and thanking everyone for coming. We had to squeeze Limp into the backseat. Mark warned him not to throw up in his car. After he received the big bootie blond chick's number, we left.

I was happy as hell. I'd finally gotten to speak with Carla. But my happiness came to and abrupt end when Limp threw up on everybody in the car. We were only ten minutes away from home. Mark, Clarke and I cursed him out, as he tried to apologize. Mark was heated, he threatened to whip Limp's ass.

I was the first one he dropped off, Thank God. I couldn't take the smell anymore. I ran into the crib and took me a hot shower. Then I jumped into bed and popped in a porno, *"Black Ass City."*

I did my daily jerking off, and went to sleep thinking about Carla, my wife to be.

SHANA
7

"Take your time, baby." I whispered to Tyrone as we fucked in the back seat of his BMW. We were parked by the Verrazano Bridge in Brooklyn. It was going on one a.m. I was sitting on his lap with his chocolate erection thrusting hard into me. I clamped my arms around his neck as he gripped my butt tightly.

"Damn, you feel so fucking good, Shana." He said.

There were about eight cars parked around us. A couple parked next to us tried to observe our actions. We didn't give a fuck who was watching; we continued on with our business. He was about to make me cum, my body quivered as I moved my hips in a forward to backward motion. My jeans lay across the backseat, his pants around his ankles. The circumference of his dick filled every gap in my vagina, expanded it to capacity. I felt him everywhere. He kissed and licked on my hardened nipples. He played with my butt as he thrust himself strongly into me. The windows were all fogged up from our breaths and the cold outside and visibility was at a minimum. I cried out. I was definitely feeling it coming. Definitely riding the wave, just as he was.

"Give it to me, Ty baby, give it to me." I cried out.

He shook furiously, as I felt him bust into me. His neck snapped back, his eyes rolled to the back of his head. He pushed my buttocks in strongly with his powerful hands. His dick felt larger as he let off a nutt inside me. His legs pushed up; making me almost hit my head on the car ceiling. I felt mines coming, too. I told him to keep it in me. His hard-on was still strong and he still continued to thrust it deeply into me, making me climax explosively. I screamed out as I shook rapidly and out of control. I dug my nails into his back and slumped my head over his shoulders. It felt so fucking good.

"Damn, you got some good mutha-fuckin' pussy." Tyrone told me.

We remained close for a few more minutes. I just wanted his dick to sit in me for a while.

"I needed that, boo." I said, kissing him around his ears.

"Jakim never gave it to you that good?" He asked.

"Yeah, but you're better. You be making me go into mutha-fuckin' convulsions and shit. What the fuck do you be feeding that thing anyway?"

"Brunettes, Blondes, Asians, Blacks…you name it, he'll eat it."

"Just don't stuff yourself too much. I can't be having it get too fat on me, then shit will no longer be able to fit."

"Then I'll just have to force it in." He said.

I laughed. "Please, it can barely fit now."

I got off the dick and started to put my clothes on. Tyrone started to do the same. I wiped the sweat from my forehead and face, then climb over the front seat and sat down in the passenger seat. I rolled down the window to let a little air circulate through the car. Tyrone didn't bother to climb over the seats. He opens the back door, with his shirt still open, chest exposed, and walks around the car to the driver's seat.

"You ready to go?" He asks.

I nod. He starts up the car and we pull out of the spot.

He explained why he didn't come through after my second fight with Sasha. He told me that he was out of town on business. He was gone for four days. He slid his right hand between my legs and rests it between my thighs, controlling the steering wheel with the left. I placed my hand over his and let it rest there with his.

"You hungry?" He asks.

I nod, yes, and we soon pull into a 24-hour burger joint. I'm constantly staring over at him. I think I'm falling in love with him. I try to keep my emotions for him hidden and pretend it's only about the sex. But the more I try, the more I desire the man. I also want to get back with Jakim. We've been separated for too long, almost three months now. He is constantly stopping by, giving me flowers, candy, writing poems, trying express how much he is missing me and I'm falling for it. Jakim claims to have not been with another woman in weeks. He says if we get back together, that it's going to be different this time. No more mistakes like before. He says he will always put us first. And I'm falling for his words.

Yet, what I have with Tyrone, I really don't want to give it up. He's rocking my world from day to day. The dick has never been this good. I mean Jakim was doing his thing, too, but damn, Tyrone works it like he created pussy. I don't have one bad thing to say about his actions when it comes to his fucking. That niggah gets a 10 times10 on my scale.

I'm all confused.

We pull up to the burger joint. It's kind of crowded for a late night. We head inside where there is only one line working with one cashier. I'm not too fond of standing on lines, so I take a seat in one of the booths. Tyrone remains on line. I smile and stare at him in his black leather bomber and beige Timberlands, with his brown and white Colombian collar shirt. He is definitely a sexy man.

I notice a few of the brothers on line are clocking me closely. They whisper to their homies and stare. I don't even smile back.

The line soon starts to diminish. A group of about four young brothers step into the joint. Tyrone is next to order. They're very loud as they enter the building. I know one of them. I used to talk to him when I was a freshman. His name is Terry. We dated for a few months. I broke up with him because I felt that I needed to move on. He tried to get back with me. Eventually he moved south and got some girl pregnant. We've remained friends over the years; sometimes he would hook a sista up, and wire me some cash when I depleted my funds. He would call and write. He even sent me pictures of his newborn baby girl—Riana. The last I heard about him, he had gotten into some beef with his baby mama. I hadn't heard from him since. It's been three years now.

I tried to turn my head to the right, hoping that he wouldn't recognize me. He stood on line and talked to his buddies. I wanted to get up and change booths to where I wasn't so easily seen. It was too late, he already saw me.

"Shana?" He called out.

Tyrone turned around to see who was calling me. Then he looked over at me. I gave him a thin smile,while I remained seated.

"Oh, shit, Shana, it is you." Terry said, "What's up girl? I ain't seen you in a minute."

He came at me with open arms, expecting a hug. I wanted to ignore him, but I really couldn't. His boys still stood on line and watched. I glanced at Tyrone as he waited on line. I was nervous, but I couldn't pin point the reason why? Tyrone wasn't my man and Terry was just an old boyfriend/friend from the past who just happened to be in the burger joint that night. But Tyrone's eyes beaded straight at him.

"Damn, you're still looking fine as ever, Shana" Terry said.

"Long time, Terry." I said, leaving just enough room between him and I.

Before I could even look back over at Tyrone, he was already standing behind Terry. My eyes widened. Terry turned around and it looked like he had seen a ghost. He took a quick step back, bumping into me slightly. His boys on line curiously stared on.

"Tyrone." Terry murmured.

"Yeah, mutha-fucka', it's me. Where you been and where the fuck is my money?" Tyrone shouted.

"Look. I ran into some problems." He tried to explain.

I was dumbfounded. How did Tyrone know Terry? I thought. They both went to separate schools and every time I was around Tyrone with Jakim, I'd never seen Terry hanging around.

Terry looked scared shitless as he stood standing in front of Tyrone. His movements made him look so pussy. He looked over at his boys. He glanced over at me, and I looked confused just like everyone else that was around.

"Tyrone, look..."

"Shut the fuck up!" Tyrone screamed out.

He stared into Terry's eyes without even blinking.

"Tyrone, I, man, you see what happened was..." He didn't even get to finish his sentence. Tyrone knocked him across his head with his closed fist, causing Terry to stumble back against the table. Everyone's attention was now on the situation. Tyrone then pulled out a gun and started pistol-whipping him in front of my eyes.

"Tyrone, what the fuck are you doing?" I shouted.

He paid me no attention. Terry's boys tried to rush over to his aid, but when Tyrone turned around and pointed the gun at them, they all froze in their tracks.

"What the fuck y'all gonna do? Help out your pussy ass boy?" He shouted, with the gun aimed directly at them.

Everyone in the place started to panic. Some people ran out of the restaurant, while others ducked behind tables and counters. Terry's boys didn't know what to do as they stared down the barrel in terror. I was in the same shock. I just stood there and watched one of my ex-boyfriends get beat down by someone I was fucking. Terry lay across the table, beaten and bleeding.

He looked helpless.

Tyrone then went over to Terry and continued to terrorize him. He pushed the barrel of the gun to his temple and threatened to shoot him if he didn't come up with his money soon. Terry begged for his life.

"I'm giving you until next week. I want my fuckin' money, or I'm gonna blow your fuckin' brains out." Tyrone shouted.

He then shoved Terry down to the floor. Terry looked up at me, his eye was badly bruised and closed. His nose looked like it was broken and blood covered his mouth, chin and neck. He was a fuckin' mess.

"C'mon, Shana." Tyrone yelled, grabbing me by my arm. I stood there, contemplating if should I get in the car with him. He called for me again. "C'mon Shana, get in the fuckin' car."

I was so scared. I thought about poor Terry. I felt sorry for him. What has he gotten himself into? Back in high school he was such a nice guy. Now he was getting tormented and beat down by a street thug. A street thug that I was having sex with on a regular basis. Terry was on the Varsity football team and was voted the most likely to succeed. He was even on the debate team. Now his life was looking like shit.

Tyrone blew the horn repeatedly. I could hear sirens in the distance. I wanted to help and comfort Terry, but my mind was telling me to get in the car with Tyrone. I looked around nervously.

"Shana, if you don't get your fuckin' ass in this car, then I'm gone, bitch."

I needed to leave the scene. I couldn't afford to stay and hang around not knowing what I was getting myself into. The cops might arrest me, thinking that I was somehow associated with what just happened to Terry. They might want to interrogate me.

I jumped into the car. Tyrone sped off down the street. He didn't even give me the chance to shut the door properly. For the next ten minutes, he drove like a mad man, doing eighty on the side streets until he hit the parkway. He remained quiet. He didn't even look at me or try to explain what happened until we were a few miles away. I wanted to say something, but I kept my mouth shut.

"You love me?" He suddenly blurted out.

My eyes got big as I glanced over at him. What the fuck was he talking about? I thought. He wasn't going to explain what just happened? He just beat my ex-boyfriend nearly to death with me standing there. What was with this you love me question? I kept my mouth shut. I couldn't answer him. I was scared to.

He sped down the Belt Parkway. I had my hands folded in my lap. I wanted to say something, but I didn't.

"Look, I'm sorry about what happened back there, but that was just business. Don't let it interfere with what we have. You cool?" He asked, actually sounding concerned.

Then he rested his hand on my thigh and started to massage it lightly.

"I'm cool." I quietly said to him.

He gave me a quick smile. I felt really uncomfortable. I didn't move his hand off my thigh even though I wanted to. He started to slide his hand in between my legs but that's where I stopped him.

"C'mon Tyrone, you expect me to be feeling romantic after what just happened?"

"Shana, don't worry about what happened back there, that's my business." He said.

"I used to go out with him, did you know that?" I asked.

He slowed the car down. "You were fucking that asshole?"

"It was a long time ago. How do you know Terry?" I asked. I couldn't hold the question any longer. I needed to know.

"Look, all you need to know is that we did business together and he owes me a lot of money."

Tyrone wasn't big about giving out information or letting you know his business. He was a very discreet niggah. As I recall from Jakim, he would disappear for days, maybe weeks at a time, and you wouldn't know anything about his whereabouts. He would just suddenly turn up in the neighborhood again with no explanation. He put fear into a lot of niggah's hearts. The man was only twenty-two, with a decent size bank account, his own crib and driving a fancy car. He was both feared and respected by everybody he came into contact with.

I couldn't turn myself away from him. Even after tonight, I knew that I was going to still be involved with him. He was like a drug and Tyrone was my supplier. I knew he could become violent at times, it came with the job—it was the way he was. But he never flipped on me, and that was the main point. Even when I was with Jakim, and he was around, he always treated me kind and with respect. To be honest, I wanted to get with Tyrone before I ever got involved with Jakim. But Jakim and I hooked up, and I let my little crush on Tyrone fade away—until now.

Tyrone said he preferred that we drop the subject and just forget about it—what was done, was done. So like his bitch, I remained quiet and dropped it. He didn't give a fuck about me once dating Terry. We left it at that. My fear then turned into lust for the man. He could definitely hold it down.

We parked in front of my crib for a few minutes, where he tongue-kissed me goodnight. I stepped out of his car. Once inside I took a quick shower and went straight to bed.

It's been three days since Tyrone beat down Terry in the all night Burger joint. I kept the incident a secret to myself, telling no one about it. Yesterday, Tyrone surprised me with a gift. He bought me a diamond bracelet from Tiffany's in Manhattan. I nearly cried when he clamped it around my wrist. He refused to tell me the price of the bracelet.

I flaunted the expensive bracelet in front of Naja and Latish . We were over Naja's crib, chilling and playing cards. Naja lived with her man Bosco. He was one of Tyrone's business associates. Naja liked the bracelet so much, that she said she was going to press Bosco into buying her one. He was making enough cash to afford it.

"So what's up with you and Jakim now?" Latish asked.

"What do you mean what's up with me and him? We're still cool." I responded.

"But I thought you were planning on getting back together with him?" Naja added.

"Please, girl.... Jakim can wait it out a little while longer...it's my decision." I said.

"Why you messing with that boys head? Shana, you know he loves you and you're out fucking his man. That's some cold shit." Latish said.

"First of all, Latish, he fucked up with me and I'll give my pussy to whoever I wish. Jakim don't own this." I said, pointing down to my shit, "this is my treasure. I was just loaning it to him."

"Now you know you're frontin'." Naja said loudly, "Jakim had you in love. It was always Jakim this, Jakim that. I love me some Jakim. Your relationship was like an emotional roller coaster."

"Please, ain't like y'all never cried over no dick." I said.

"Yeah, I be crying." Latish said, "when that dick be hitting the spot just the right way."

Naja and I started to laugh, as we slapped each other five.

"Yo, I got this niggah named, Bent. They call him that because when he gets hard, his shit bends three inches to the side, looks like he got a hook at the end of his shit, but anyway, he could work some mutha-fuckin' pussy girl." Latish said. "That niggah be hooking on to my shit, and starts to drag me all across the room with his hook dick."

"You are so stupid." Naja said.

"So, Shana, let me ask you a personal question, who got a bigger dick, Jakim or Tyrone?" Latish asked.

I hesitated to answer.

"Yeah, for real, whose is bigger?" Naja wanted to know.

"Why y'all wanna be all up in a girl's business." I said to them. "They're both big."

"Tyrone!" They both said.

"What makes you think its Tyrone?" I curiously asked.

"Because, I can see it in your eyes--plus you ain't gotta answer. The way you've been carrying on about Tyrone, I'm surprise you just don't marry the man and have his babies." Naja said.

"And leave a fine man like Jakim out in the cold, girl you must be crazy. You gonna fuck around and have some other hoe pick up your leftovers, Shana." Latish cautioned.

I couldn't trust Latish around any of my men. She would fuck them in a heartbeat. It made me wonder how I managed to befriend her and stay cool with her for so long. I still had my doubts about her and Jakim being together. Sometimes, the way she looked at me made me feel uncomfortable, like she knew something I didn't.

"Shana, what's the deal with you and Sasha? Y'all been friends for so long, ever since the eighth grade." Latish suddenly bought up.

"Fuck her!" was my answer to her.

"I heard she tried to cut you." Naja said.

"Yeah, on Jamaica Ave a few weeks back. Can you believe that shit? She's gonna get hers one day." I said.

"Well I saw her the other day in the mall with some guy. She told me that you actually started the whole thing." Latish said.

"You gonna believe that bitch's lies?" I responded. "She set me up with the most ugliest person y'all could think of and expected to me to be on my best behavior. That bitch knows my standards. Then she had the nerve to beef about it in front of my crib the next day and shit. So I had to slap her!"

"Y'all just need to kiss and make up." Naja said.

"Can we just drop the conversation about that dumb bitch. Damn, don't stress it, just fuck that bitch and let it be!" I yelled.

The both of them just stared at me.

We went back to playing cards. The room was silent for a quick minute. They were a upset about my outburst.

"Look, I'm sorry about my reaction. Y'all know that y'all are still my girls." I apologized.

They smiled, and we got back into our friendly game of cards and girl talk.

The next morning, I got a call from Jakim. He wanted me to accompany him down to the studio in Flatbush, Brooklyn. He practically begged for me to come. I looked at the time. It was going on eleven. He said he would be here around one to pick me up.

I heard a knock on my bedroom door. My Aunt Tina peeped her head into my room. "Wake up sleepy head." She said.

"What you want?" I asked.

"What you doing tonight?" She asked.

"Why you wanna know?"

"Because, I got tickets to the Baller's Jam at the Convention Club in Manhattan for tonight."

"Say word!" I hollered, jumping out of my bed and running up to her. "That shit's been sold out for weeks, how the fuck did you get them?"

"I got my ways girl."

She definitely did!

Every major playa in the city was going to be there tonight. The girls and I have been trying to call up for tickets for weeks now and been unsuccessful. They announced that artists from Def Jam, Arista, Bad Boy and Death row were going to be attending this party. So you know I had to be up in the joint somehow.

I wanted to kiss my Aunt.

"So, you rolling tonight or what?"

Like she had to ask. I never gave it a second thought. Of course I was going. My Aunt had her ways in getting things. She didn't care whose dick she had to suck or who she had to fuck. She knew what she had between her legs was precious and she used it to her advantage--making these men out here buy, beg borrow and steal for her. I wondered why she was still living with my moms and me when all she had to do was fuck the right man and have him buy her a house. I remember this one Italian guy who owned his own car dealership. He owned ten different lots in eight major cities across the country. He bought her a brand new car, a white BMW 740IL, a $53,000 car. She crashed it in three weeks, totaled the car. She suffered a fractured hip, sprained ankle and a few cuts and bruises. Her friend Ebony, who was also in the car, came out with minor injuries. Eddie, her boyfriend at the time wanted to kill her. Needless to say, they broke up and he ended up paying for all the damages. The car, the insurance, everything was in his name.

My Aunt fucked up big time with that one, but she recovered and moved on to the next luxury dick. During the three weeks she had that car, we used to have a ball driving around. She even let me push the car twice.

"Be ready by eight, James is coming to pick us up at nine." She said.

"How many are going?"

"Just you and me."

Damn, I wish I could have bought Naja and Latish with me. None the clothes in my closet weren't going to cut it for tonight. I needed something special that was an eye catcher and sexy as hell. Something that would have all the males at that party craving to holler at me. I needed to get my hair done too. I knew Sandra would hook me up and fit me into her busy schedule. She was my home girl. She would definitely look out. She works at a hair salon on Merrick Blvd. It was eleven thirty and there were a lot of things I had to rush and get done before I went to this party.

I called up Sandra and explained my situation. She told me to come in around five. She wasn't too busy around that time. I needed to go shopping. I only had two-hundred dollars and the other day, I saw this phat dress in Macy's in Green Acres Mall. The price tag was $350, and I needed an extra $65 for Sandra to do my hair, not to mention, spending money for tonight. Although I can always con some guy into buying me drinks, it's good to have your own little cash stashed away just for emergencies.

Damn, why did my Aunt tell me she had tickets to this event so late. Now I had to run around and get things done like a chicken with its head cut off. I could ask my moms, Danny was always giving her loot or I could ask him myself. I knew he was here, I saw his jeep parked outside. Then I thought about Tyrone, I knew he would front me the cash, but how long would it take for him to get over here? Plus, I really didn't feel like seeing him. He might try to mess up my plans.

I took a quick shower and thought about my options. I've decided to ask Danny. I stepped out of the shower and wrapped a towel around myself. I walked into the living room skin glistening from the water and my hair still wet. I remember Jakim once told me that a female looks her best when taking a shower. He said watching me used to turn him on. We would then fuck on the bathroom floor..

I wanted to see if my being wet, coming out of the shower would have the same effect on Danny as it did on Jakim.

He was on the couch watching TV. I stood in front of him.

"Where's my mother?" I asked, feeling his eyes studying every inch of my body.

"She's in the bedroom." He said with his sexy voice.

I walked towards the bedroom, peeked in and saw that my mother was still asleep. I smiled and softly shut the door. My eyes made their way back to Danny. His eyes never left my body. He played it cool though. I wanted him to fuck me so bad, that it hurt.

"Danny, I need a favor from you." I said so soothingly.

"What is it, baby girl?" He asked.

I took a seat next to him on the couch still wrapped tightly in the towel and placed my hand on his lap. The towel stopped mid thigh. I gazed into his eyes. "I need to borrow three hundred dollars."

"That's a small favor." He responded.

He reached into his pocket and pulled out a wad of hundreds. I tried to keep cool, but being next to him with all that money in his hand combined with the fact that he looked so good, nearly made me lose control and jump his dick. I wanted to take him into my mouth, suck him so good, he'll forget about my mother and work his miracles on me. I wanted to drop this towel to the floor and show him how young and lovely my body was. A view of my body did wonders for all of my old boyfriends, they never got tired of it. I only got tired of them.

"Here you go, baby girl." He said, handing me four hundred dollars. "Here's an extra hundred just in case."

God, I hated my mother for having such a wonderful and fine man. He could hit this morning, noon and night! I gave him a quick kiss on his cheek, and then got up from the couch. I slowly strolled down the hall to my bedroom, then I did the craziest thing, I dropped the towel down to the floor, giving Danny a clear glimpse of me from the back, butt naked. I bent over to pick up the towel with my legs parted slightly and retreated to my bedroom. I didn't even turn around to see his reaction. I already knew his reaction.

Who needed a job, when I was getting dollars from the fellas? I threw on my black Guess jeans, my blue and gray George-Town sweater and my fresh new beige Timberlands. I wrapped my hair into a ponytail, put on a little lip gloss. Then I called Naja to see if she wanted to go to the mall to do a little Saturday afternoon shopping. I called Tyrone, but he wasn't home. I paged him but he never returned it.

At 12:30, the doorbell rang, it was Jakim. I had totally forgotten about promising him that I would go down to the studio and chill for the day. I'd gotten so excited about the party tonight. He stood in front of the door and asked, "You ready to go?"

"Shit, Jakim...I forgot about this afternoon." I said.

"What you mean you forgot about this afternoon. I just spoke to you a couple of hours ago." He sounded pissed.

"Yeah, but something came up."

"Like what?"

I turned around and saw that Danny was all in our business, so I calmly stepped outside and shut the door.

"Look, Jakim, I'd promised my Aunt that I would help her with something today. She just reminded me about it after I hung up with you."

"That's some cold shit, Shana. You got me all excited about spending the day with you, now you wanna blow me off to go and hang out with your Aunt?"

"It ain't even like that, Jakim."

"Why you're doing this to me? Why are you playing me?"

"I'm not doing this on purpose." I gently said.

Then it came to me. He could take me shopping. I knew he wanted to go down to the studio and all, but with the right encouragement, that can easily change. I pressed myself softly against him and gave him a sweet and gentle kiss on his lips.

"Look Baby...you want to hang out with me today?" I said sweetly in his ear.

"You know I do, Shana." He spoke back.

To put my plan into effect. I licked the corner of his ear, then whispered, "Can you ride me around then? I need to take care of a few things." I placed my hand over his heart and felt it beating rapidly. I knew the ear thing would excite him.

"But I was planning on going down to the studio today." He said.

"Well can it wait?" I asked, snuggling up to him. "I need a ride, baby." I added.

I could feel him caving in, so I turned up the pressure by cupping my hand over his dick and whispered softly in his ear, "You miss my lovin' boo? Do me this favor and I promise tomorrow night, it will all be back to you...with interest."

"How long you gonna be?" He asked.

"Does it matter? You're gonna be spending the day with me."

"Alright, then, let me make this quick run to Greg's crib, get my shit and I'll be right back."

"Don't take too long."

He rushed to his car, hard as a rock. He was still my heart. I watched him pull off, then turned around to go back inside. That's when I saw Danny peeping at me through the window. I walked back in the house and headed towards my room. Danny's eyes were on me the whole time.

Around two, Jakim came back around to pick me up. We went straight to the mall, where I picked up this phat Matte jersey dress. I also picked up some shoes. Jakim shopped around with me. He also helped me pick out a few things. He even took me out to get something to eat. By the time we were done, it was going on four o'clock. I still had a five o clock appointment at the hair salon.

"Shana, you must think that I'm stupid." He blurted out as he drove down Sunrise Highway.

Stunned by his words, I gazed at him and asked, "What?"

"You're doing all of this shopping and shit. Now you're about to go and get your hair done. Who you seeing tonight?"

"What are you talking about, Jakim? I told you that I'm hanging out with my Aunt tonight."

"You told me she asked you do something for her."

"Yeah, to hang out."

"So you gotta get all dressed up and shit." He responded.

The day was going so good, and now here he comes with this attitude shit. But I promised myself that I wasn't going to get upset today, especially over no bullshit. I glanced out of the car window, then turned to Jakim and flipped the script, "Look, mutha-fucka', did you or did you not forget that we are separated, as in no longer together, apart. I can see or fuck whomever I want! So don't step to me with your bullshit attitude worrying about my business. You ain't see me all up in your business when you was fucking that big headed bimbo down the block. Don't think I don't know."

He gripped the steering wheel and said, "Look, Shana, all I'm saying is stop teasing me. I'm sorry about that, but I feel that I've been punished too long for it. I'm no fucking puppet. You just can't keep stringing me along whenever you feel like it. Shit, you always talk about your feelings. What about mine?"

I didn't even answer him because I'd promised myself not to get upset. I calmly looked over at Jakim, as he focused his eyes on the road. He was looking as cute as ever, slanted back in his seat, one hand on the steering wheel just pimping it. "Jakim, I will always love you, no matter what. I just need some time to myself. I'm not going to lie to you, yes I'm seeing other people. Maybe someday we'll get back together, and maybe we won't. But we'll have to let time tell." I said it so smooth and so calm.

"Well, I'm still in love with you, Shana, and I'm still missing you. If we can't be lovers, then I feel that we can't be friends."

The rest of the ride to the hair salon was mostly quiet, small talk here and there. I told him to just drop me off and I'll catch a cab home, no telling how long I was going to be there.

When I walked into the salon, there were about six girls inside and only four ladies doing hair. I saw my girl, Sandra, finishing up one of her client's. She waved at me, and I walked over to her.

"What's up girl?" She hollered.

"Nothing. What's up with you?"

We gave each other hugs and then I took a seat in the empty chair next to her. It took her ten more minutes to finish the lady's hair, and then she got started on mine. I just wanted it straight and permed. We gossiped while she worked on my hair. She was telling me what was going on around the way and with her life. She dumped her man, who she's been with for six years. She found him cheating on her with her cousin, who he'd gotten pregnant. Damn, talk about drama.

"I whooped that bitch's ass, Shana. How she gonna play me like that and fuck my man behind my fucking back?" She asked.

"I would've killed the bitch." I said just to have something to say.

Sandra always had news or dirt on other people. That was one of the main reasons I went to her, to get the low down on other people. She also brought up my little beef with Sasha, wondering what was going on with that. I explained to her what, when and how it went down. She was 100% on my side.

"She was in here the other day." Sandra informed me.

"Fuck that bitch." I blurted out.

I was done around a quarter to seven. I paid Sandra her usual fee, tipping her a twenty on the side. We gave each other hugs and promised to hook up some night and go out to the club. Then I called a cab.

Around eight, I was dressed and ready to go to The Baller's Jam. I was looking so fly in my new dress. It showed every curve of my phenomenal body. My butt was looking too good from the back, it was like an onion, guaranteed to make a niggah cry. I moved my hands over my body and stared in the mirror.

"Girl, you is looking too good." I praised myself.

I looked at the time. It was eight-thirty. I was home alone, waiting for my Aunt to arrive with her date. I sat quietly on the living room couch watching television. Naja gave me a call, and I told her of my plans for tonight. She was hating. She wanted me to beg my Aunt for another ticket, but I told her that I'd received the last one. Tyrone called too, but I didn't pick up the phone. He left a message.

It was ten after nine when my Aunt Tina came to get me. Her date was driving a black Hummer. She was dressed in a beige leather mini skirt and a blue sheer mesh shirt.

"Shana, you ready?" She hollered for me.

"Been ready." I said.

I met her date outside. He wasn't all that cute, but you could work with him. He was stocky, about 5'8, with a thick beard and two gold earrings. He had braids and sported a very nice gray Italian suit. His name was Kendell. He was an A&R for Arista records.

We arrived at the Baller's Jam a little after ten. The crowd outside was ridiculous. Every style and make of luxury car was parked out on the street. Lexus', Benz, BMW's, Porsches, town cars and stretch limousines as far as the eye can see. Everyone tried to get in. They even tried to rush the door, but security was strapped and not having it.

We drove by a barricade for VIP only. We got out the Hummer and Kendell escorted us to a private entrance. He gave several people dap as we passed, letting us know he was well known.

"Damn!" I heard someone shout out. I knew they were talking about me.

We enter the party, and the first person that I bump into, is Nas. He's standing there with a bottle of Crystall in his hand. My eyes light up with excitement. Ohmigod! He is too fine.

My Aunt notices him too, and she comes trotting over with excitement asking for an autograph. I tell you, Latish and Naja would be hating right now if they knew that I ran into Nas. Aunt Tina is all over him, smiling and flirting, and I'm standing off to the side thinking, what a groupie she is.

The place is jammed pack with celebrities, athletes, fans, groupies, managers and producers. The DJ is rocking the house. Kendell buys me a drink. I stare into the room. There were so many fine men in the house, I felt like a child in a candy factory.

"Can I buy you another drink?" A fine gentleman asked. He was dressed down in Armani, had short curly hair, and was fine enough to be related to Denzel Washington, my future husband. He just didn't know it yet. He had gorgeous brown eyes and the softest looking lips.

"It depends." I softly said.

"Depends on what?" He asked.

"Depends on if you tell me your name."

"Barry…Barry Jones." He introduced himself, taking the half-finished glass of Alize out of my hand and placing it down on the bar. "Let's get rid of this old drink, and allow me to order you a fresh one."

He ordered my drink and paid the bartender. He then escorted me over to the VIP area, where Puff Daddy was sitting down at a table.

"So, I never caught your name." he said.

"That's because I never threw it at you."

"So, are you going to pitch it to me before this party is over?"

I paused, gazed into his lovely brown eyes, while wondering how big his dick was, "Its Shana." I told him.

"You are beautiful, Shana. Have you ever thought about a career in the entertainment industry?"

"No, not really."

"Well, if you do, here's my card." He said, placing it into my hands, "I'm a music manager." He added.

I stuffed it into my purse and sipped on my drink. We talked and danced for about an hour. Eventually he asked me back to the hotel. He said it had a Jacuzzi, 24hour room service and satin sheets. It was tempting, but I declined.

Aunt Tina was having a good old time. Men were approaching her left and right. She must have forgot that she came with a date.

By two, I felt so exhausted that I took a seat in one of the lounging chairs and nearly fell asleep. I had danced and talked to so many men that I could barely keep my eyes open.

I felt someone plop down on the seat next to me. It was Kendell. He sat down next to me hunched over resting his elbow on his thighs.

"Shana, what's up after the party?" He asked.

"Huh?"

"A couple of the fellas are throwing a little after party at the Sheraton, and they want you to roll along."

I gave him a blank stare. He placed his hand on my lap and just let it rest there like it was a fuckin' truck stop. I glanced around for my Aunt, but she was nowhere in my sight.

"So, you rollin' with us or what?" Something in his tone told me to turn this offer down.

"Nah, Kendell, I'm gonna pass. I'm tired." I explained.

He gave me a disappointed look, and grasped my leg even tighter, rubbing my inner thighs with his fingers. I saw him look over at one of his homies as he gave him a nod.

"But yo, mad heads are rollin' with us, including your Aunt. I'm saying, we got like fifty people coming. We got the liquor, the weed, and the music."

He moved his hand slightly up my inner thigh, creeping his fingers near my precious Kitty Kat. "Kendell, do I look like one of these groupies to you?" I blurted out.

He gave me a smug look. "Nah, Shana, why you ask that?"

"Cause you got your hand on my thigh, reaching for my shit like I owe you something. So I would appreciate it if you move your hand from off my fucking thigh."

He slowly moved it away, carefully, so he wouldn't look like a fool in front of his boys. If he 'd jerked it away too fast, then his boys would know I shot his ass down. "And no, I'm not rolling to no hotel with y'all." I added.

There was a slight pause as he looked at me. By the expression on his grill, I knew he wasn't too happy with my little answer. Before he got up, he whispered in my ear, "If you ain't rollin', then take the subway home stupid bitch!" Then he got his ass off the couch and walked over to one of his boys.

No he didn't, I thought. I really wanted to slap the shit out of that ignorant mutha-fucka', I didn't give a flying fuck who he was. That mutha-fucka did not have the right to disrespect me.

I was ready to go home. I got up, and searched for my Aunt. What Kendell said to me got me too fuckin' upset. I was about ready to fight up in here.

I saw my Aunt standing next to Kendell, arm in arm. My face screwed up. I quickly step over to her and that bastard. His boys were also standing around. They saw me coming over and started smiling from ear to ear.

"I see you changed your mind." Kendell's ignorant ass said.

"No, fuck you, I came over to get my Aunt." I said, pulling her to the side.

"What's da matter?" My Aunt asked.

"Your new man's a dick head, and I'm about ready to leave."

"But I'm about to go over to the after party with Kendell." she said. "Plus, he's our ride home."

"Fuck him Aunt Tina. I'll take the subway home." I shouted out loud enough for that asshole to hear.

He gave me a dumb smirk, standing and drinking next to his whack ass crew. They thought that they were the shit.

"I'm not taking the subway." Aunt Tina stated.

"Kendell tried to hit on me." I said.

"Shana, stop lying! Why you gotta hate on me because my man got money and can get us into fine places? Every niggah in da world don't want you."

I was in shock! Did this niggah brainwash her? Kendell and his crew heard my Aunt's words and were in their little huddle laughing at me. I was furious. I could kill that muthafucka.

"I'm going with Kendell, you can leave by yourself, if you want to." She said.

I wanted to smack her, for being so naïve and stupid. She gets a rich piece of dick and starts to think that muthafucka is gonna treat her like she's the Queen of England. She was better off with her past losers.

She strolled her sorry ass back over to Kendell. They started drinking, laughing and carrying on. Kendell threw his arm around my Aunt and flipped me the bird. My temper was at its highest point. It was all good.

I went over and retrieved someone's unfinished drink from the bar. I walked towards Kendell. He stared at me. I stood directly in front of him, while he was standing beside my Aunt.

"If you got something to say, then say it you dumb bastard."

"Get away from me you dumb bitch." He said.

I threw the drink in his face and slapped him across the face so hard everyone around heard it. "Who's looking like the dumb bitch now?" I shouted.

"Shana!" My Aunt shouted.

Kendell wiped the drink off his face, looking shocked as hell. His boys chuckled and stared at me. They knew what time it was. My Aunt tried to help and clean him up, at the same time looking over at me, stunned. I flipped her the bird and stormed out of the place, hearing Kendell cursing and hollering. That made me feel so fucking good.

I took the subway home that night, even though I had ten offers from guys willing to take me. I wasn't feeling the male attention. I had enough for the night.

I arrived home around four in the morning. There was a message on the answering machine, I pressed the speaker button to hear.

"Hello, Shana, it's Naja, sorry I'm calling so late, but I thought you might want to hear this as soon as possible...Terry's dead, they found his body last night. Call me when you get this."

I stood there. I had to replay the message to be clear if I heard her right. One of my ex-boyfriends was dead. First the incident with that asshole at the club, now coming home to hear someone you knew and cared for—was dead.

Terry was dead!

SPANKY
8

At eleven-o clock at night, I found myself driving around searching for a prostitute. I was so fuckin' horny. I was in the Bronx over by Hunts Point. A co-worker from my job told me about this place. One day at work a few males were in a huddle discussing females and pussy. They were all bragging about how much pussy they were getting and exchanging great sex stories. Here I was, with no story to brag about. But I smiled, and still slapped fives with the fellas, frontin'. I was weak in the jeans, with two bitches under my belt. And the two that I had under my belt were only five minutes combined. I couldn't brag about that shit.

The fellas in the office were just running their mouths. One dude said he was fuckin' this one bitch for so long, that his dick became numb. Another said that he fucked this bitch for three hours straight and made her have multiple orgasms. They talked about getting blowjobs and fucking bitches in public places.

The two that had a lot to tell, were Michael and Johnny. They were bragging like they experienced it all, fucked in every position in every place and that they had had every female from every race. Michael even bought Carla's name into the conversation. He bragged about how close he came to hittin' that one night. That was one story that the fellas couldn't believe. He tried to go into detail, but they weren't hearing that.

I never felt so fuckin' envious in my life. My Johnson was as dry as a 100-year-old nun. When they asked if I had anything to say, I buckled and told them that I had to use the rest room. I wanted to have great sex too. I wanted to brag about it to the fellas. It was bad enough that I had to hear this from Limp, Clarke, Tommy and the rest, now I was hearing this shit at work. I was a fuckin' embarrassment to myself and my dick. I wouldn't be surprised if it packed up and left me because I wasn't feeding him properly. All I did was jerk my shit off almost every night. And I was getting tired of doing that. I needed a woman so fuckin' bad, that I was willing to drive way out to the Bronx and pay for one.

I was driving down Hunts Point Ave waiting to come across one. I was already hard knowing what I was about to do. The streets looked quiet, a few people here and there. I continue to drive around in search of a hooker. I was so horny, that I pulled my dick out and started masturbating. My eyes diverted left to right, carefully searching down every street and dark corner seeing if I could spot out one. I saw two fat ladies in spandex standing in front of a bodega. Good lord, I hope they ain't working, I thought to myself. It was horrible just thinking about it.

I saw one cutie standing alone. She had on a brown leather jacket, some nice tight jeans, and her hair pinned up in a bun. She was Spanish, with a phat ass. I got excited, slowed the car and rolled my window down. She glanced over at me. I was nervous. Before I could say anything, a man came from around the corner, hugging up on her.

I was getting desperate and it was getting late. Shit, I was getting so desperate that I was about to roll back over to where I saw them two nasty fat bitches, and ask how much?. My man from work told me that this was the spot to go to if you wanted some pussy. But I couldn't find a hoe in sight. Maybe because it was cold out. But I refuse to give up the search. I circled around the neighborhood for ten minutes.. If I couldn't find a hoe soon, then I was going to park this car, and beat off my shit. I made a quick U-turn and headed back towards the highway. I was just throbbing for some pussy. Just when I was about to give it up, I glanced to my right and saw this woman walking in the street. She was in a brown mini skirt, some stiletto heels, and a short brown leather jacket. She looked like a hooker to me. I put the car in reverse and backed up. I was nervous as hell. She stood half way in the street, waiting for a date. When I was near her, I shouted, "Hey, how you're doing?"

She peered into the car, squinting her eyes to see who I was. She came closer to my vehicle, hunched over and asked, "You looking for a date, Sweetie?"

I nodded my head.

"It's twenty for a blow and forty for sex. If you want both, then it's fifty-five."

I made the suggestion for her to get in. I definitely wanted a date tonight. She quickly glanced around, and then hopped into my ride. I too glanced around and saw no one in sight. I put the car in drive and drove forward. She was brown skinned with big luscious lips, good for sucking dick, I thought but had no way of knowing.

"So, what is it that you're looking for, a suck or a fuck?" She asked.

"How about, both?"

"Aw'ght, then that's fifty-five."

"Is there anywhere we can go to?"

"If you want to go do this in a motel, then that's a hundred and ten, sweetie. If that's too much, then there's an alley just around this corner here, it's dark and it's quiet."

I knew that I wasn't paying a $110 for no motel, so the alley was my best choice. I agreed, and she directed me to the place. I made a left, drove three blocks down until we came up to the alley, and she was right, it was definitely dark. It also looked dangerous, but even danger couldn't stop me now.

I made a left turn and drove to the end of the alley. There were three abandon cars on the block and one gray van that looked empty. I parked the car in a dark place, not wanting to be seen by anyone. But the smell of garbage almost made it hard for me to do my thing.

"That'll be fifty-five." She said, waiting for me to hand her the money so we can get down to it.

I reached into my pocket and pulled out three twenties, passing it over to her in her hand. She checked each twenty, like it was counterfeit money or something. She then stashed the loot into her purse.

"What about my change?" I asked.

"I don't have any change on me." She said annoyed.

"But you said fifty-five, I gave you sixty."

"Sweetie, you wanna argue about five dollars, or do you want to fuck me?" She said, lifting her hips and pulling up her mini skirt. She wore no panties underneath. Her shit was clean-shaven down below, not one piece of pubic hair visible. My mouth watered and my dick got hard again. She unzipped my pants and pulled them down around my ankles.

"I see you're ready to go." She said.

Just feeling her hands around my dick made me want to explode. She gripped it with force and put her lips to my dick. Her mouth felt so warm. She sucked and stroked me at the same time, making my shit harder. I gripped the back of the passenger seat, I knew it was coming, I pleaded for it not to happen so soon. Her head proceeded to bob up and down, sucking me like she was born to do this. I wanted to cry it felt so good.

I looked at my watch, and so far it has only been a minute. I tried to hold on, I tried, but with her big lips around my dick, in no time I exploded into her jaws. I quivered, grabbing the back of her head, shaking my dick into her mouth.

"Damn, you're fast." She stated. "But that's how I like them' nice and quick."

I couldn't feel any more embarrassed than I already was. I paid her fifty-five for a blowjob and a fuck, and I couldn't even get past the first stage. She stood up and fixed her clothes.

"I'm saying, I didn't get to fuck you, so I should get at least thirty back."

"It doesn't work that way, sweetie." She said.

It was a waste of time and money. I came out here to fuck, and was unsuccessful in doing that. There was nothing that I could do about it. I was too pussy to even attempt to snatch my dough from her and jet, leaving her stranded in the alley.

I cried in the car on my way home.

The next morning, I heard laugher and two women's voices coming from downstairs in the kitchen. Curious to see who was in the house, I took a quick shower and threw on my bathrobe. I walked into the kitchen, stunned to see Adina and my mother cooking breakfast together.

"You're finally up sleepy head." My mother nagged.

"Hi, Jamal." Adina said.

"Why are you here?" I asked.

"Jamal, she's my guest. She's helping me prepare breakfast. You got a problem with that?"

"No."

"All right. Adina put those biscuits in the oven for me, baby."

I just went back upstairs into my bedroom. Adina was in my home chilling with my moms, but it wasn't anything new to me. We practically grew up together. I've known Adina since the second grade. Her moms was really strict and kept her daughter on lockdown. But since her moms and my moms were really good friends, she would let her daughter come over to play. We were tight until we started junior high school, that's when being cool and popular really mattered.

During the end of seventh grade, my friends started teasing me because I used to hang out with her. They said she was the ugliest thing in the school. I would argue and fight with them, until one day I got tired of standing up and protecting Adina's name. Adina and I went our different ways. Some days I would join in with my friends and joke on her, but it was because I was trying to fit in. I really didn't mean it. She felt betrayed and met up with me one day after school and cursed me out. I just told her to stay the fuck away from me. From that day on we were in our own different worlds. In high school, she was treated like an outcast. They taunted, teased, and even tried to jump on her, but she kept her spirits up and her mind strong. Adina graduated from high school with a 4.0 GPA and a full scholarship.

My moms came up to my room to tell me that breakfast was ready. I went downstairs and saw that Adina was still present in my home. She was taking the biscuits out of the oven. I grabbed myself a plate.

"Mrs. Day, I have to go now." Adina said, untying her apron.

"You sure you don't want to stay for breakfast, I mean we cooked plenty." My mother offered.

"No, that's Okay. I told my mother that I would help her clean the attic."

"Ok, but you know that you're always welcome here. Don't be a stranger." My moms said, escorting Adina to the door.

I could finally eat my breakfast in peace.

My mother came back into the kitchen, smiling and saying, "Jamal, That's a very nice girl. Whatever happened between y'all two? I mean y'all used to be such good friends."

"I moved on, mom."

"Um, um, whatever. You sure none of your friends got nothing to do with it."

"Man, my friends are cool." I replied.

"She is a very sweet and lovely young woman. She's going to make something out of her life one day. Yeah, she may be a little on the weird side, but I would rather have a weird woman, than a stupid one."

"Good for you mom."

"Oh, I forgot, you like them young, sexy, stupid and voluptuous. You want to marry a woman for her body and her looks, not her personality and attitude."

"Whoever said that I was getting married?"

"Jamal, wake up, If I was you, I would push up on that…."

"And think about how your grandkids are going to turn out…just as ugly and weird as she is."

"My grandkids would be respectable and intelligent with manners. Not one of these hoodlum thugs or sluts running out in these streets, having sex twenty-four seven and shooting everything up. Adina would make a great mother to her kids. Look at your father, he was one of these pretty, playboy, sweet-talking, Mac daddies, with the fly car, nice jewelry and stylish looks. I was young and I fell into that. He turned out to be an abuser. He mistreated me. I cried myself to sleep every night when I was with that man. When I was pregnant with you, he would run off and screw every woman he could put his dick into, then would want to come home and beat and mistreat me. He treated me more like a hoe, than his woman. The only thing good that came out of that relationship, was you."

I just sat there, listening to her tell the story about my no good father. Yeah, it made me angry, made me want to go and hunt the man down, but he was still my father.

My moms came over to me and placed her hand on my shoulder. "Jamal, all I'm saying to you, is just be careful out there. Use the condoms I give you, make wise decisions about the women you sleep with. Just because it looks good, doesn't mean it is good. A shell is just a covering, like they say, you can't judge a book by its cover, and you can't judge a good woman by her appearance. You only see Adina for her outer self and what your friends think and see of her. I bet they don't know a damn thing about her. If you keep judging a woman by what your friends think, then you're going to miss out on a lot in life."

My stepfather came trotting into the kitchen, interrupting our conversation. "What's cooking, baby?" He asked. The two of them were so in love. He was the opposite of my father. He wasn't into the exotic cars, jewelry, playing out women or making fast money. He was a hard working, black man, who supported his family the best way he could.

The two of them got to hugging and feeling on each other. I damn near lost my appetite again. I had to take my plate upstairs into my room and eat.

Later that evening, I got a call from Clarke who told me that Tommy was supposed to bring some bitches to his crib later on.

It was Limp, Clarke, Abney, Peter and me chilling down in Clarke's basement. We were watching some lame movie on channel five. For the first time in a while, everyone was quiet. There were no mamma jokes and no pranks. We were all just chilling. I guess everyone was waiting for Tommy to come through with the women. He told Clark that there were about five of them.

"Yo, anybody ever saw these bitches that Tommy is bringing through?" Limp asked.

"Nah, dawg...but you know Tommy stay with dime bitches."

My eyes stayed glued to the TV, as I calculated the math in my head. Five bitches and there would be about six of us. I guess if an orgy got started, someone would be left out.   That somebody would probably be me. For the first time ever, I can say that I was bored. There wasn't any laughter; nobody was bugging out like we usually do when all of us are just chilling. It was just smoking and passing. I was on my third pull, when the doorbell rang.

"Tommy finally showed his ass up. He better have the bitches with him." Limp said.

Clarke took his time getting up from his seat. He passed Peter the L and traveled his high ass up the stairs to answer the door. Everyone else just sat around, quiet and in their own thoughts. I couldn't front, I was excited. After my little escapade last night, I needed a round two to try and redeem myself from the humiliation. I was a one minute brotha' and that was the one thing that bitches didn't tolerate. I needed practice.

"Yo, what's up with that niggah Mark? I ain't seen him in a minute." Abney said.

"That niggah chilling with some new pussy." Peter responded.

Clarke came back down the stairs with Tommy and three bitches that were from Uptown. He was two hoes short. As soon as they entered the basement, all eyes and attention were on them. The three ladies just stood there, quiet and probably waiting to get introduced. Abney started grinning wildly. Peter just sat back on the couch, pimp style; legs spread open, one arm lying across the back of the couch. Limp licked his lips like he was hungry.

"Fellas, what's up?" Tommy shouted, giving everyone high five.

I had to admit that they were cute. They were average height. Two of them had really short haircuts like Halle Berry, and the third had braids. They were all brown skinned; wearing the hell out some tight fitted Guess jeans, and one in particular had the phattest ass on the planet. She caught my attention the most. Their names were Tamika, Monica, and Mindy. Mindy was the one with the phattest ass, and the biggest fuckin' titties. Tommy came through. I knew these bitches were down to get into something tonight. They wouldn't have traveled all the way to Queens if they weren't.

After about twenty minutes, everyone got settled and Clarke rolled up another L.   We smoked, talked, joked, watched television and clowned the night away. The place really livened up after the girls arrived. We started watching porno's and that's when all freakiness broke loose.   The girls didn't mind; they were down for whatever. Abney left, saying that he had things to do, and Peter was damn near falling asleep. He was so high that he took comfort on the floor and shut his eyes.

Tommy was sitting next to Tamika and I was sitting opposite across from Mindy. Clarke supplied the liquor from his grandfather's bar upstairs, and the trees kept on burning. The conversation downstairs soon turned into sex, with **Black Dat Ass Up!**" playing on the tube.   One female was catching it in her butt and her pussy. Then another female was swallowing two dicks into her mouth. I was getting turned on.   Leave it to Limp to say some fucked up shit before the night was over.

"Y'all bitches be doing that shit?" He blurted out.

"No he didn't!" Mindy responded.

"I'm just keeping it real, cause that's how I be." Limp said, high from the weed.

Clarke laughed, and Tommy just shrugged his shoulders. I just looked over at Mindy.

"Do you eat pussy?" Tamika asked Limp.

"Do you suck dick?" Limp asked back.

"Limp chill out." I begged. I didn't want him to get them offended and have them leave. It wasn't supposed to work like that.

"I do whatever I want to do." Tamika said.

"Oh, please, most of y'all bitches be frontin', y'all be saying one thing, then back out of it the next."

"Please mutha-fucka' I ain't even like that. Don't get me confused with those cheap hoes you be fuckin' with out here." Tamika stated.

"Well I know I be going down for mines." Limp added.

I thought that them two were about to start brawling down here. Limp was straight real and always spoke what was on his mind.

"Yo, Spanky, put in another movie." Tommy said, as the one we were watching was about to end.

"That's your movie, Spanky?" Monica teasingly asked.

"Yeah, why?"

"Nuthin' just asking."

I didn't like the way she was asking, like I was some kind of homebody, who stayed home and watched pornos and jerked off all day long. It was only at night. Limp and Tamika engaged more in their conversation. They insulted and teased each other. Both of them had sharp and wicked tongues. I just sat there listening to them. But it was hilarious. Things got really funny when Tamika mentioned if we knew anything about the *rainbow kiss.*

"What the fuck is a rainbow kiss?" Limp asked.

"See, Y'all from Queens, y'all Queens niggahs don't know nuthin' about that." Tamika said. "That's an Uptown thing."

"Please bitch, you ain't test these waters yet." Limp replied.

Tamika rolled her eyes at him and sat back down and crossed her legs.

"So, what is a rainbow kiss?" Clarke asked.

Tamika's girlfriends looked on in curiosity, they too looked like they had no idea what their girlfriend was talking about.

"It's when your man eats you out while you're on your period."

"What the fuck?" Limp shouted.

"That's nasty, bitch!" Clarke said.

"Yo, that ain't freaky, that shit is disgusting." Limp stated.

"You're a sick bitch." Tommy said.

"Please, my ex-man used to do it to me all the time." Tamika said.

"Then that niggah's nasty as you, and y'all both need help. Eating a bitch out while she's on her period. Whoever started that shit needs to get shot." Limp proclaimed.

Tamika flipped him the bird.

"Tamika, then you probably was tasting other bitches periods while why you were with your man." Limp said.

"What you mean?" She asked.

"If your ex-man used to do that shit on you, then you know you probably weren't the first."

The look on her face wasn't too pleasing. "Yo, Spanky, put in another porno, fuckin' bitch talking about rainbow kisses, all y'all Uptown bitches are sick in the head!" Limp shouted.

"Excuse me!" Monica exclaimed.

"You heard me, Monica. Your girl over here talking about rainbow kisses, Queens niggahs don't be doing that shit, that's them Uptown fools coming up with some shit like that."

Tamika sat there and kept her mouth quiet for a while. I guess she was too embarrassed to speak. I placed *"Hella ass 2!"* in the VCR and for the next ten minutes, everyone just sat there quietly and watched the movie.

After about ten minutes, things got crazy again. We were smokin' our fourth maybe fifth joint, and going through the second bottle of Barcardi Limon. The girl's eyes were glued to the screen, as they watched this niggah with an 8" dick ram it into this woman's pussy.

"Damn, he got a big dick." Tamika said smiling.

"Please, bitch, you never probably even had it that big before." Limp said.

"Niggah, you don't know what my pussy be taking in. I don't be fuckin' with tickle dick mutha-fuckas like yourself." She said staring hard at Limp.

Everyone started laughing. Limp just remained seated, cracking a thin smile over at Tamika. I waited. I knew he had to come back.

"Oh, so you calling me a tickle dick." He said, slowly rising up from out of his seat.

"Please, I wonder why they be calling you Limp, is it because you be having a little problem down below in the jeans?" She dissed.

"So, you think that I'm packin' a limp dick?" Limp had his hand on the front of his pants and stood right in front of her. Tamika stared up at him.

"Please, you ain't bout it like that." She said.

"Please, bitch, if I pull out my shit right now, you would be scared to even touch it." He said, still moving in closer towards her. "All y'all bitches do is front!"

"Oh, so you think I be frontin? I'll show you how much I be frontin'." Tamika said, staring up at Limp with a patronizing look

Everyone else was looking on. Were they still bickering at each other, or were they throwing each other subliminal love messages. Limp threw out a quick conniving smile, and then he went and unzipped his shit. He dropped his pants to his ankles and exposed his erect dick. "Go ahead, bitch. Prove to me that you ain't scared to touch it." He spoke.

"Niggah, what the fuck! Nobody wanna see that nasty shit." Clarke shouted.

"Limp, put your clothes back on." Tommy begged.

I just buried my face into my palm and shook my head in disbelief. Mindy and Monica's eyes widened, as they looked on and smiled. Tamika smiles as she leans forward and puts her lips to the tip and starts sucking.

"Say word, your friend is loose like that?" Clarke hollered.

Them two did not give a fuck. Limp had his hands placed on his hips like he was some kind of Superman action figure, and Tamika continued to deep throat that son of a bitch! I didn't know whether to watch the movie on screen or them two. I knew for sure, that I wanted a piece of the action.

For the next five minutes, all eyes and attention were on those two freaks. Watching her suck on his dick made me want to go and try something with Mindy. I just had to try, but I got scared because the fellas were around, and I couldn't humiliate myself in front of them. Tommy placed his hand in between Monica legs and started rubbing his hands up her thighs. She didn't even attempt to stop him. Next thing I knew, her jeans were off and on the floor, and Tommy was eating her out on the couch—that left, Mindy. She just sat there; calm and relaxed, acting like an orgy wasn't taking place around her. Peter finally woke his ass up, and became bug eyed when he saw what was happening.

"What the fuck! Yo, I'm saying, how can a niggah get down?" He asked, sounding all disoriented.

Clarke moved in closer towards Mindy. He slowly placed his hand on her stomach, then started to put his tongue in her ear. Mindy placed her hand over his erect dick, and started squeezing his shit through his jeans. Peter and I just stupidly looked on. I wanted to go over and get something going on with her too, but my stupid ass always hesitates. After about five minutes, Clarke had her shirt unbuttoned and her bra exposed, and they were all over each other like white on rice.

Suddenly Clarke just stopped what he was doing to her, looked over at Peter and me, and said, "Yo, Y'all two niggahs is gonna have to get the fuck out!"

"What?" I shouted.

"I'm saying, y'all my boys and all, but there ain't enough of this to go 'round."

Limp and Tommy didn't even pay us any attention. "C'mon, son, bounce yo." He faintly said, as he pushed Mindy's head down into his lap.

"Yo, that's that bullshit." Peter said enraged.

I couldn't help but to envy those three mutha-fuckas. Peter and I just stormed outta the place, cursing and hating. "Fuck y'all bitch ass niggahs." Peter shouted.

Outside, Peter cursed them some more, then stormed away, without evening saying goodbye. He was really upset. What was I to do? I was ass out. Maybe it was for the best, God knows how terrible I am when it comes to having sex.

So I went home and did the next best thing, I popped in a porno and whacked off.

A few days later, the joke was on them, Tommy, Clarke, and Limp. Come to find out that them girls were only sixteen and seventeen years old—Jailbait.

SHANA
9

There were numerous bitches at Terry's funeral. I came to pay my respects with Naja. Terry had so many women shredding tears over his death that it was unbelievable. His baby's mother flew in from North Carolina. Come to find out that Terry had four different baby mothers. He had a total of six kids. He was engaged three times, and cheated on all of them. His mother flew in from Trinidad; she was hysterical over her son's death. I greeted his mother. I was surprised that she still recognized me.

I was dressed in a black skirt and cream blouse, wearing all black was not my thing. There were a handful of mourners dressed down in all black, but the majority of the people that attended his wake came in everyday gear. She even held my hand for comfort. It was an open casket viewing. He looked so peaceful in his gray pin striped three-piece suit. When I went up to view the body, I nearly broke down in tears. It hurt me to see him like this, but it disturbed me even more knowing that I was probably fucking the man who may be a prime suspect in his murder. No one knew for sure who Terry's killer was. He was found in an abandoned car shot three times, once in the neck and twice his chest. Naja stood there next to me.

"You ok, Shana?" She softly asked, as she wiped away a tear with her free hand.

I just nodded my head and continued to gaze at him. He was my second love. We stood over his casket, paid our respects and headed towards the back.

"How you doing, Shana?" A slim, dark-skinned gentleman asked as he came up to Naja and I. At first I didn't recognize him. Then I greeted him with a hug. It was Terry's best friend, Terrance. It's been three years since I last saw him. He looked different. We stared at each other for a few seconds, then he broke the silence. "I miss him, that was my fucking boy."

I gave him another hug, comforting him the best that I could. I was speechless. I never told anyone that I last saw him get beat down by Tyrone in a burger joint. I dreaded that night. I could feel my tears about to break free again as I held Terrance in my arms. Back in high school they were inseparable. They did everything together. While Terrance was messing with Sasha, Terry was my sweetheart. We had some wild and crazy nights together.

"Do they know who killed him?" Naja asked.

"Nah, the police don't have any suspects right now." He said. "The crew is wilding out though, they about ready to murder someone."

When he meant the crew, he meant Terry's cousins and their boys. They were a rowdy and ruthless bunch of hoodlums and thugs. When we were together, Terry would always talk about his cousins and how wild and fucked up they were. He told me one night; they robbed a gas station clerk and shot him in the foot so he wouldn't chase them as they just walked out with armloads of his stuff. They went to school 10% of the time, and when they were in school, all they did was fight, harass other students, and gamble in the hallways.

Terrance left our side and went to view the body. He looked reluctant to do it. It was tearing him apart to see his boy lying there dead. I just stood there and folded my arms over my chest, trying to relax myself.

Sasha arrived with a few friends of hers. When I saw her enter the building, I started to cry. All of this drama was to much for me. I started to reminisce about the past, on how things used to be. Now everything was changing.

Sasha looked over at me. I met her gaze. It would be peace between us tonight. The death of Terry set our differences aside. I even tried to give her a smile, but it just wasn't happening. I remember that bitch tried to cut me.

Naja came from the bathroom. She saw Sasha, and asked, "You ready to go?"

I nodded my head. Everything is gonna be all right, I thought. We headed for the exit, saying our good-byes to friends that we passed along the way. When we got outside, my eyes came across a group of young men, who were standing together, talking and smoking. I threw my hand over my mouth, remembering two faces. One of them looked my way and tapped his man on the shoulder. He too turned around and stared over at me. Scared, I hurried by them, rushing my ass to the car, Naja tried to keep up.

"What's da matter girl?" She shouted.

"Nuthin'." I said.

When we got into the car, I quickly locked my door and slumped down into the seat. I peeped out the window at them as we drove by. They were still watching me. They were two of the guys who were in the burger restaurant the night Terry got his ass whipped. I knew that they knew my face. I was fuckin' petrified.

When Naja pulled up in front of my place, I was looking like I had just seen a ghost. Naja kept asking me what was wrong. I blamed it on the funeral and gave her a hug. I then ran my ass inside the house. My mother was home, thank God for that, because I wasn't feeling too safe being alone in the house tonight.

The next morning, Jakim stopped by. He told me that he was sorry about what happened to Terry as he tried to console me. It felt so good being in his arms. I wanted to tell him about what'd happened to Terry in the restaurant, about how I was there and witnessed everything up close, but I couldn't. I also wanted to confess to him everything that was going on with Tyrone and I. Common sense told me not to.

I didn't want him to start flipping and create another fucked up incident to have on my conscious.

Jakim held me in his arms, as we lay propped up against a few pillows on my bed. He massaged my shoulders, played with my hair, and whispered words of comfort in my ear. Telling me that everything was gonna be all right. I smiled, turned around and gave him a quick kiss on his cheeks. I stared into his lovely brown eyes, then gave him another short kiss on his lips and asked, "Do you still love me?"

"Of course I do." He quickly answered. We started to tongue each other down. He held me tightly; the taste of his breath heated my panties. I wanted to feel him inside me. I kissed him all around his neck, as he explored my body with his hands. He pulled off my jeans, and I unbuttoned his shirt, tickling his chest with my fingers. In no time, we were completely naked. He climbed on top of me and slowly reintroduced himself to something he'd been missing for quite a while. I cried out, "Jakim!" As he slowly started stroking it.

"Everything is going to be ok, Shana, I promise." He gently said.

I closed my eyes, and gave him my body.

It felt so good, but then I started feeling guilty about being with Tyrone.

After we were done, we both fell asleep I was still wrapped up in his arms.

When Jakim woke up that afternoon, he was happy as ever. I was already dressed. He was still naked on my bed.

"You ok, baby?" He asked, getting up out of the bed.

"I need for you to leave, Jakim." I said.

"Why? What's the matter?" He asked, coming towards me still undressed.

"I can't explain why. I just need for you to go."

He looked at me. I just stood next to the doorway watching him as he searched around for his stuff.

"You know, Shana, I don't fuckin' get you. Let me know what's happening between us, because you're buggin' me the fuck out right now." He said as he fastened his jeans.

I just remained silent. It wasn't that I didn't want to answer him; I just couldn't because I didn't really know what was going on with me. After he was dressed, he stormed by me, almost knocking me down. He got to the door, turned around and gave me one cold look. "You're fuckin' someone else, aren't you?" He asked.

I didn't answer him.

Later that evening, I was walking home from the store when Tyrone's BMW pulled up on the curve. I freaked out. I started to quickstep, nearly jogging to my home. Tyrone stepped out and called out, "Shana, hold up. I wanna talk to you!"

Hearing his voice made me freeze in my tracks. I was in no mood to see him right now. When he called out my name, my body just stopped, like I was playing freeze tag. I gripped the bag of groceries to my chest and slowly turned around to see that he was already a few feet behind me. He looked serious, maybe a little too serious. I just stood there, watching him. I wasn't terrified of him, I just didn't know what he was capable of doing.

"Shana, I just wanna talk to you." He said, in a low and calm voice. "C'mon, lets go for a ride." He suggested, reaching out his hand to me.

"I gotta take this bag of groceries home." I said.

"It can't wait? This is really important."

"No, Tyrone, my mother is waiting on me for this stuff." I said, taking two steps back.

"All right, then let me give you a ride to your crib." I knew that he wasn't going to take no for an answer, so I went along and let him drive me home. During the ride, he remained quiet, focusing his attention on the road. I just stared out of the passenger window. I wanted to ask if he had something to do with Terry's death, but felt hesitant to do so. We pulled up in front of my home, and I slowly stepped out. He grabs me by my coat, and says, "Shana, promise me that you're gonna come right back. This is something really important."

I nod my head, and he lets go of my coat. Once inside, I place the bag on the kitchen counter, walk back to the front, and peer out of the window at Tyrone's car. I feel reluctant going back out there, but I promised that I would.

My mother came out of her bedroom wrapped in her bathrobe, about ready to light a cigarette. "You got my stuff?" She asks.

I just point to the kitchen, still peering out of the window. I knew she just finished riding Danny's dick, her hair was looking atrocious, plus I glanced in her room and saw him lying on her bed.

"What you looking at?" She asks.

"Nuthin', I'll be back." I tell her as I exit out the door.

I cautiously approach Tyrone's car. I'm a bit nervous. I didn't know what to expect. I get in on the passenger side, and close his door.

"What's so important, Tyrone?" I ask.

"I haven't seen you in a few days."

"I've been really busy."

"C'mon, lets go for a quick ride." He suggests, turning the ignition and starting up the car.

"Go where, Tyrone? I got things to do today. I can't be driving all over Queens and Brooklyn with you."

"Shana, why you trippin'? Is it because of that fool's death?" He asks.

"It might be, you tell me." I say to him folding my arms across my chest.

"You think I was the one that smoked him, don't you?"

"Well the way you beat him down the other night was a clear sign that you two didn't get along." I turn my head away from him, glancing out the window at a few kids play wrestling on someone's front lawn.

"Shana, look at me...look at me!" He shouts. I slowly turn myself toward his direction, staring him straight into his eyes. "I didn't smoke Terry, believe me, yo, and if you're thinking that I did, then get the thought of it out of your fuckin' head."

"Well, if you didn't, then who did?"

"I don't fuckin know! That niggah had enemies." He says.

"Terry?"

"Shana, let me tell you something about your boy. Yeah, he owed me money, and didn't pay up. But he owed a lot more money to people that are far more vicious and dangerous than me. Why the fuck do you think he got up and just left for North Carolina, to evade paying his debts. Yo, your boy Terry was foul!"

I couldn't believe him. Terry wasn't that kind of person. He was an honor student for god sake! He was one of those pretty boys, who got manicures, shopped more than me, and got his haircut twice a week every week. I remember one time he got pulled over for speeding, and was so nervous speaking to the police, that he started stuttering.

"Shana, why you trippin' over his death anyway, ain't like y'all was still together." Tyrone said.

"That's not the point. He was my friend. How much did he owe you anyway?"

"Yo, Shana, I don't wanna discuss that sorry mutha-fuckas debt right now, let it be."

"Why?"

"Shana, just let it be!"

I hated this. I hated when he omits vital information about himself, his life, and his experiences. I mean, I was fuckin' him, the least he could do was open up some. If he didn't do it, I'm sure he knew who did. Tyrone knew almost every thug, killer and hood in Queens and Brooklyn.

I peered over at Tyrone. I knew he knew something, he just wasn't saying. I didn't know what it was with him. I just couldn't figure the man out. Or maybe he wasn't meant to be figured out.

"Shana, look, I'm falling in love with you, and I would never do anything to hurt you." He said, as he leaned forward, placing his hand on my thigh.

He pressed his lips against mine, trying to pry open my mouth with his tongue. Then I felt his hand deep in between my legs. "Tyrone, not now." I begged, slowly moving his hand away.

"What's da matter? You don't want me?"

"Its just that I got a lot on my mind right now, Tyrone. I just need to be by myself for a while."

He continued to look at me, then slowly moved back into his seat. "Shana, don't be stressing your ex's death. I'm saying life moves on, and I wanna move on with you." He took my hand in his. I knew this was a side of Tyrone that people rarely saw. A sweet, loving and romantic Tyrone, not the usual shoot them up roughneck. I believed every word he said to me. He leaned forward and tried to give me another kiss, I went along with this one.

His pager went off, breaking the spell. He looked at the number, placed it back on his hip, and gave me another quick kiss.

"I gotta go, Shana, this is important." He said, restarting the car. "I'll give you a call sometime tonight."

I stepped out of the car and watched him pull off. The temperature dropped rapidly. I was shivering and wondered if this was a sign. I ran my ass back into the house where I remained for the rest of the night.

Two weeks had passed since Terry's funeral and my escapades with Tyrone were becoming frequent. I even stayed a few days over at his place. He had the gift of gab. I swear, he could talk the panties off of a nun. He made me dinner, took me shopping, he even ate my pussy out for hours.

I stopped asking questions about Terry's death, Anyway, it was obvious that Tyrone wasn't going to break and say anything, so why keep trying. So, taking his advice, I got over it.

One day I went out shopping with Naja and Latish. We were looking for outfits to wear to a party that night. Tyrone had given me $500. We headed towards Manhattan.

The girls and I decided that it would be best for everyone to meet up later and get dressed over at my place.

That evening we were all buggin' out, talking and watching "*Boyz n' the Hood*" on cable when Latish asked, "So Shana, what's going on with you and Tyrone? I mean, y'all been pretty tight these past few days now."

"We're doing our thing!" I responded.

"So, is it really over with between you and Jakim?" Latish asked.

"No, he's still my boo."

Naja shook her head and said. "Shana, you know you're playing with fire, right?"

"Please, Naja, I got the heat under control. And like I said before, Jakim and I are not officially together, so I can spread my legs to whoever I want to." I said, laying back on the bed, and parting my legs.

Latish started laughing.

As I propped myself back up in a sitting position, the doorbell rang. Both girls looked over at me. I shrugged my shoulders. I wasn't expecting company.

"Could it be Tyrone's sexy ass?" Latish teased.

I went to see who was at the door. I glanced out the window and saw Jakim's car parked outside. I sighed and slowly opened the door.

"What's up?" He said, stepping inside.

"What's going on?" I asked.

"I'm saying, I ain't been through in a minute." He said, taking off his coat like I asked him to stay.

"Well, me and the girls are about to go out tonight, so you can't stay long."

He probably wanted some pussy tonight. He got a little taste of it again and wanted seconds. I knew he was horny, I could see it in his eyes, antsy mutha-fucka'. He came closer to me, reaching his arms around my waist, trying to kiss me on my neck. I pulled away from him, smelling the liquor on his breath.

"What's da matter? A brotha can't get any love?"

"Jakim, you're drunk, go home."

"I'm not drunk boo."

I picked up his coat and passed it to him. He came towards me again with open arms. I just pushed him back. Hearing laughter coming from my bedroom, he quickly turned his head, and asked, "Who you got in there with you?"

"My friends, Jakim."

He rushed by me, hurrying to my bedroom. I followed behind him. He pushed open my bedroom door to see Naja and Latish sitting on my bed half-naked, getting ready for the party. Startled, Naja ran and covered herself with a towel hanging over the back of a chair, but Latish just remained seated on my bed in her panties and T-shirt.

"Sorry ladies." He apologized.

"Hi, Jakim." Latish said with a broad smile on her face.

"Jakim, get out of here!" Naja screamed, embarrassed he saw her with nearly nothing on.

"Jakim, can you please leave!" I yelled.

He walked back into the living room, stood by the door and said, "I'm saying, Shana, when you and me gonna really get together and hook up again?"

"I don't know, Jakim."

He started to say something but thought better of it and walked through the door..

I locked the door behind him and went back into the bedroom with the girls

Latish laughed and said, "Girl, he got it bad for you. You better hang on to him."

"Lets just get ready for this party tonight." I told them.

It took us two hours to get dressed. Naja spent nearly an hour in the bathroom. Latish took more time applying her make-up and doing her hair than getting dressed. It was almost 10pm when we left the house.

We arrived at the *Executive* around 10:40. The Executive was a famous club in Queens located on Linden Blvd. Every Saturday night they had something going down. Often famous rapper or celebrity would stop by to get their party on. The line was getting long, so we had to hurry and park Naja's four door blue Pontiac somewhere on the street.

We stepped up to the line and it seemed like every male was breaking their necks to howl and whistle at us. Of course, once again, the bitches were hating.

Once we were inside, the room was blasting Wu Tang . The house was nearly filled to capacity.

I glanced around. There were a few cuties in the place. This one guy with a bald head caught my attention. He was looking too good. While I was eyeing him, this guy with a fucked up bowl cut and buckteeth came up trying to holla at me. He offered me a drink. I refused. He gave me a smile. I shot him down with an ice cold stare. Then he tried to talk to Naja, she turned his ugly ass down. Then he had the nerve to try and talk to Latish. She played nicer to him than the rest of us. He bought her two drinks and then she told him to step off.

When my song, *"It Ain't Hard To Tell."* by my boy *Nasty Nas* blasted over the speakers, I went crazy. I love that song! I grabbed the closest cutie next to me and started grinding up all over him. The mutha-fucka didn't have any rhythm. So I dismissed him and moved on to the next fine man who wasn't cursed with having two left feet.

"My name's Charlie." this next one whispered in my ear.

I gave him a strange look. I didn't care for his name. I just wanted to dance. I moved on to the next guy. Naja was laughing as her and Latish were noticing everything.

The third guy was cute. He had curly hair, brown eyes, a goatee, and a nice build. We were grooving together nicely. He had a real smooth groove and he kept his mouth shut. After my joint came to an end, I needed to take a breather. We headed to the bar, where he offered to buy me a drink. He didn't say anything, he just used hand gestures.

"Damn, boo, don't hurt nobody tonight." Some idiot told me as he passed by. I just ignored him.

I told the bartender my preferred drink, then took a seat on one of the stools next to my male company. I wondered why he wasn't talking? I mean now when you want a guy to talk, he keeps his mouth shut. So I just smiled and sipped on my drink.

"So, what's your name?" I asked, taking my drink and sipping.

"Cory."

"You're not getting yourself a drink, Cory?" I asked.

He shook his head no. "So, Cory, you're not gonna ask me for my name?"

He smiled, hesitated in speaking, but eventually stammered.

"Wwwhaaat...isssss, your...nammme?"

I covered my mouth with my hand. Holy shit! I thought to myself. It took him almost a minute to ask my name. He just looked at me as I started to chuckle and felt tears of laughter coming to me eyes. He was cute and all but the speech impediment ruined it. I gulped down the remainder of my drink.

"Caaaannnn...I, bbbbuy you...aaannnoootheer one?" He asked.

The lady that was sitting next to me was cracking up. I shook my head no. I didn't even tell him my name. Ohmigod! The cutest one and he had a serious speech problem. "Shana." I blurted out.

"Huh?"

"Remember you asked for my name, well my name is Shana." I said to him.

He was so fine he deserved to know my name, even though he couldn't speak for shit. Latish and Naja came over admiring Cory. They stared him down, looking him all in his grill.

"Damn, he's fine!" Latish whispered in my ear.

Yeah, he was fine all right. But they didn't know his downfall.

I passed Cory my home phone number and he passed me his. I gave him a kiss on his cheek, and whispered in his ear, "I'll call you and we'll hook up later."

He smiled. What he lacked in words, he made up for on the dance floor.

Latish was drunk as usual. She was slumped over by the bar. Naja was getting her party on with some fine brotha with dreads. I went in search of the ladies room. As I made my way through the tight crowd, I felt someone bump into me and curse, "Fuckin' bitch!" I couldn't see who said it, or else I would have scratched their fuckin' eyes out. So I just blew it off and continued to make my way towards the bathroom

While I was running the comb through my hair, three ladies entered. I paid them no attention, just continued to freshen up.

"Your name's Shana right?" one of the girls asked. She was about my height, with chinky brown eyes, corn rows, and an attitude. I had to give her props. She was beautiful. Almost as stunning as me.

I turned my head to her and asked, "Why? Who wants to know?"

Her girls had her back. They surrounded me, one to my left and one to my right. I knew this situation far too well. We used to beat bitches down in Jamaica like this, catching them while they were in the bathroom. We called it *the web* because it was impossible for a girl to run or escape. You had to accept your ass whooping. Now here I was being put in the same predicament.

"Stay the fuck away from my man, bitch!" The chinky-eyed girl threatened.

"Excuse me." I replied. "I don't even know your fuckin' man."

"Yo, Chinky, fuck this bitch up!" The girl on my left shouted. I shot her down with a wicked stare.

Chinky, I knew the name. It travels around the way. Chinky was supposed to be a ruthless bitch from the Jamaica housing area, called 40 Projects. She ran with a ruthless crew. They were known for slashing bitches with box cutters across their faces leaving permanent and disfiguring scars. Almost everyone who ran across her feared her, like she was God almighty! They called her Chinky because of her eyes. They were small and slanted like she was Japanese. It was like every niggah was sweating her and bitches were scared of her. I had only heard of her. I had never met her, until now.

"Bitch, do not fuckin play stupid with me." Chinky yelled out, as she reached in her right pocket.

"Who is your man?" I demanded to know.

"Tyrone!" She said.

"What?" I couldn't believe it.

"Yo, fuck that bitch up, Chinky." The same girl to my left shouted out. I was about getting tired of her ass.

"That's my kids father and it's my understanding that you're fucking him!" She continued to stare at me with ice-cold eyes.

"I didn't even know Tyrone had kids..."

"He got two, by me, bitch!" She yelled.

My first instinct told me to just throw the first punch and set it off. Why waste any time? I wasn't about to become a victim of hers in this club tonight. Both of my homegirls were outside partying. They had no idea that I was about to get jumped.

My situation went from hectic to critical, when Chinky pulled out a small box cutter, and so did her friend on my left. Here I was, about to get my shit sliced because Tyrone neglected to mention to me that he had two children by this crazy bitch. I prayed for someone to enter the bathroom and help me out. Now was a good time to have Sasha by my side. She could definitely throw down. I just clinched my fists together and prepared for the worst to happen.

I screamed out, "Fuckin bitch!" And lunged forward at her with a quickness, hitting across her head before she could attempt to cut me with that box cutter. Her friend, the one that was talking so much shit, came to Chinky's aid as did the one on my right. I managed to knock both of their weapons out of their hands, thank God! But I fell to the floor in the process, and was getting stomped and kicked by all three.

"Fuck that bitch up! Fuck that bitch up!" I heard one of the girls.

Chinky grabbed me by the hair, and dragged me across the bathroom floor like I was some kind of rag doll. I was screaming, kicking and cursing.

I managed to kick Chinky in her shin, crippling her for a few seconds, but I couldn't get her two girlfriends off of me. I looked around for one of the box cutters while I was getting beat down, and saw that I had knocked one under a bathroom stall next to the toilet. I tried to reach for it but that tall bitch was too strong. She yoked me up in some wrestling move.

The second bitch gave me a serious scratch across my eye. Chinky retrieved one of the box cutters and came swinging. Her friend held me from behind. I threw up both my legs and started kicking her. There was no way my face was going to be looking like a jigsaw puzzle. I screamed as I kicked ferociously. The music outside the ladies room was playing so loud no one could hear me screaming for help.

I managed to kick Chinky in her face, striking her across her mouth with the heel of my boot. The tall bitch finally let me go seeing her friend's mouth filled with blood. Chinky threw both her hands over her mouth, screaming. She was in serious pain. That didn't stop the other two from fucking me up on the floor. I found myself folded into a tight ball.

They went buck wild on me. I never hurt so bad in my entire life. These bitches from the 40 projects, stomped, kicked, punched, slapped, and even spit on me. I knew for sure that they must have yanked a handful of my hair out. I was nuthin but a helpless bitch. What seemed to have went on for hours, really only lasted about two minutes. Security finally arrived in the ladies room.

It was a scene. It seemed like the entire club was present in the ladies bathroom. Everyone wanting to see what was going on. The club's security tried to get everything under control. They tried to give Chinky medical aid but she was bleeding from her mouth and cursing me out something terrible. Yelling, "It's on bitch! I'm gonna kill that fuckin' bitch! I'm gonna kill that stupid fuckin' bitch!"

"Whatever, stupid bitch!" I shouted in return as security held me from plunging towards her.

They took everyone out of the bathroom. The crowd parted to make room for our exit. I saw Naja. She looked stunned. "I know that ain't my girl, Shana! Shana, what happened?"

Then she looked over at Chinky and her girls with fire. "I'm gonna fuck you up, bitch!" Naja shouted at Chinky.

It took about twenty minutes for everything to return to normal. Unfortunately they shut the club down for the night and called the police. Eight squad cars arrived at the scene. The EMS workers came for Chinky. They had to fight with her to put her in the ambulance. I had to ride down to the precinct with those bitches that jumped me. Naja said that she would come down to the precinct with me. It looked like she would have to drag Latish's drunk ass along.

I should have just left with Cory when I had the chance, I reflected.

It was around eight in the morning when I finally left the precinct. I gave 'them my description of what happened in the bathroom. They still had them two stink bitches in custody for assault with that razor.

Naja and Latish had waited around for me. They looked dog-tired having sat almost all night on them hard wooden, nasty and dirty benches in the precinct. When I came out, I gave the both of them a hug. I explained everything to them in the car as Naja drove home. She was so fuckin hyped she was ready to kill Chinky. I was ok. I had a few bruises and scratches, but Chinky caught the worse of it. I busted her fuckin jaw with the bottom of my boot, knocking two of her teeth out. I let her know that she was fuckin' with the wrong bitch!

My real beef was with Tyrone. He should have told me that he was fuckin' with Chinky and that he fathered two of her children. But then Naja bought up a point in the car, saying the bitch was probably lying about Tyrone. She was straight up trifling anyway. I knew I had to get to the bottom of things. I was planning on having a few words with Tyrone as soon as possible. I didn't care if I had to go down to his apartment and knock down his front door.

After Naja dropped me off, I gave her a hug and thanked her. She told me to give her a call. We were going to handle this situation even if we had to get a crew together and travel down to the 40 projects to whip that bitch's ass.

I went into the house and saw that my Aunt and moms were already up cooking breakfast. They noticed the bruises and scratches on my face and went hysterical, shouting, "Shana, what the fuck happened to you?"

I told them about my little brawl with Chinky and her crew. They were ready to start making phone calls and hunt the Chinky bitch down. I had to love them for that but I told them it wasn't necessary.

My moms fixed me a plate of grits and fish. She tried to pamper me the best that she could, treating me like I was still her baby girl.

The next morning, I took a cab over to Tyrone's apartment in Rochdale. I tried to call his house number and his cell, but he wasn't picking up either.

I banged on his apartment door for about five minutes until his roommate, Evay, came to the door.

"Why you come banging on my door so fuckin' early in the morning like you the po-lease or something." He hollered.

"Where's Tyrone?" I demanded to know, as I stormed by him making my way into the apartment.

"He ain't here."

"Then where is he?"

"He's been gone for a week; went out of town to do business with some peeps."

I didn't believe him. Evay could be covering for his man's whereabouts. Tyrone practically told him what to do. He controlled him like he was a worthless and brainless zombie.

"I'm saying, Shana, he bounced sometime around yesterday, him and this other dude...you know that niggah don't really tell me shit."

"Whatever!"

I went into Tyrone's room and looked around. His bed was still made. I searched in his closet and noticed a few clothes missing, along with a small suitcase he keeps in the corner of his closet. I guess Evay was really telling the truth.

"C'mon, Shana, you know you can't be in here while he's away." Evay pleaded

"I'm his woman, I can go anywhere I fuckin' please." I chided.

He just looked at me, with his sorry ass, standing by the doorway. "Do you know this bitch name Chinky?" I asked him. The expression on his face told me he knew something.

"Chinky?"

"Yeah, Chinky. You see my fuckin' face? That bitch tried to jump me in a club the other night."

"Word!"

"Yes, word. So is Tyrone still fuckin with her?"

"I don't know nuthin' about that." He said, looking down at the floor.

I was heated. "That bitch told me that Tyrone's her babies father."

"Word, she told you that?" He responded.

"So, I wanna know if it's true or not."

"C'mon, Shana, that his business. I can't be telling you his business like that when he ain't even here."

"Why not?"

"'Cause Ty's my man. He trusts me."

I just stood there and stared at him, thinking about doing the impossible. Evay knew what was up with Chinky and Tyrone, but he feared Tyrone so much he was scared to tell. You cannot live with a man and not know some details about him. I just wanted to know something. So I went up to him, and softly grabbed his dick through his dirty sweats. I slowly massaged his shit with my hand and softly whispered in his ear, "If you tell me everything I need to know, I'll suck your little dick right here in this room."

He stared at me and starting smiling as his dick got hard in my hand. I put on a phony and seductive smile, squeezed his dick tighter, and he cracked like a walnut.

After he was done singing to me like a bird, telling me everything that I needed to know, he dropped his sweats to the floor, exposing himself and waited for his reward. I looked down and laughed. His dick was a little bigger that I thought, but I still wasn't sucking it. It nearly turned my stomach just seeing him naked, his fat belly falling over his dick. I'd have to lift his stomach up just to get to it. It wasn't happening. Not in this lifetime. He remained standing there, waiting for my precious lips to touch his shit. I just sighed, walked off, and left him standing there harder than the man of steel himself.

"Shana, what's up?" He yelled, chasing behind me pulling up his sweats. He came and grabbed my shoulder from behind.

"Don't touch me." I yelled, knocking his hand off of me.

"I'm saying, you ain't gonna suck my dick?"

"Hell no mutha-fucka. What do I look like to your ass?."

"Oh, that's fucked up, bitch!" He shouted, looking like he wanted to knock me the fuck out. He knew better if he loved and valued his life. "You ain't nuthin' but a trifling ass hoe. Stink ass bitch--You ain't all that!" He shouted at me as I waited for the elevator.

I flipped him the bird and gave him a nasty smirk. Then to tease him even more, I stuck out my tongue in a seductive way, licking my lips and grabbing one of my breasts. He was so mad he slammed the door.

It was true. Tyrone was the father of Chinky's kids. Come to find out, she was also two months pregnant him, which meant he was still messing with her. The way Evay was explaining it, Chinky was his wifey, his main hoe. If that was the case then what the fuck was I to him? Evay told me that they'd been together for seven years now. Tyrone's twenty-three. Evay also told me that Tyrone had another eighteen-month-old boy by some hoe out in New Jersey. My ass was hurt.

When I arrived at my crib, Jakim was waiting out front. We embraced hello.

Shit, here his man was playing me out, he was in love with me and I was in love with the asshole.

I mean, at first it was just a sex thing with Tyrone, but then I let my feelings get involved. I should have just kept it sexual. The dick was too just good.

Jakim asked if I wanted to go for a ride. I said yes. I needed to get out of here and go some fuckin' where. Anywhere was better than being here at this moment. We went to the studio.

As I sat on one of the spinning stools, listening to him rhyme over the mic, I smiled. He had true talent. Listening to him made me forget about everything that was going on with Tyrone. Heck, I even got on the mic, singing and acting like I was some kind of diva.

After we left the studio, we went back over to his crib in Jamaica Queens, by Baisley Park. He lived with his father, while his mother, a struggling actress was living in Los Angles. He saw his mother maybe five or six times a year--Christmas, Thanksgiving, Birthdays, etc. He showed me a picture of her once. She was definitely beautiful.

We retreated to Jakim's room where I fucked the shit outta him.

I ended up spending the night over at his house. The next morning, I told myself to leave Tyrone alone and focus all of my energy and time on my ex, Jakim.

Easier said than done.

SHANA
10

It was three days until Thanksgiving. My mother planned to have dinner at our house, inviting family and friends. The last time I had heard from Tyrone was almost two weeks ago. Jakim and I were hitting it off. Nothing was official yet though.

I was still laid up in my bed recovering from a wicked hangover. The girls and I had gone out partying the night before. I met a few cuties, but they weren't anything to make a big fuss over. I ain't get in the house until six in the morning. Shit, I was still in my skirt, blouse and stockings when I woke up to the sounding of bedpost knocking against my mother's wall. She was moaning and calling out Danny's name. I tried to go back to sleep, but hearing them having sex in the next room was keeping me awake. I wondered if the dick was really that good? I got out of bed, went into the bathroom and took a nice hot shower.

I was in the shower washing every detail and inch of my body. I let the water cascade off my nipples and in between my legs. I thought I heard movement in the bathroom. I peeped from behind the shower curtain, and saw Danny standing over the toilet butt ass naked taking a piss. My eyes widened as I gazed down at his dick. Damn, he was hung. I could now understand why my mother was howling so loud. He continued to pee like I wasn't even there. I knew he felt me watching.

"You left the bathroom door open." He stated simply.

"Oh." I replied.

"It's cool." He said.

I closed the curtain and took a deep breath. I was both in shock and aroused.

"You all right?" He asked, looking over at me, as I continued to peek at him from behind the shower curtain.

"Yeah, I'm cool."

"This doesn't bother you?" He asked.

"Nah, it don't, it really don't."

God, he has a big dick. I watched him shake his dick and flush the toilet. He went over to the sink, washed his hands, and started to brush his teeth. I was still looking at him like I wasn't in the shower with the water still running.

"You gonna be in there all day?" He asked.

"No." I responded, at a lost for words.

I turned off the shower and stepped out of the tub. Danny glanced over at me and smiled. I reached for my towel. I wasn't uncomfortable being naked in front of him. I wanted him to see me naked. I stared over at Danny while I dried myself off. He just stood there watching me, hard as a rock.

My heart beat rapidly. My pussy was moist and I could feel my nipples hardening. I wanted some dick. I wanted him in me. I wanted to taste him and feel him in my mouth. I couldn't care less if he was dating my mother at that point. All I knew is that they weren't married so that left the door open for plenty of opportunity. Temptation was just burning in me something terrible.

"Where's my mom?" I asked.

"In the room, sleep."

I continued to look at him, as he stood over by the sink, with his dick in full view. That shit was just hanging, looking big and black. I knew he wanted the same thing that I wanted, if not, then he would've left the bathroom a long time ago. I wanted him so bad that my pussy was throbbing with excitement. I threw one leg up on the toilet and wiped myself from toe to thigh in a sensual motion. He smiled as I teased him by wiping the towel in between my pussy and letting out a soft moan. He threw me a sinister grin.

"What's all that about?" I teasingly asked as I looked at his dick.

"It's liking what it's seeing." He responded. "But what's all that about?" He nodded his head towards me.

"What? I'm drying myself off. Is there a problem?" I asked.

"Don't know a woman to dry herself off like that, all sexy and shit."

"Well, it's the way I do it. I take my sweet time with whatever I do."

"Word!"

"Word!" I responded back.

My eyes were focused on his dick. My pussy was getting wetter by the second. I swear I had a river flowing between my legs. It was either now or never. I took a seat on the toilet and spread my legs exposing everything. I leaned back slightly and started fingering myself.

Danny was hyped. "It's like that!" He said, all excited and shit.

"If you want it to be." I said, slut that I was.

Danny locked the bathroom door and came over to me. He got down on his knees, buried his face between my legs and started to eat my pussy.

"See, nice and clean for you." I said to him, playing with his dreads as he ate me out on the toilet.

His tongue action was something fierce. I was moaning and groaning so loud. He sucked on my pussy, stuck his tongue in my ass, and kissed all in between my thighs. He had to tell me to shut up a couple of times. Afterwards, he had me bend over the toilet. When he put it in me, it took everything in my power not to cry out. The dick was so fuckin' good, Shiiitttt!

He made me cum quick as hell but he wasn't done, until he let off a roaring nutt, gripping my butt and making me hit my head against the toilet.

After we were done, I threw on a towel and ducked into my room. Was I feeling guilty about what just happened? Hell no! In fact, I was looking forward to round two. It was the way I dreamed it would be, even better. My mother was such a fuckin lucky bitch to be getting dick from a man like him on the regular.

Early that evening, Jakim stopped by. He was in the mood for some, but I resisted. I had gotten mine just this morning, and like all men when they don't get any pussy, he caught an attitude. He told me he "got needs". So I told him to go get his needs taken care of somewhere else. He tried to persuade me into giving him a blowjob, but that was a no, no. My mind was still on Danny and how good his dick was.

The day before Thanksgiving, I hung out with my girls, Naja and Latish. We did a little shopping on Jamaica Ave and went to the movies. I got my nails and hair done, since my moms was having family and friends over for the holiday.

My day was going good until homicide Detective Brisco approached me.

Him and his partner were waiting for me outside of my mother's home in a black caprice. I was carrying three shopping bags filled with gifts and clothes at the time, and was about to get ready to go out tonight with Naja. But my plans changed soon as he stepped to me wanting to ask questions.

"Excuse me, are you Shana Banks?" Detective Brisco asked. He was about 5'9 and a little stocky, wearing a leather jacket, glasses and a beard.

His partner followed him, stepping out of the car with a cup of coffee in his hand. He was taller and younger. He also wore a leather jacket and had a goatee, with a gold earring in his ear.

"Who wants to know?" I asked.

"I'm Detective Brisco, Homicide. This is my partner, Detective Rice. We would like to ask you a few questions about the death of Terry Miles."

"What?" I was stunned.

"We would like for you to come down to the station with us, Ms Banks." Detective Brisco said..

"Am I under arrest?" I asked.

"No." He said.

"Then I don't see a reason for me to roll with y'all."

"Ms. Banks, we can do this the easy way or do it the hard way, it's your choice." His partner, Detective Rice stated.

I just stared at the both of them. Tomorrow was Thanksgiving Day and here they were coming to me with this bullshit. I knew nothing. I wasn't even sure that it was Tyrone who killed Terry. I sighed and agreed to go with them. There was no need for officers to come and break down my front door over some silliness.

They escorted me to their car. The ride was quiet to the 105th precinct in Queens. I just sat in the back, wondering how soon it would be over.

When we arrived, the detectives escorted me into a small gray room with a wooden table and two chairs. They left me there to sit for about twenty minutes. I nervous as hell.

Detective Brisco and Rice finally entered the room.

"Ms. Banks, I want to ask you a few questions about your boyfriend, Tyrone." Detective Brisco spoke, taking a seat in the chair opposite me.

"He's not my boyfriend."

"Then what is he to you?" Detective Rice spoke.

"Just a guy I'm fucking." I bluntly said.

Detective Rice put out the cigarette in the ashtray on the table and continued to peer at me.

"The reason you're here, Ms. Banks…"

"Damn, would you please stop calling me Ms. Banks! Fuck!" I shouted.

"Then Shana, the reason you're here is, witnesses placed you at the scene of an assault the night Tyrone assaulted and nearly killed Tyrone Miles in a fast food restaurant." Rice informed.

"What?"

"Your lover is our prime suspect in this case." Brisco said. "Do you know of his whereabouts?"

"I haven't seen or heard from Tyrone in weeks. He just fucks me, then leaves, fucks me, then leaves."

They wanted to know how long we were going out, how long I'd known Tyrone. Who were his friends? Did I know where he hangs out? I'm surprised they didn't want to know how long his dick was.

After spending about fifteen minutes with them, I started to get really agitated and annoyed. I yelled out, "Look, am I gonna be placed under arrest. Do I need a fuckin' lawyer?"

"No!" Detective Rice answered.

"Then can I just fuckin' leave. I don't know nuthin' about the man, he didn't tell me shit about his life. We just fuck and that's it!" I added.

Detective Brisco annoyed with my attitude, just waved his hand and announced "Let her go!"

Detective Rice looked like he was neglectful to do so, maybe seeing my beauty was the highlight of his day. "Come with me." He said.

Before I stepped out of the door, Detective Brisco stood up and said, "Shana, if he contacts you, call us." He passed me his card.

How was I supposed to get home, I thought. While in the hall, I saw Tyrone's roommate, Evay, handcuffed and sitting down on the bench with his head slumped over looking like he was feeling sorry for himself. I turned my head, not wanting him to recognize me. I wondered why he was here.

Detective Rice offered to give me a ride home. I accepted. He tried to rap to me in the car. He had some nerve. They wasted a good portion of my day, and now he thinks I'm gonna to give him my phone number.

As soon as I arrived home, I took a hot shower. I was trying to get the precinct smell off me. Afterwards, I gave Naja a call. She'd left two messages on the answering machine. In the first message she said that she and Latish was coming over for Thanksgiving. In the second message she was telling me to be ready by nine. We were going out once again.

When I gave her a call back, her boyfriend picked up. God, I hated hearing his voice. He sounded like a little kid. That niggah was twenty-seven and his voice sounded like he was thirteen. When Naja finally came to the phone, she sounded all tired and exhausted.

"Were you having sex?"

"Yeah, I gotta get mines too. What's up?"

"I need to talk to you."

"About what?"

"Just get over here girl. This is important."

"Shana, you can't tell me over the phone. Shit, I'm in the middle of some good dick here."

"Then break his dick off in your pussy and bring it with you." I said.

"No, see, you're wrong, bitch. Just give me a half-hour. I'll be there soon."

"Hurry, girl."

After our conversation, I threw on my robe and went into the kitchen to make myself a snack. My mind was on Tyrone and his situation. He told me himself that he had nothing to do with Terry's death. And I somewhat believed him. But then again, he was out of town for a while now. Maybe he was on the run.

I went into the living room with my cheese sandwich and soda, turned on the television and plopped down on the sofa. It was time like these that I felt like getting high, just roll myself a phat ass L. The house was quiet, a little too quiet. It felt like I was in one of those horror movies, where the young female is home alone and there's a killer stalking around town. But there ain't no serial killers in New York, much less, in Hollis, Queens. The only thing out here is trouble; gangs, chicken-heads, wanna be's Thugs and Playa's and fake ass bitches.

When Naja finally arrived I told her about the two detectives coming to see me. I told her I was with Tyrone when he beat down Terry. Naja went crazy; thinking that Tyrone actually killed Terry. Then she asked me why did he do it. I told her that it was over money.

"Bitch, why didn't you tell me this before?" She asked looking upset.

I had no explanation for her. I guess I was too scared to tell anyone else. She told me to leave Tyrone alone from now on, but I disagreed. I felt he really needed me now. I told her that I was too in love with him to let him go. She looked at me like I was crazy. Then she started asking about Jakim, and what was going on with him. I told her the truth, about the sex, how we were talking about maybe getting back together someday. I even told her that I love him too.

The bitch called me confused. She said I didn't know true love from good dick, and asked how could I care for that asshole, in light of the Chinky incident.

That wasn't true. I knew what true love was. I knew how it felt to be in love. I told her that I was in love with the both of them, but a girl still gotta get her freak on once in a while. It isn't like I was married to either of them. And as for that dumb bitch, Chinky, the hoe couldn't be trusted.

I was tempted to tell her about Danny but I decided to keep my mouth shut about that one. That was to much information to be exposing.

Naja stayed over my house the remainder of the evening. We changed our minds about going out. Instead, we rented movies, called Latish and helped my mother out in the kitchen with Thanksgiving dinner.

That little meeting with the detectives was kept a secret between Naja and I. She made a vow not to tell anyone about what I'd told her. I trusted her.

Thanksgiving Day, we had over twenty relatives and friends come over. My day was planned from morning to night. First, I was to have dinner with my family. Then, my girlfriends and I planned to head out to Newark, N.J. where there was a huge party jumping off. We were definitely going.

My moms cooked some mashed potatoes, string beans, rice and peas, macaroni, collard greens, yams, roast beef, stuffing, fish, and a huge turkey. She also baked five sweet potatoes pies and one large chocolate cake. Even though my moms could act ghetto, she could definitely cook. My grandmother was one of the greatest cooks in the South and she passed that gift on to my mother.

My two uncles, Jimbo and Jimmy arrived. They were the two who'd gotten into a fistfight four years at my Aunt's Christmas party in Jersey. My mother said she was going to throw them both out if they didn't behave themselves this year.

My cousin, Pamela showed up with her third husband in four years. My cousin Sharice showed up with her three badass little boys. My Uncle Leone showed up with his gold-digging girlfriend. That bitch had on more jewelry than Mr. T from the A-Team. Then there was my Aunt Samantha, who was more promiscuous than my Aunt Tina, my mother and myself combined. She came dressed in some old fashioned eighties fishnet stocking? some bamboo earrings, a mini skirt and a sultry attitude. Then there was my perverted uncle Penny and my always-staying drunk uncle Jake. I could go on and on about my dysfunctional family.

My Uncle Penny kept trying to hit on Naja, talking about she got pretty legs. He was an embarrassment. Both of my Uncles, Jimbo and Jimmy kept trying to get into Latish's pants, and she played along and kept flirting with them. They're my family and all, but them two are disgusting. They both are unemployed and unattractive men with no kind of ambition at all.

"Damn, girl, why you lookin' so fine, wit' yo beautiful self." My cousin, Ellis said to me.

I gave him a little smile and chuckled. He was funny to me. He came up from Delaware, with his butt ugly girlfriend, Shannon. That bitch was so ugly she made dogs scream and howl. "Shana, get your perverted Uncle, Penny away from me." Naja begged.

"What da matter, girl? You don't like to have a good time?" My crazy nasty and drunk uncle Penny said to Naja.

"Uncle Penny, will you please leave my friends alone." I begged.

"What da matter, Shana, she a lesbian or sumthin'?" He asked, looking at her strangely.

"Oh, no he didn't." Naja replied. "Shana, do something with him, before I have to smack him."

"I will." I promised her.

She walked away peering over her shoulders making sure Uncle Penny wasn't following her. I started to push Uncle Penny in the opposite direction, assuring he wouldn't come anywhere near Naja.

Minutes later, Naja came back out to get me with this bugged out expression on her face. "Shana, come here and look at this shit." She said, leading me to my bedroom.

I followed her. When I reached my bedroom and opened my door, I couldn't believe my eyes. I saw Latish making out with both of my uncles. Jimbo and Jimmy on my fuckin' bed. Was she crazy? I thought.

"Bitch, you crazy?" I shouted, startling them.

"Oh, shit, I thought y'all locked the door." Latish said, rising up from between them, looking surprised.

I was about ready to kill that bitch along with both of my Uncles. Naja stood by my side just shaking her head in disbelief. Latish had her skirt hiked up, shirt unbuttoned, and her hair was looking a wreck. Both my Uncles had their pants off. I stepped into the room and slammed the door behind me. All three just stared at me, probably too shocked to say anything.

"Shana, let me explain." Latish tried to speak.

"Explain what? That you're a nasty bitch."

Both my Uncles retrieved their jeans from the floor. I felt like I was going to vomit. It was a horrendous sight and caught me totally off guard.

"Shana, I'll wait for you out in the hallway." Naja said, leaving the room.

"First of all, y'all need to get the fuck up out of my room." I said. "And second, y'all need to get the fuck up outta this house."

"C'mon, Shana, we were just having some fun." My Uncle Jimbo said, buttoning his jeans.

"Not in my fuckin' house, and especially not in this fuckin' room. All three of y'all must've been smoking crack." I shouted.

Soon afterwards, my mother walked into my room, with Naja following not too far behind. She looked around and already knew what was going down.

"I know both my brothers must be crazy to think that they were going to fuck in my daughter's room?"

"C'mon, sis' it ain't even like that." Uncle Jimmy responded.

"And Latish, I'm surprised at you." My moms said "I thought you had much better taste than them two."

"But, Ms. Banks, they paid me." Latish informed.

"What?" My mother and I both shouted at the same time.

"Y'all think I'm running some fuckin' brothel in my house?" My moms shouted.

By now, the whole family started hearing the ruckus that was taking place in my room. They gathered around the door peering inside to see what was going on. They saw my mother going crazy, throwing things at her brothers and trying to smack them across their heads. Naja was holding her hand over her mouth trying to hide her laughter. Latish embarrassed, just rushed out the room, I followed behind her. She reached the doorway and I grabbed her by her shoulder and spun her around.

"Where you going, bitch? This shit ain't over." I shouted.

"Shana, I'm sorry, but they forced me to."

"My Uncles ain't force you to do shit!" I yelled, with my fist tightly clenched, I was bout' ready to knock this bitch out for disrespecting me and my home.

She stared at me, looking petrified. I decided not to hit her. It wouldn't be worth it. She already had two strikes against her. One for fuckin' my man, even though they both were denying it, and now this. One more and I was definitely going to fuck this bitch up.

Thanksgiving was officially ruined thanks to my uncles Jimbo and Jimmy

"You know what...everyone get the fuck out!" My moms shouted.

"C'mon, sis, don't spoil it for everyone." Uncle Jimmy said.

"You shut the fuck up. I'm bout to kill both of y'all." My mother threatened.

Before I could even turn around, Latish was already out the door and gone. Naja came up to me and said, "Girl, your family's crazy, I'm gone. You still down for tonight?"

I just looked at her. Minutes later, everyone started collecting their things and leaving the house one by one. My moms retreated to her bedroom mad as hell. Once again, her brothers ruined it for everyone.

Jakim came by after everyone left. He saw how upset I was and tried to comfort me the best that he could, but it just wasn't working. He even volunteered to help me and my mother clean the house. When I told him about Latish he had nothing good to say about her. He called her a nasty slut.

After all the cleaning and rearranging was done, Jakim and I settled in my room for the night where I thanked him personally.

SPANKY
11

The day before Thanksgiving, the guys and I were playing a game of spades over at Mark's crib in Jamaica, Queens. He lived with his mother and older sister, Bettina. She's a dime piece. I lost count on how many times I've asked Mark to hook me up with her, and so did the fellas. But he would tell us forget about it, because none of us were her type. She likes older men with financial security. That description apply to any of us.

Mark's moms owns a fly ass three bedroom home decorated with leather furniture, sculptures and paintings. Every time we went over to his home, we had to take our shoes off at the door and hang our coats up in the hall. She didn't play when it came to her home. She kept that bitch in tiptop shape.

We were all in Mark's room, where he had the table set up for us to play cards. That niggah room was off the hook. He had a 27" television in his room, with a DVD player. He had his playstation 2 hooked up to it. Mark had a phat Sony stereo system with a CD player next to his waterbed. Since he was a huge Chicago Bulls fan, his wall was plastered with posters of but Michael Jordan and the Bulls, featuring Scottie Pippin and Horace Grant. It's too bad Jordan's retired.

Mark and I were partners against Limp and Abney. Clarke and Tommy were seated on his waterbed watching a bootleg copy of *"The House On Haunted Hill."* Mark and I were down by a hundred points, while Limp and Abney were talking shit.

"Yo, Limp, where you get this fucked up copy from?" Clarke asked.

"Niggah, just watch the movie." Limp scolded.

"Niggah, don't get mad." Clarke said.

Limp just flipped him the bird. Once in a while I would get distracted and glance at the movie. Mark would tell me to pay attention to the game. He was a person who took playing cards very seriously.

Mark's mother entered the room without knocking. "You can't knock, ma?" He blurted out.

"Boy, shut up. Don't get embarrassed in front of your friends." She said. "I want you to take the garbage out of the kitchen."

"A'aight, I'll do it later."

"I would like you to get to it now. That garbage stinks, Mark."

"Why you can't do it? I'm in the middle of a game."

"Mark, don't get smart with me. I'll kick your friends out of my house." She threatened.

"Mark, listen to your mother and take out that garbage." Clarke said, playing kiss up to her.

She looked at each of us, then stepped outta the room shutting the door.

As soon as she was gone, Limp says, "Damn, your moms got some big ass titties."

"Shut up, Limp." Mark muttered.

"I'm saying, she do. Your pops was a lucky mutha-fucka' to be running up in that." Limp said.

Mark just stared at him, not too pleased with Limp running off his mouth about his mother. But then Abney joined in the conversation saying, "For real, though, she do. Yo, Mark, your moms looks good."

I started chuckling, as did Clarke and Tommy.

"Nah, I wanna get with his sister, Bettina." Tommy said.

"I'm saying, what's the deal with that, Mark? You still can't hook a brotha up?" Limp asked.

Mark, looking fed up, just threw his cards across the table and shouted, "Would y'all ignorant mutha-fucka's just back off my damn family. Y'all niggahs act like y'all ain't never had no pussy before."

"Why you getting' all loud? I'm saying, we're just paying you a compliment about your fam, dawg, you got a good looking home." Limp spoke.

Mark cut his eyes at him, then gave him a smile and laughed. He knew Limp was a fool, shit, we all did. There was no changing Limp and the way he was. He just sometimes kept it a little too real.

"I'm saying, Mark, give me one night with your moms and I'll give you a little brother." Limp said, having everyone bust out laughing.

"Yo, that's fucked up Limp!" Clarke said.

That little comment killed our spades game completely. I couldn't believe Limp just said that. He was definitely a fool. Every one just threw their cards on the table. Limp got up and grabbed his crotch and said, "This shit right here will knock ten years off your mother's life."

"You're a rude mutha-fucker, Limp." Abney said.

"Niggah, your moms so stupid, when you were younger, she took you to a Clippers game so you could get a free haircut." Mark joked.

"Niggah, I'll put my dick so far up your mother's ass she'll be spitting cum for a month." Limp said.

Now it seemed that it was getting a little too personal. Mark wasn't so thrilled about that little comment about his moms and shit. He stared at Limp.

"Yo, Limp, c'mon, that's enough." I said.

"Nah, it's all good. He can't even come within a foot of my sister without her dissin' his ugly ass." Mark replied.

"Yeah, whatever, dawg, I'm about to make you a nephew too." Limp continued to joke, "Niggah, I'm about to add some branches to your family tree."

"See, now let's not talk about your black ass mama. That bitch's so black, she can get into a tub and make tea." Mark retaliated.

"Mark!" his mother shouted out from the hallway. "Take out the damn garbage. I'm starting to smell that shit up here."

"It's probably her pussy that's smelling so stink." Limp said.

Mark cut his eyes at him, "Fuck you!" He shouted.

"Enough!" I shouted. "Y'all niggahs need to chill off the mama jokes for a minute. It's getting a little too personal."

They both just stared at me like I'd just lost my damn mind. But I didn't want them to start throwing blows at each other. We were all friends up in here and Limp was pushing his friendship with Mark a little too much. I knew that Limp was starting to boil Mark's nerves, so before shit went to fuckin' far, I felt I had to say something.

"Yo, Mark, lets go downstairs in the basement and play pool or sumthin'." Clarke suggested.

We all headed downstairs towards the basement to get a game of pool started. Mark took out the garbage, then joined us.

When Clarke was about to make his shot, he was interrupted by Mark's sister, Bettina coming downstairs in some tight blue Levi's jeans and a tight white shirt. We all gawked at her. "What the fuck y'all losers looking at?" She asked with a snobbish attitude.

"Damn, Bettina, you're making my dick very happy right now." Limp said.

She cut her eyes at him, then walked by all of us, acting like we weren't even present. She went into the laundry room.

"She got a phat ass." Limp said, jerking the pool stick.

"You're sick!" Abney said.

"It's still your shot, Clarke." Mark said, getting aggravated that the game was disturbed because his sister was catching mad attention from all of us.

"Yo, c'mon what's the deal, Mark, hook a brotha up." Tommy begged.

"Don't embarrass yourself." Mark warned.

Bettina came out of the laundry room looking upset. "Mark, did mommy wash my red Polo shirt?" She asked.

"I don't know!" He shouted.

"What you need washed baby? I'll clean your shit with my tongue." Limp came out of his mouth and said.

She sucked her teeth and went back into the laundry room.

"Clarke, shoot." Mark said.

Bettina came out holding some clothes in her arms causing the game to stop again.

"You need help with that, boo?" Limp asked.

"NO!" She made clear.

"You wanna hold my dick in your mouth then." He mumbled, which I'm sure everyone heard, because we all started giggling.

She cut her eyes at him, sucked her teeth and then proceeded to head back upstairs. Limp just stood there smiling. Mark just looked at him. I had a slight hard on from her presence myself. All I could think about was her in them tight jeans and that sexy tight white shirt. She made me horny.

"Yo, Mark, can I use your bathroom?" I asked.

"Go ahead."

Even though there was a bathroom in the basement, I chose to go upstairs. No one noticed. I crept upstairs into the bathroom and took me a quick minute piss. Afterwards, I started to massage myself over the toilet, thinking about Mark's sister and moms. I even took it to the extreme taking a pair of his sister's panties that were hanging up to dry and started sniffing them. I did the same to a pair of his mother's. I was being fucking perverted.

I continued to jerk off holding both pair of panties in my hand. When I finished I placed both pairs of panties back where I got them, and stepped out of the bathroom still fuckin' horny as hell. As I was about to head back down stairs, I noticed that his sister door was cracked open. I went from being a pervert to a peeping Tom. I took a quick glance into her room and saw that she was in a blue thong prancing around. I got so excited that I almost fell. I squatted down close to the floor and continued to look into her room. She had the radio playing loud so she didn't hear me outside of her door. She walked towards her bedroom window where I caught a better glimpse of her ass. My god, she was hot. I was so hard that I thought I would rip through my jeans.

I was waiting for her to pull down her panties. I really wanted to see how bushy her shit was. I looked at my watch but hesitated in heading back downstairs. This was much more exciting than playing a game of pool. Besides, I knew the guys wouldn't miss me being gone for a while.

I continued to peer into her room as her radio blasted 98.7. She started to dance around and pulled out a dress from her closet. She placed it neatly on her bed then walked towards my direction. I started to panic, as I quickly stood up and took a few steps back. Her bedroom door opened, and there I was, standing just a few feet away. I startled her.

"What the fuck are you doing up here?" She asked.

"Using the bathroom." I answered back.

"Ain't there a bathroom downstairs in the basement for you to use?"

"Yeah, but that one's already occupied."

"Ma!" She called out.

I nearly panicked as I headed for the stairs. Her moms came out of her bedroom and looked from me to

Bettina. She screwed up her face as she saw her daughter standing there in her robe and me standing there with a hard on in my jeans.

"What's going on?" She demanded to know.

"This pervert was peeking in my room." Bettina said.

"No I wasn't." I proclaimed.

"Yes he was, look at his hard on."

"Boy, are you crazy!" Mark's mother shouted.

"I wasn't peeking at your daughter." I said in my defense.

"Yes he was, mom, I saw him watching me." She said, gazing at me with her ice-cold eyes.

Now I was sweating and in a serious panic. There was no way she saw me watching her. She didn't once look my way. I tried to cover my hard on. It didn't help much, so I stood there with a serious boner.

"Call Mark." Her mother said.

"Mark! Mark!" Bettina called out. She retreated down the stairs and came back up with Mark next to her side.

"Mark, I want your friends out of my house." his mother said.

"Why?" He asked.

"Because, I saw this one peeping in your sister's bedroom while she was getting dressed."

Mark gave me a disgusted look, then glanced over at his sister. As for myself, I never felt so embarrassed in my life. I couldn't even look him in the eye.

"I want them out, now!" his mother shouted.

"Yo, that's fucked up, Spanky." He said sounding angry and disappointed.

"Yo, but she's lying."

"Is she? Then why didn't you use the bathroom in the basement?" He wanted to know.

There was nothing I could say to justify my being upstairs, so I just kept my mouth shut. We returned to the basement where the fellas were still playing pool. Mark interrupted them by telling them that they had to leave. He didn't reveal the reason. He just explained that his mother told him that it was getting late and that they had to go. So everyone gathered up their stuff and headed towards the front door. It seemed that something was bothering Mark all night and now this little incident really did him in. As we all walked out the door, he didn't even tell us goodbye or happy Thanksgiving. He just slammed the door behind the last person.

Thanksgiving Day included my mother, stepfather, Aunt Helen and myself. My moms cooked up everything she could think of--macaroni, string beans, collard greens, fish and black eye peas, sweet potatoes, catfish, turkey, and a ham. She also made her wonderful sweet potato pie. After dinner, my stepfather and I sat in the living room and watched football games. My mother and my Aunt were in the kitchen washing dishes and talking. I didn't have much family, so Thanksgiving wasn't a big deal. I had three cousins, who I barely know and my Aunt Helen, who I see twice a year.

After the game, I went upstairs to rest. I had a stuffed belly and wanted to lay down. You know what they say about black people after they eat a big meal. I popped in a porno movie and by five o'clock I was fast asleep.

My sleep was interrupted when my Aunt came into my bedroom and turned off my television. I slowly opened my eyes to see her standing over me with this disgusting look on her face.

"What the hell were you watching?" She asked, placing her hands on her hips.

I stared at her looking disoriented trying to think of what the hell she was talking about. Then it dawned on me that, I had left the porno tape playing in the VCR when I fell asleep.

"Why are you watching this smut, Jamal?" She demanded to know.

I've been watching pornos since I was ten, and now here comes my Aunt acting like she caught me committing a crime.

"Do your parent's know that you watch this sort of thing?"

Did my parents know? Did my parents know? Shit my stepfather supplied the movies. And my mother, my Aunt had no clue as to the things her sister was getting into with her husband.

My Aunt ejected the tape from the VCR and walked out of the room with it in her hand. Oh no she didn't, I thought. I got up from my bed and followed her into the hall, down the stairs and into the kitchen, where my parents were playing kissing games with each other against the kitchen counter.

"Um, excuse me." My Aunt interrupted them.

They turned around. I just stood in the doorway like a lost boy.

"What kind of example are you trying to set for Jamal, getting kinky with each other while your son's still around."

"The boys twenty-one." My stepfather protested.

"I don't care if he was eighty. Parents should not show that kind of sexual behavior in front of their children."

"What sexual behavior? We were just kissing, Helen." My mother said.

"Yes, and kissing leads to other things that your son doesn't need to be around." Aunt Helen said.

"The boys twenty-one and out of school, Helen." My stepfather spoke.

"I'm surprised at you. Our mother taught as better than that." My Aunt Helen said to my mother.

"Excuse me, Helen. This is my house. What I do in my house with my husband in front of my son is none of your business."

"Well maybe it needs to be my business. Because maybe I wouldn't have caught your son watching this smut in his room." Aunt Helen said, showing them the tape she had in her hand.

My stepfather just smirked as he looked at the tape. "Oh, *Extreme Cream*, I was wondering where that movie went."

"You mean, this is your movie, Leroy?" Aunt Helen said in shock.

"Yeah, me and your sister watch it all the time."

Aunt Helen looked like she was about to catch a heart attack. She couldn't believe what she had just heard. "Still, a boy of his age shouldn't be watching smut like this. His mind should be on his future."

What the fuck was she talking about? This from a lady whose son, is doing ten years upstate for assault, sexual abuse and rape. Her other son is a high school dropout, who's unemployed and got four kids from three different women. Now here she is, trying to get all in my family's business.

"Excuse me, sis, for a woman who's kids aren't the greatest, you need not talk about my son." My mother challenged.

"Well, you need to learn from mistakes. I don't want my nephew to become some stupid, uneducated slob with an around the clock hard on."

"What?"

"Yes, dear sis, you need to get on your job and raise your kid up right." My Aunt pushed the limit. I could tell, cause my mothers eyes went bloodshot red.

"Oh, no see, Jamal, go upstairs, you too Leroy. I need to have a few words with my older sister."

Leroy and I knew what time it was. We didn't stand around to ask questions. We just both left the kitchen in a hurry. I could hear my mother shouting, screaming and cursing my Aunt out. She had crossed the line.

After everything cooled down, I headed back down the stairs to find my Aunt Helen gone. When I asked where she went, my mother said back home. She told me that she wasn't welcome here until she knew how to talk and treat people with respect. That's why her kids came out to be so fucked up. She never respected them. She'd always looked and talked down to them as if they were still children.

That wasn't the problem with my mother. She gave me all the respect in the world. She knew I was twenty-one and an adult. She gave me my freedom. She didn't pressure me to attend college right after high school like most parents do to their kids. She said it was my life and my decision. I loved her for that.

When I returned to work the following Monday, everyone in the office looked like they have gained twenty pounds. Not Carla. She was looking finer than ever. I still had a crush on her. She came into the office in a denim mini skirt, knee high boots and a white blouse.

"Eat enough Turkey, Jamal?" Elaine asked. She was always in everyone's business. She wasn't attractive. Ok looking if you've been locked up for twenty years. Rumors around the office were that she was easy. I'd heard about many late night encounter with her. One guy bragged that she sucked his dick under his desk in the office.

"More than enough." I said, not even making eye contact with her, pretending I was busy.

Michael came over and flirted with Elaine. It was a game to him. She wasn't his type.

"Hi, Michael." Elaine spoke with such enthusiasm. She has had a crush on Michael for the longest, but he never gave her the time of day. "How was your Thanksgiving, Michael?"

"It was cool. I spent my holiday with these gorgeous set of twins from California." He said.

"Word!" I said, sounding excited.

Elaine gazed up at Michael, as he had his arm placed around her shoulders. He snuggled her up against his body, then bragged about his experience with the twins. Seeing this pitiful look on Elaine's face as Michael went on and on about his sexual experience over the Thanksgiving holiday made me just wanna tell him to shut the fuck up. He was definitely hurting Elaine's feelings.

"It's good to hear that you had a really good time, Michael." Elaine said. The sound of her voice made her seem like she was about to cry. "Well, I got work to do, see you guys later."

As she walked away, Michael said, "If she had a body, I would hit that. It would definitely make up for her face."

"You're wrong. Why do you do that to her. You know she likes you, but you're forever teasing her."

"That's my job, Jamal. I'm the closet to real dick she'll ever get. I gotta make her feel good about something."

"You shouldn't tease her. It fucks with her head."

"Well, at least some part of her is getting screwed."

I sighed and walked away from him. It wasn't fair. He even attracted the ugly ones too. While I Mr. Nice guy stay getting dissed by females. He had no respect for women. I showed more respect for them than he did but his dick action was always busy. It just didn't add up to me.

After I finished talking to Michael, Johnny, the black man trapped in a white man's body, came up to me. He once told me that he loved everything about a black woman.

"What up, Jamal?" He greeted.

"What's going on, Johnny."

"Yo, dawg, I had this fine sista chilling with me on Thanksgiving night."

"You fucked her?" I asked.

"Nah, she wasn't down with that yet. But yo, I'm gettin' there." He said.

I just looked at him in disbelief. Johnny had game, but I just didn't believe he was fuckin' all the sistas he was bragging about. He was a pretty white boy who always dressed in suits and wore the hell out of men's cologne. But a lot of sistas around my way didn't fall for that kind of stuff. Sad thing was they weren't falling for me either.

"Yo, you see what Carla got on?" Johnny nodded over at her.

"Yeah." I responded.

"Yo, I don't give a fuck what Michael says. Our little bet still stands. He just knows that I'm about to fuck her first that's why he called it off."

I don't know the reason Michael called off the bet between him and Johnny. Maybe he felt a loss with this one. He didn't push up on Carla as much as he did when she first arrived. I thought that benefited me more. Carla was starting to acknowledge me. She would tell me good morning, good night, and ask how my day was. That made me feel good. We even had small conversations with each other here and there. She made me feel alive!

Now all I had to do was gather up enough courage to ask her out. Whenever I started to, my nerves got the best of me. I would start to stutter and stumble knocking over things and dropping stuff.

At the end of the day, some of the guys said that they were going to a bar on Hillside Ave. to have a few drinks. They invited me to come along. At first, I said no. I wanted to try and walk Carla to the bus stop. Carla said she was staying late at work, so I reconsidered and went along.

There were five of us at the bar. Greg ordered drinks for everyone, One of the guys asked what was the special occasion with Greg, since he was buying everyone drinks. He responded by saying that he was getting married. He proposed to his girlfriend of two-years on Thanksgiving night and she accepted.

Whoa, Marriage, I thought. That was a big step. At my age, I wasn't trying to see marriage. Besides, if I was to ever get married, then it would be to Carla, she was the wife type. I knew that I was in love with that woman.

Greg continued to talk about his wonderful wife to be. He said the wedding would take place sometime next year. Johnny thought Greg was going crazy.

"Damn, Greg, marriage? Shit you're only twenty-seven."

"Yeah, Johnny, I'm only twenty-seven, and done been through so many women that I feel it's time for me to settle down and take it easy. This is the woman I love. All those others were just preparing me for her."

"So, Mr. Ex Playa, how many women have you been with in your life?" Ronald asked.

"Too many." Greg responded.

I just sat there with a beer in my hand curious to know the answer. Greg was a built fellow, who always dressed nice and was clean-shaven. He was also a nice guy, and very handsome. The women in the office adored him.

"Care to share the number?" Johnny asked.

"Y'all really want to know?" Greg replied, taking a sip from his beer. "All right then. I've been with over a hundred women in my time."

I nearly choked on my beer. He had sex with over a hundred females. Oh, how I wish I were him. That meant over a hundred females gave themselves to him. They offered their most valuable and prized possession between their legs to him. I couldn't see myself having sex with over a hundred women. Shit, I couldn't see myself having sex with over ten women. It was pitiful.

Ever since I've known Greg I've never heard the word bitch come out of his mouth. Nor have I seen him disrespect any of the ladies in the office. Him having sex with over a hundred women was possible.

Johnny tried to compare numbers by saying he had sex with over thirty women in one year. It was like he wanted to compete with Greg. But Greg didn't let that bother him. "Women are not trophies." Greg told Johnny. "They're angels put on this planet to help life reproduce and take care of man."

"Yeah, Greg's talking that shit now cause he done had enough pussy to last him two life times." Terry joked.

The fellows laughed and another round of beer was ordered.

Around seven, some fine young sistas walked into the bar. They looked like they were in their early twenties. Heads turned, lips drooled, and hard-ons were born, as they took seats near the back.

"Yo, you see that?" Johnny excitingly said.

"Damn, all of them are fine." Terry added.

It wouldn't take long for somebody in here to approach them.

"Jamal, go ahead and do your thing. Go get yourself a piece of that." Johnny spoke.

My eyes widened. "What?"

"C'mon, dawg. I never see you talk to any ladies. I'm starting to wonder about you." Johnny said, embarrassing me.

"I'm saying, I'm not in the mood right now."

"What, you're scared of pussy?" Johnny gloated

The rest of the guys just stared at me, probably wondering what my answer would be.

"Nah, never, you know me, Johnny."

"Nah, I really don't. I never see you around any ladies, Jamal. You don't even fuckin' brag about pussy."

I was being put in a tight spot. I was too scared to go over and approach all six of them ladies, by myself, anyway. At the same time, I couldn't play myself in front of my co-workers. They may think I'm some kind of little boy scared shitless. Johnny continued to harass me to go over and make conversation. I was so fuckin' nervous that I felt like I was about to pass out.

"Go ahead, Jamal, show us your mack daddy skills." Ronald instigated.

I glanced over at the young ladies, as they laughed and talked amongst each other. One girl in particular caught my eye. She was brown skinned with long curly black hair. She had the nicest lips. I just sat there on the barstool, gazing over at her.

"This guy here's scared of pussy." Johnny said.

"No I'm not." I said in my weak defense.

"Then why are you taking so long?"

"I'm just thinking of a game plan."

My palms were sweaty and my throat was dry. This had to be one of the worst days of my life. I was in a no win situation. All attention was on me. "Please, God, help me with this one." I mumbled under my breath. I took a deep breath and slowly got off the stool. I was still wet behind the ears with this talking to women thing. Then I thought about Greg having sex with over a hundred women. That boosted my confidence a little. If he did it, maybe I could too. He was an nice guy just like me. Then I started to second-guess myself. I wasn't Greg, or Johnny, I was just me, Jamal, a.k.a. Spanky. I wouldn't know the first thing to say to any of the ladies over there.

I slowly crept their way, feeling like I was about to pee on myself. I turned around and all the fellows were encouraging me to proceed. I forged ahead. When I got within conversation distance two guys came out of nowhere introducing themselves. I myself never felt so relieved. I wasn't going to cock block them. That wasn't my thing. So I turned around and walked back to the bar, smiling.

"Jamal, you were scared, you fronted." Johnny said. "Just admit to us that you're scared of pussy and I'll leave it alone."

"Please, I ain't scared of a damn thing." I said.

"You looked scared to me." Ronny said.

"Leave the boy alone, y'all." Greg said, "Maybe he's still a virgin, and is waiting to give himself to his bride on his wedding day."

What Greg said, cut through me like a knife. How can he think that I was still a virgin? I thought. I wasn't a virgin. It shamed me to have him think that I was. I didn't tell him that I wasn't. I just let him assumed that I was. I could have tried to defend my sexuality and told him about my two, well, two and a half past experiences with females. But then again, that would have been even more embarrassing. I looked at my co-workers. All of them had great sex stories to tell. I was still the lonely fuckin' asshole left out in the cold.

"I respect that, Jamal." Greg spoke, "You still being a virgin. Don't rush sex. There are too many diseases out there. You wait and marry that special woman one-day. Believe me, the best wedding gift you can give to her, is yourself."

I wasn't a damn virgin. God, my life sucks, I thought.

Johnny was just standing there with this smirk on his face, like he was laughing and taunting me inside his head. The others just remained silent. I felt like leaving the place. I peered over at the table where those six beautiful ladies were seated, and they were getting along quite well with those two gentlemen. Why can't that be me, I thought.

"Y'all ready to go?" Greg asked.

"Yeah, I guess so." Terry reluctantly said.

"You're in a rush to leave, Greg?" Johnny asked.

"Yeah. I promised Stacy that I'll be home by eight." Greg said.

"Damn, you ain't even married yet, and she already got you on a set time schedule." Johnny said.

Greg laughed. "Hey, that's life. That's soon to be marriage."

"Well, not me, never. I'll be a playa until the day that I die." Johnny bragged.

We got ready to leave the bar, all except Johnny. He stayed. He wanted to get acquainted with some young female that was sitting alone for the past ten minutes.

"You should stay and watch to see how it's done, Jamal." He said

When I arrived home I just fell across my bed, thinking about my pitiful sex life. It had to change. Muthafucka's in this world were going to stop thinking I was a virgin, and start seeing me as a playa.

I was going change my ways and my approach. There was going to be a new me. There was too much pussy out there for me not to be getting any.

SHANA
12

I lay on my back, with my legs split in the air, as Danny sticks his tongue so deep into me that it feels like a hard dick. I clutch his dreads and moan and moan. I glance at the time, and it's three in the afternoon. My mother had a doctor's appointment so she took his jeep and left him here with me. His whole mouth just swallowing up my sweet pussy. I tell him to lie on his back; then take him into my mouth, gulping his dick down to the balls. He grunts, lying butt naked on my bed with the body of a God. I suck him off so well that he tells me to stop while pulling my head away.

"Lay on your back." He orders, and I quickly do.

He gets on top and stuffs his dick into me, forcing my legs wide open, because his frame is so large and muscular. I passionately scream out his name, feeling his dick ramming and swelling in me. My juices flow with every stroke. He calls me his little wildcat because I stay scratching up his back when we be fucking. He don't care, because my mother be doing the same when they go at it.

We're into it for about fifteen minutes, sweating, bumping and grunting. He starts tearing it up from the back. I clutch onto the headboard strong, as he goes at it hard. Suddenly, we hear a car door slam.

"Shit!" Danny shouts, as he jumps out of the pussy and runs to the window. "It's your mother, get dressed."

I dash out of bed, run to my closet and quickly throw on a pair of blue jeans and a T-shirt. Danny rushes out of my room, forgetting his clothes and runs into the bathroom. I shove his clothes under my bed and start spraying air freshener around my room to get rid of the smell of sex. I hear her coming down the hall, towards my room. Damn she moves quick, I thought. I hop back into bed, pick up the phone, and pretend I'm talking on the line. I hear the shower going off in the bathroom. My pussy's throbbing so hard because I didn't get to finish.

My mother walks into my bedroom. She sees me chatting over the phone. "Why you're home so early?" I asked.

"The doctor wasn't that crowded." She answers, peering around my room. "Who you on the phone with?"

"Naja."

"Where's Danny?"

"You don't hear him taking a shower?"

"At three in the afternoon?"

"That's your strange fuckin' man." I say, pretending to speak to Naja over the phone.

She was looking strange and acting like something was wrong with her. She insisted on going to see the doctor alone this afternoon. Come to think of it, all week my mother's been acting strange.

"You all right, ma?" I asked.

"Yeah, everything's okay, Shana."

I just shrugged my shoulders and continued on with my phony conversation. My mother leaves my room slowly closing the door. As soon as she was gone I hung up the phone. I heard her banging on the bathroom door calling for Danny. This mutha-fucka takes a shower. He could have quickly gotten dressed in the bathroom and pretended like he was taking a shit or sumthin'. Instead, he jumps in the shower. I swear, men don't think nuthin' like women. They do things backwards. They just be looking to get busted.

I peep out into the hallway, watching my mother in front of the bathroom door. Danny finally comes out, with a towel wrapped around him, dripping wet. "Hi, baby." He greets, giving her a quick kiss. "When did you get home?"

"I need to talk to you." My mother says.

I was thinking, how was he gonna retrieve his clothes from out of my bedroom? I know he didn't bring an extra set with him. He follows my mother towards the bedroom. He looks at me like what should we do. I just point to the bathroom, hoping he gets the idea that I was going to place all of his clothes in there after they enter the room.

The second they leave my sight. I grab every piece of his clothing, run out my room and throw everything on the bathroom floor. Minutes later I hear movement in the hall. Curious, I open my door, to see Danny still in a towel, quickly coming towards my door. I step out and point to the bathroom. There ain't no need for him to come to my room. A few seconds later my mother comes out of her bedroom crying. I get nervous, thinking what could be wrong? Did she know that I was fuckin' her man? If she had any suspicion she would have confronted me about it. My mother doesn't play when it comes to her boyfriends. She'd be ready to scratch a bitches eyes out in a second, then cut her man's dick off. You best to believe she would be up in my face like I was some stranger in the street, fighting for her man-- daughter or no daughter.

I followed behind my mother, as she went into the kitchen. "Ma, what's wrong?" I asked.

She just ignores me, taking a seat at the kitchen table. Danny comes walking into the kitchen, fully dressed. I burst out at him, "Mutha-fucka, what you do to her?"

"I gotta go." He says, calm and cool.

"What? What the fuck happened?" I scream out.

Feeling lost, I followed Danny to the door, grabbing him by his shirt, and say, "What did you tell her?"

"I ain't tell her shit about you and me, she's dealing with a different problem." He informs, then walks out the door.

I slowly walk back into the kitchen, where she's still sobbing at the table. I pass her a few pieces of tissue and take a seat next to her. "Ma, what's the matter? You alright?"

She takes a deep breath, then says, "Shana, I'm fuckin' pregnant!"

"What! Is it Danny's?"

"Of course!" She yells.

"Damn! So what he say about it?"

"He told me to go get a paternity test taken."

"What?" I couldn't believe it. My mother was pregnant. And this mutha-fucka had the nerve to try and deny it when he was running up in her twenty-four seven. I tried to comfort her. But I feel guilty because I was fuckin' her man a few minutes ago.

"So, what you gonna do? You gonna keep it or what?" I asked.

"I don't know, maybe." She softly responded.

"How far along are you?"

"The doctor told me five weeks."

She dried her tears, as I passed her some more tissue. I brought her a glass of water, and helped her to her bedroom. I stayed with her the remainder of the day, making sure that she was ok. Damn, being pregnant must be really fucked up, I thought. You get fat, moody, loose your shape, and you no longer fit any of your clothing, while being constantly tired and sleepy. Shit, having children definitely wasn't for me. Kids can wait!

Christmas was soon to come, which meant gifts. I sometimes receive cards with money inside. The most money I'd ever received in a card was $500 from a man who used to ride the bus with me every morning when I was in high school. I never knew or met him. I used to see him gawking at me every morning on the bus, probably catching a hard on. A week before Christmas, he approached me, giving me a white envelope with ***please read, sexy***, written across it.

I arrived at school and opened the envelope during my third period class. The Christmas card had five, crisp hundred-dollar bills inside. I nearly fainted when I saw the money. I read the card:

Dear sexy,

I don't know your name, but you can know mines. It's Kyle, and I'm forty-five. I watch you everyday on the bus, and your beauty has just blown my heart away. You're the most beautiful woman that I ever laid eyes on. I know you're young, but age doesn't matter when it comes to beauty like yours. Give me the chance, and I'll marry you within a heartbeat. What's mines in this world, I'll give to you within the blink of an eye. I give this money to you just to prove that I'm not a lie. You're definitely worth a lot more, but this is all I can afford! The next time you see me traveling on the MTA, please speak, and remember Kyle's my name.

He also wrote his numbers down. I ripped up the card and kept the money. How stupid can you be, I thought, giving a total stranger you never met $500. From that day on, I took a different bus to school. I didn't want to risk running into him. With the money I bought Jakim a leather jacket and purchased a few outfits for myself.

I was on Jamaica Ave doing my Christmas shopping with Naja.

"So, what your moms gonna do?" Naja asked. I had told her of my mother's condition.

"She don't know. She might have it."

"Damn, Shana, you might be having a little brother or sister."

"Yup!"

"How do you feel about it?" She asked.

"I don't know."

As we walked towards 165th street I couldn't help but wonder what I would do if that was me. I wasn't trying to ruin my wonderful figure by having some assholes baby. I think my mom should get an abortion. Aunt Tina told her the same thing. She wasn't for it. She loves Danny. And even though he was acting like an asshole, my mother wasn't going to kill his baby.

Best of luck to her trying to get me to baby-sit. I love my moms, but I had a life, and watching kids all day long was not part of the plan.

As we walked down 165th street, towards the Coliseum shopping center, Naja pointed out a black BMW to me. "Ain't that Tyrone's whip?" She asked.

Yes it was. I knew his car like I knew my period. I had not seen or spoken to him in weeks. I had a serious bone to pick with him about Chinky and my little scrap with her in the bathroom. This bitch tried to cut me because of him. Then there was the thing with the detectives coming to speak to me about him.

"You wanna go the other way?" Naja asked, as we stood there, staring at his car.

"Nah, I wanna ask him some questions." I told Naja, walking towards his car.

"C'mon, Shana, it's Christmas. You don't need to be dealing with this shit right now! Deal with him some other time."

But I ignored her and walked straight toward his car. There was some dude sitting in the passenger seat. Tyrone was nowhere in sight.

I looked at him, and asked, "Where's Tyrone?"

He leaned up from his seat being reclined so far back and looked up at me. "Damn, boo, why you lookin' for him when you already found me?" He said.

Naja came and stood behind me, disappointed in my decision. "Where's Tyrone?" I asked again.

"He's in the record shop." His friend answered. "But I'm sayin' boo, what's your name?"

I walked towards the record shop with Naja close behind. I stopped at the glass door and peered inside. He was chatting with some hoochie looking female. She was smiling and laughing. She was all over him like flies on shit.

"C'mon, Shana, fuck him! You got Jakim back in your life now." Naja tried reminding me.

She was right. Jakim and I were bonding again. But seeing Tyrone chatting with that girl set me off. Here I was ready to curse him out, but caught feelings for him when I saw him talking and huggin' up on someone else. Once again I was confused.

"C'mon, lets go." Naja said, pulling me by my arm away from the record shop. I wanted to resist, but didn't. I wanted to approach Tyrone, smack that bitch, and yell get the fuck away from my man. I wanted to curse him out, hate him and try to still love him at the same time. I also wanted the truth from him about his relationship with Chinky, his children, and about us!

We walked away from the record shop. I wanted so much to turn around and seriously confront Tyrone. But Naja encouraged me to move along.

As we waited for the bus, Tyrone's car pulled up to the curve where we were standing. I sighed, and turned my head. Naja sucked her teeth.

"Shana, I need to talk to you." Tyrone shouted from the driver's seat.

"What do you want?" I asked, feeling somewhat glad that he showed up.

He stepped out of the car, wearing a black hoodie and a gold chain draped around his neck. His man remained seated in the car, staring hard over at Naja.

"Naja, watch my bags." I said, as I placed them next to her.

I tried to calm my nerve, I didn't know if I wanted to smack and curse him out or just fuck and love him. It didn't matter that he was wrong. He was for me. He pulled me to the side, out of everyone's hearing range. I back up against a brick wall as he's just stands inches from my face.

"So, what's up?" He asks.

"What's up with you?" I responded back.

"I was in jail for a few days."

"Why?"

"You know why. Because of that Terry situation. Fuckin cops trying to blame me for his murder. What you tell them, Shana?"

"I ain't tell them shit, Tyrone."

"You sure?"

I just looked at him. "They asked me a few questions about you, as if I knew anything about your whereabouts. All I told them was that we were just fuckin'!"

He chuckled. "That's my girl. They ain't got shit on me because I didn't do it. I ain't touch that mutha-fucka since that night I was with you. You believe me right?"

I didn't answer him.

"You believe me, Shana?" He repeated.

"Yeah. I do." I slowly answered.

He smiled. "Don't sweat it! So, where are you and Naja headed?"

"Home!"

"I'll take y'all." He volunteered.

"No. You need to answer me a few questions."

"Like what?"

"Who the fuck is Chinky?"

"What?" He stammered.

"Don't fuckin' play games with me, Tyrone. That bitch jumped me in the club. She claims that you're her man, her babies daddy and shit!"

"Don't believe that dizzy bitch, Shana."

"Why not, it's the truth, ain't it?"

"Nah, we ain't together. Yo, fuck that bitch!"

"Tyrone, don't bullshit me, Evay already told me all about y'all. He told me y'all been together for seven years. He told me you got some other bitch pregnant out in Jersey."

"Yo, you gonna believe that fat fuck, Shana!" He shouted. "That niggah just jealous. You know he likes you."

"But why he gotta lie?"

"Because he's hating on a brotha!"

"Nah, see, you need to take care of that bitch Chinky. Her and her home girls nearly sliced my face open…"

"I'll take care of it." He interrupted.

I stared at him with doubting eyes. I so much wanted to believe him but it was hard for me. I've been hearing so many things about him. It's hard for me to know what's a lie and what's not.

"I'm not gonna lie, Shana. Yes I do have kids by her. But we ain't together no more. I thought you knew this, everyone does." He said, sounding so convincing.

"What about that bitch in Jersey?"

"What bitch in Jersey? Shana, don't believe a word that fat mutha-fucka told you. I'll deal with him later."

"Shana, the bus is coming!" Naja shouted out.

"We'll catch the next one." I shouted back.

She didn't look too pleased standing there, while Tyrone's friend was trying to kick it to her.

"What about that bitch I saw you huggin' up on in the store a few minutes ago?"

"Shana, that bitch ain't nobody. I just ran into her. We used to talk a while back."

"So am I just another bitch in your life, Tyrone?"

He came closer to me. So close that I could feel his breath against mine. He pulled me against him. His scent brushed against my nostrils. "Don't be letting these jealous mutha-fucka's out here brainwash you with all these stupid rumors. I want you to be my woman. It's about me and you."

"So why you never act like it, Tyrone? I mean, you're always leaving town without me knowing. I don' hear from you for weeks, then...."

"Sshhhhh. Come here." He said, slowly pressing his lips against mine. I knew Naja was watching. I felt her eyes on me. I knew she would be pissed. But who cares. This was my life. I knew what I was doing.

"I'm taking y'all home." Tyrone insisted.

"I thought we were catching the bus, Shana?"

"Nah, Tyrone's gonna take us home."

She rolled her eyes, and sucked her teeth.

"Damn, boo, it's Christmas, Santa ain't bringing you no dick this year?" Tyrone's friend said.

"Check your mutt, Tyrone." She cursed.

"Chill, Pipe." Tyrone told him.

While riding in the car, Tyrone was constantly checking me out through his rearview mirror, smiling. I smiled and flirted back. Naja just sat next to me, mad. She ain't say one word during the whole ride home.

He pulled up in front of my home. Naja got out. I gave her my keys to go inside.

"So, what are you doing tonight?" Tyrone asked me.

"Nuthin', why?" I said, sounding like putty.

"I thought we could go out to dinner or sumthin'."

"That sounds good. Then what?"

"Then, we can chill over at my place. I'm about to evict that niggah Evay for good. I missed you, Shana." He said.

"I missed you too."

"I'll pick you up around nine, cool?"

"I'll be ready." I said, backing slowly towards the door, staring at him as he walked back to his car.

When I entered the house, I knew I had a few words coming from Naja. "Why you playing yourself out like that, Shana?"

"What you talking about?"

"I mean, why are you still fuckin' with him. You know he's wrong for you."

"What, you're my mother now? You're gonna preach to   me?"

"No! I'm just trying to look out for you. You've seen him huggin' up on that bitch in the store. Then his baby mother tried to cut you in the club. The detectives come to your crib asking you questions about Terry's death after you witnessed him pistol whip Terry a while back over money. Tell me you don't believe he didn't do it?"

"He said he didn't."

"Open your eyes Shana. Tyrone's putting you in bad situations. He's gonna get you hurt or killed. What happened to you Shana? You were stronger than this back in high school. You could see right through a guy's bullshit. Now you're acting like a fuckin' floozy."

"You don't know what you're talking about, Naja. I can take care of myself."

"I'm telling you, leave Tyrone alone."

"Or what, Naja?"

"What about, Jakim? I thought y'all were getting back together?"

"We were."

"So you're just gonna let him go? Dump him for Tyrone?"

My answer was silence. I gave her a smirking look as I slowly turned my head away from her. She had her arms folded across her chest, not once taking her eyes off me.

"You gonna play Jakim like that?" She continued.

"Fuck him." I exclaimed.

"Oh, that's wrong, Shana. You know he loves you! Now here comes Tyrone creeping back into your life after you ain't seen or heard from him in weeks. And you ready to go play make up with him."

"Please, it's my life!"

"And you're just gonna dump Jakim for his best friend!"

"So! I don't feel for him like I feel for Tyrone."

"You talk all this shit about Jakim being your love, your heart. You're playing with fire, girl, and it's gonna blow up in your face. You can't be switching back and forth between two best friends like that."

"Well, I'm not. I'm with Tyrone now, and Jakim's gonna have to understand."

"You gonna tell him?"

"Yup!"

"You know he ain't gonna take that shit lightly." Naja warned.

"Yeah, I know, but he won't have a choice!" I proclaimed.

Naja just sighed, unhappy with my decision. But it was my life and my choice. Jakim was a sweetheart. It just that when I'm with Jakim, sparks didn't fly for me. My panties didn't get moist. I didn't get aroused like I used to get when we were together. It's different with Tyrone. He was like a cigarette. You know it's bad for your health, but you smoke them anyway.

I knew that I had to tell Jakim about Tyrone—if he hasn't heard already. But I didn't know how. I knew once I told him, he would be upset. That's the way life is. You have to accept the good along with the bad. The bad being that I was screwing him over for his best friend. All week, it's been nothing but Tyrone and I. He took me to see a Broadway play. We ate at *Slyvia's* in Harlem and he took me shopping.

I knew what Tyrone and I shared was love. I was the only female in his life. That's why I satisfied my man, orally, anally. Whatever he wanted. A week before Christmas, he asked me to move in with him. The day after he asked, Tyrone had a small van in front of my mom's crib, with a few fellas helping to move my things. I didn't have much to move, except for my clothes, my shoes and my television.

When I told Naja, she thought I'd lost my mind. Aunt Tina hated to see me go, but she understood. I couldn't pass this opportunity up.

Word around the hood, was that Jakim knew about Tyrone and I, and he was threatening to cause Tyrone harm. Tyrone didn't take his threats to the heart. He understood that the boy was hurt. I knew I should have told Jakim about Tyrone. It probably would have been better for him to hear about us from my lips, rather than on the streets. God knows how they put it to him? But now that he knew, It felt like a burden had been lifted from me.

Christmas day was the best. Tyrone and I woke up around eight. We made love on the bed and then again in the shower. We had a real tree set up in the living room near the balcony. I made breakfast then we tore open gifts. I received a diamond ring, a necklace, a leather jacket, a Gucci purse and some lingerie.

"Why so much?" I asked.

"Business been good this year." He responded, smiling.

I bought him some sexy silk boxers, a coat, some beige Timberlands and a ring.

After the gifts, we cuddled on the floor watching movies together. He was sending chills down my spine when he started to nibble on my ear while whispering romantic things to me, and tickling my body softly with his fingers—oh my Lord—my baby had me open. Being warm and romantic is one of his special qualities that he hides so well. One that only his woman would know about. Tyrone is also a very clean and meticulous person. He puts everything in its place. And he takes his time with whatever he does—extra points in the bedroom. He doesn't like to rush things. He's also smart. He has a collection of novels, biographies, autobiographies, and non-fiction books. I never met a black male who loves to read so much. Despite his street life, you would think he's a Harvard student the way he sometimes carrys himself—very professional and well mannered. Some brothas out here try to hide their intelligence—if they have any. They think you must always act, talk, and be rugged, to survive in the streets. But it ain't even about that. Some of the most notorious kingpins were very intelligent, and weren't afraid to show it. Shit, you gotta be a smart man if you don't wanna do twenty-five to life, and wanna try and keep your business. But after moving in with Tyrone, I've learned so many great things about him.

Tyrone wanted me to try on one of the pieces of lingerie he bought me. I dashed into the bedroom and slipped into an animal printed piece and some stiletto heels. I came back out into the living room, and by the gigantic smile on his face, I knew that I was looking good.

"Come here!" He ordered.

I obeyed.

After our third sexual encounter, his cousin Aaron, stopped by around eleven that morning. He was a cutie too. But my man was better. This was my first time meeting him, and by the way he looked at me, I knew he liked what he saw. Tyrone told me to get dressed because we were going out. I stayed in the bedroom, getting dressed, while he discussed business in the kitchen with his cousin.

I wore my new white mink coat, along with my diamond ring and necklace. I was looking and feeling like a superstar as I stepped out of the car, getting ready to head into Lassie's. A very elegant and upscale restaurant located on the Lower East Side of Manhattan. We walked hand in hand towards the restaurant.

"You're looking stunning tonight." Tyrone complimented.

I blushed, and felt proud to be with him tonight. It was Christmas, and there was nothing that I loved more than being with my man on Christmas day. I was lookin' fine and he was lookin' fine too, dressed in a black Armani sweater, black slacks, and black alligator shoes.

The waiter escorted us to our table. We fit right in with the crowd which were mostly old white fogies. Tyrone, being the gentleman that he is, pulled out my chair for me. Then he took his seat opposite me. The environment in the restaurant was so welcoming and gentile. You could feel the Christmas spirit as soon as you stepped in. They had mistle toe's draped all around the place. A small band of three, played Christmas carols on their stringed instruments. Our waiter wore a red and white Santa hat. Even our table was decorated with a small Christmas tree as a centerpiece.

Tyrone reached over and gave me a courtly kiss. I smiled. "What's that for?" I asked.

"Look up." He pointed.

I looked up, and saw a small sprig of mistle toe hanging over my head. I chuckled and even blushed. He continued to stare at me, smiling.

"Damn, you're beautiful...Merry Christmas." He meekly said.

"Thank you." I cordially responded, as I smiled sheepishly.

My night could not get any better. I felt like I was in heaven. I was with my dream man on a dream date. I had to pinch myself to make sure that everything was real. I mean, a woman like myself couldn't ask for anything more. We had our own apartment—a very nice apartment. He had money to burn, so he wasn't cheap with expenses. He always dressed nice, and smelled good, thank God for that.

And the sex was UN-fuckin' believable. I had no complaints, and thank you Lord for that! My life was the bomb!

After dinner, we went on one of those horse & carriage ride through Central Park. We made out in the carriage the whole ride. He fondled me through my dress, as I also blessed him with that thing I do. The night was a little breezy, but it wasn't brick ass cold outside. But the cool air felt good blowing in between my opened legs.

This was the best day of my life. After we got home, we chilled in front of the television, watching more movies, and sexing each other—cuddling in his arms, as he held and caressed me gently. I felt like Cinderella, and he was my handsome prince, and this spacious apartment was our kingdom. I felt that no man or woman could break up what we had. I felt that this was it. He would be my man or maybe my husband for life. No one could oppose on what we have.

I felt that, and I even dreamed it.

SPANKY
13

I` was in village, shopping and decided to go into one of those stores that sell sex toys. I was at the table eyeing two products, a cream and a bottle of pills that guaranteed a hard dick.

"How much for that bottle right there?" I asked, pointing to the internal one.

"For you my man, forty dollars." The cashier said.

"Forty, damn."

"Yo, you'll love me for this. I get no complaints when brothas pick this up."

"And what about that one?" I pointed to the cream.

"Thirty."

"What's the difference?"

"Yo, get the forty-dollar bottle." He suggested, shoving it into my hand. " It comes with a hundred tablets. You take a half hour before you have sex, and then you'll be able to fuck your woman all night long." He sung in a melody.

"What about the other one?"

"Yo, all you gotta do with that one, is rub a little on your shit, and that mutha-fucka is gonna have you harder than rock itself. But I suggest you go with the forty-dollar bottle, because from what I hear, it gives you better results and shit."

I needed results. My sexual stamina was too damn short, and these little pick me up pills might just do the trick for me. Shit, they better if I was paying thirty or forty bucks.

"Yo, trust me, they'll work. I haven't had one complaint about these pills since I've started selling them. These mutha-fucka's be selling like pussy itself."

I passed him the forty, and he placed the merchandise in a small plastic bag.

"You've made the right decision, my man. These here are gonna do wonders for your sex life."

Now I just needed some pussy.

It was a Saturday, and I called up some of the fellows to see if they wanted to go back to that underground strip joint. Clarke was the only one down.

I picked up Clarke around nine. And we headed out. I had two pills wrapped up in foil, in my front pocket. We pulled up to the spot and after securing my vehicle, we stepped inside. I had $250 in my pocket, and was ready to spend it well. Since we arrived early, shit wasn't jumping off yet. There were a few girls in the place, but none weren't dancing, stripping, or doing VIP yet.

I ordered me a Corona, and Clarke ordered himself a rum, mixed with a little Coke. We sat at the bar, watching the Lakers play the Knicks on the MSG channel. The Knicks were losing by twelve in the third quarter. And being the huge Knick fan that I am; I was pretty upset. It was an intense game.

"The Knicks are fuckin' garbage." A man, in a blue suit insulted.

I turned and looked at him. How dare he diss my team like that, I thought.

"Houston's a bum, Camby's a bum, they should eliminate that whole fuckin' team from the NBA. I mean, c'mon, how you loose to the Rockets in the Championship game, back when they could have finally won themselves a fuckin' ring," He continued, speaking the to bartender.

The bartender laughed, as he turned and glanced at the television. I had confidence in my team. Yeah, they lost the championship game, but they still won the eastern conference title, and the Rockets were a pretty good team to play against, back then with Sam Cassell and Olajuwon playing center.

"Watch Houston miss this shot." The guy said, with his eyes glued to the TV. "See, what I tell ya'" He added. Houston shot the three pointer, but it missed, bouncing off the rim right into the Rocket's hands.

I kept my comments to myself. He ain't know shit about my team, or basketball. I took a sip of my beer, as I continued to watch the game, hoping that my team would make a comeback during the fourth quarter.

"Why don't they just trade that non-ball playing Houston? He ain't no good to the team anyway, shooting like he scared of the ball. I've seen kindergartens with better shots than him." He continued on. "Mutha-fuckin' bum!"

"You musta lost money, Jimmy." The bartender said, referring to the man dissin' my team.

"Yeah, I lost money. Those fuckin' Knicks cost me $500. That team should burn in hell. They're paying this little weasel looking coach all this money for coaching, and they can't even win a fuckin' Champion game...not one."

Damn, he lost five hundred dollars, I feel his pain, I thought, sitting there drinking my Corona. I was never that stupid to bet that much money on the Knicks. I mean, they're my team and all, but when betting that much doe, you gotta go with the facts, and the fact being, that they weren't doing good this year."

At the end of the third quarter, the Knicks were trailing by ten. The guy ordered himself another beer, and sat there watching, and still cursing at the game.

Clarke tapped me on my shoulder, gesturing for me to turn around, and look at the door. I did, and saw three black sistas walk into the place, looking fine as hell. They were carrying small duffle bags in their hands, and talking to the bouncer. One of them turned around, and she had a phat ass, so phat that you can see it from the front.

AH, man, I wanted to demonstrate my pill on one of them. If I could go the full twelve rounds with one of those sistas, then I knew my hat was in the bag. I swallowed the last of my beer, got up, and headed into the next room where the action was suppose to take place for the night. Clarke wasn't too far behind. We walked into the poorly lit dark room, where there was a small stage set up, with one gold pole positioned in the center of it. And there was an old torn up leather couch placed in the back, which the girls used that for lap dances only. There were a few fellows standing around with beer and liquor in their hands, as they watched this bony light skinned chick dance around in her jeans on the stage. She was probably drunk.

Clarke and I leaned up against the wall. We watched the chick on stage dance from a distance.

As I stood there, I was becoming antsy, and just wanted to do my business right now at this very moment. I wanted to wait for the right girl to come along. I wasn't going to waste these two pills on just any scally-wag, hoe.

By midnight, the stage was filled with three butt naked chicks dancing, exposing their sweet spots, lap dances was being performed, and it was touchy feely all over a bitch.

I was on my third beer.

"C'mon, dog, I'm going to the back to see some bitches." Clarke said, getting off the barstool.

I was right behind him.

We stepped into the crowded back room. We made our way through the tight crowd, towards the stage, where there were two ladies, eating each other out. The men went totally berserk, as they threw money onto the stage, encouraging them for more.

"Yo, lick that pussy, baby." One guy shouted.

"Yo, bitch, I want you to suck my dick afterwards." This chubby guy yelled, holding a huge bankroll in his hand. He threw a fifty-dollar bill onto the stage, as he gazed on with excitement in his eyes.

The ladies switched up their routine, as they both straddled their legs around each other and started rubbing pussies together. The crowd went fuckin' bananas. Clarke and me got bumped and pushed, as more niggahs rushed to the stage to catch an eyeful of the action. Money was being tossed and thrown everywhere.

"Yo, these bitches is wilding!" this hood lookin' niggah shouted.

I was turned on by it. The Spanish lookin' bitch caught my full attention. I felt that she was the illest one. I started daydreaming on what it would feel like to get her alone and do my thing with her. When they were done they collected money off the stage, and walked off. I wanted to meet her. Yeah, she was the one. Ah, man, I could just imagine how good that shit was gonna feel.

I followed her, as she walked towards the room exit. But she didn't get too far, some young punk pulled her to the side and she grinded all up on him, fondling his crotch. He had his hands all over her tight little booty and in between her thighs. She didn't seem to mind. He slipped a twenty in between her breast.

I tried to be patient. I wanted to be next. I wanted her to grind all over me and have her fondle me too. I tried to be slick, and went and stood next to them. She had money's zipper open, with her hand inside, massaging him, as he leaned up against the wall. She pressed her body against his.

I just wanted to snatch her away from him, and take her somewhere private where she could freak me. She pressed her buttocks against his pelvis, massaging his shit with her tight ass. She glanced my way, smiled, and then gave me a friendly and seductive wink.

Next thing you know she was whispering in his ear, he nodded, and then they both walked off with each other. Curious, I followed. I had an idea on where they were going. She was about to give him VIP treatment. Heck, I wanted a VIP, that's what I came here for. I was hating.

Damn! I cursed myself. I've should have grabbed her as soon as she stepped of the stage. But there was nuthin' that I could do now. I reached into my pocket and pulled out my two pills wrapped inside the tin foil, contemplating if I should take one now, or later. Later, I thought.

I joined Clarke back at the party in the other room, where there now was this thick chocolate chick bouncing that ass up and down, wearing a black cowboy hat, and some cowboy boots. She swung around the pole, throwing both legs into the air, and coming down slowly. Whoa, I thought. I didn't know thick chicks could move like that.

"Yo, Limp would lose his mutha-fuckin' mind if he was up in here right now." Clarke said.

I chuckled. It was true. Pussy everywhere!

Another thick chick joined the one on stage. She wore a red thong and some heels. The first thing she did on stage, was lie down on her back, and spread her legs for the crowd to see her stuff, as she parted her thong to the side. Bushy wasn't the word for what was between her legs. She needed a serious razor. The fellows didn't mind; they tipped her, sticking dollar bills into her thong, and into her coochie. I gave that other bitch, with the cowboy boots, and hat, five dollars, just for being cute.

Twenty minutes later, my favorite female came back into show. I automatically tipped her a ten. The guy she went in the room with gave a twenty. Showoff!

She went over to him, and straddled her legs around his waist, and they humped and grind right there on the stage. He couldn't keep his hands off her.

"Yo, y'all gonna do another show?" someone shouted from afar.

She smiled, cuffed her breast, and licked her nipples very meekly. I was aroused just by the thought of her rubbing up against me. I tipped her another ten dollars. She came to me, as I placed the bill in between her breast.

"Thank you." She said, as she smiled pleasantly at me. "Do you want a dance?" She asked.

I wanted more than a dance, but a dance would do fine with me right now. I nodded, and she said, "Give me a minute."

I got so excited, that I tipped her another ten just for the hell of it. She was thrilled.

She went around collecting more tips, and entertaining the men, by sprawling across the floor on her stomach, with her legs widely spread, exposing her clit from the back. Then she went on and started fingering herself while she lay on her stomach.

After her gig, she came my way. "You still want that dance?" She asked.

I nodded. We walked arm in arm trying to find a dark and deserted corner, or wall. It was nearly impossible to find, there were so many people in the place. Every corner, wall, and space on the couch was occupied.

"Damn." I uttered, "There ain't nowhere for us to go."

"How about a VIP then." She suggested.

I smiled, Thrilled about the idea.

"How much?" I asked.

"Eighty."

She was worth it. I needed to try out this pill, and I needed to try it out on the best female that was up in here. I reached into my pocket, and pulled out one pill for me to take. This was it, I thought. I told her I had to go to the bathroom.

"You about to finally tear up some pussy." I said to myself in the mirror. Shit, I needed a half hour for this pill to take affect, Damn, I'd totally forgotten about it. I had this hot, freaky bitch outside waiting to fuck, and I needed to wait about thirty minutes.

Ok, everything's gonna be cool, I thought. I'll just buy her a drink and keep her company at the bar for about thirty minutes. Yeah, that would work. I walked out of the bathroom, to see her chatting with some other guy. Damn! I slowly make my way back to her. I'm afraid to interrupt. So like a cornball, I just stand there, hoping that she'll see me waiting. It doesn't work that way. That faggot offers to buy her a drink. So forgetting about me, she walks away with him. But I'm still cool about it, I still got twenty minutes for this pill to take affect.

They take a seat at the bar. Ten more minutes pass, and now I'm sitting at the bar, looking across at them, as they chitchat, and play touchy feely with each other, and he buys her more drinks. I slide over to the next chair, now I'm sitting right next to the guy, with her sitting on the other side of him, and I'm trying to hear every word he tells her.

"Damn, you're fuckin' fine, you're from South America."

She takes a sip of her drink, and nods her head.

"Yo, bartender, let me get another Corona." I say.

"So, do you want this VIP, or not?" She asks him.

"Of course I do, baby." He says, as I watch him slide his hand in between her thighs. "Damn, that pussy feels so wet, and so good." He tells her.

"Then let me satisfy your *guevo* with my wet *toto*." She says to him.

"What?" He responds.

"You don't speak Spanish, papi?" She asks.

"Nah, boo. I just speak tongue."

She chuckles. "C'mon, let me give you a VIP, you won't regret it." She tells him, as I watch her massage his crotch with her hand.

"Cool, then, c'mon." He says, getting up from his seat, with her doing the same. No, I shout in my head. That's my VIP. She takes his hand, and leads him towards the back rooms. Stunned, I get up, and try to follow. But I'm unsuccessful, as one of the bouncers keeps me from entering.

Clarke comes from out of the other room with one of the strippers

"Spanky, why you out here? It's off the hook up in there." He says.

"Nah, I'm just chilling."

I gawk at the girl he came out with, with her phat thighs and hips. He loves the thick, plus sized women. She's pretty though. She looks at me and smiles. I give her a friendly smile back.

"You gonna buy me that drink?" She asks him.

"Yeah, sure." Clarks answers her. "Yo, show my man what you be doing up in there." He tells her.

She turns around, and bends over, with that phat ass in the air, jiggling up and down, then she falls down to the floor into a split, with both cheeks touching the floor.

"See that shit." He says in amusement.

But I see nuthin' so spectacular about her doing a split on the floor, bitches been doing that all night.

Shorti gets up, "What about my drink?" She asks.

"Yeah, hold on, it's coming." He says, "Let me just talk to my boy real quick. He puts his arm around me, and leads me away. "Yo, this bitch think I'm gonna buy her a few drink, that bitch is dizzy. She's been giving me free lap dances and shit, because I'd promised to treat her to the bar. The bitch is an alcoholic."

After he talks to me, he ducks back into the room where the girls are, leaving the one he came out with out to dry. I walk back towards the bar, to have this bitch come up to me, and ask, "Where'd your friend go?"

I point to the room, and by the look on her face, she ain't too pleased. She storms off, shouting, "Nah, see, niggahs be playing themselves. I ain't come here to have niggahs grope on me for free."

I just shake my head and laugh. I take a seat back at the bar.

"You want another drink?" The bartender asked.

I tell him no.

Another twenty minutes later, shorti comes trotting back out. She finally sees me and comes walking my way.

She steps to me, as I try to play it cool, and stare up at the tube. "You still want that VIP?" She asks. "C'mon, Papi', I can make you feel good." She says..

I can't help but smile, as she reaches up to my crotch, and squeezes it soothingly. I face her, staring into her lovely and beautiful face. It's hard to believe that a woman who looks like her fucks for cash. I mean, she don't look like the type of woman who gets into this kind of business.

"C'mon, papi, let me fuck you." She says, taking my hand, and trying to lead me away.

And my dick agreed, and followed.

"C'mon, papi, get undressed." She said, laying down on a single gray, worn out mattress in the room that needed a serious paint job. She rested on her knees, pressed against the mattress, as she waited for me, and her money.

This pill better fuckin' work, I say to myself, as I stepped out of my jeans and underwear. My dick dangled in front of her, as she smiled, admiring what she saw.

"Where's the eighty?" She asked.

"Oh!" I reached back into my pants, and pulled out four twenties, and passed it over to her. She tossed it to the side, passed me a condom, and lay back on the mattress, parting her legs. I was fully up, harder than Bed-Stuy in Brooklyn. I slipped the condom on, walked up to her, climbed on top, and eased it in her.

"Aaaahhhh." I grunted, feeling the wetness, and softness of her vagina.

"Fuck my *toto!*" She exclaimed.

She straddled her legs tightly around me, as I vigorously pumped into action. Don't cum, don't cum, don't cum, I repeated multiple times in my head. I really needed this pill to fuckin' work for me.

"Suck me *tetas*." She said, referring to her breasts.

And I did, taking one of her breasts completely into my mouth, and sweetly sucking on her nipples, as she humped against me.

"Mmmm-hmmm, yeah!" She moans.

Don't cum, don't cum, don't cum, I repeated again, and again, because I was definitely feeling it. I looked at my wristwatch, and it's only been two-minutes. We rocked back and forth on that stained and dirty mattress, my palms flat down, as I thrust harder and harder into her. Her pussy just devouring what she called, my *guevo.*

Don't cum, don't cum, don't cum. I looked at my watch once again, and it's only been four minutes. I started to get excited. I felt that this shit was really working for me. I cocked her legs fully back over her head, stood on the balls of my feet, and pumped my *guevo* deeply into her.

"Yeah, papi', yeah, papi'." She shouted. "Doggy style, papi'."

"Hunh?" I said, sounded disoriented.

"I wanna fuck, doggy style, papi'." She repeated.

I looked at my watch, and it was going on six minutes. I was feeling like a fuckin' king, I told her to, "Turn that ass over!"

She abides, switching positions, resting on her hands and knees. I struck a pose, then rammed it into her from behind. She cried out. She rocked back and forth, as I thrust deep into her. Sweat pouring off my chest, my face drenched with excitement. This is the longest I've ever been. She clasped onto the wall, as I grasped both her buttocks, and doing my thing. I looked at my watch again, and it was going on eight minutes. Her pussy's pulsating heavy, as my dick was doing the same. I started to breathe heavy. Okay, now, I was definitely feeling it. The faster I went, the tighter it got.

"Oh my god." I cried out. "Shit, fuck, Dammmnn…muthafucka!"

She put it on me so bad. I wanted to do it in one more position before I came. But the way she'd worked it, it looked like I wasn't about to get that chance. Her breast and face were pressed against the mattress. Her arms sprawled out like an eagles' wings, as her buttocks were raised in the air, pushing back against my shit.

"C'mon, cum, papi', cum for me." She said, looking back at me.

And soon after, I surely did. Letting off a strong nutt. I sighed in relief. I looked at my watch. Ten minutes. I've lasted ten fuckin' minutes. I got up and jumped for joy. I felt like doing cartwheels. "It worked!" I shouted. "It actually works!"

"Damn, papi', my shit was really that good? See, I told you, you'd love it." She said. I stared down at my dick in amazement, proud of it. He did good for the first time ever.

She came up to me, and asked for a tip. I gave her another ten dollars. I was pumped up. She smiled.

"Can I get your number?" I asked, so maybe one day I can get a round two with her.

She grinned. "You gotta a el boli'grafo, papi'?"

"What?"

"A pen."

"Oh."

I got dressed, and pulled out a pen and small piece of paper so she can write down her number. She quickly wrote in down, and passed both items back to me.

"It was good, right?" She asked, picking up her money and clothes.

"Yeah, it was real good." I complimented

"See, papi', my *toto* is the best."

I felt like I was on cloud nine. This is how sex supposed to feel. Ten minutes, I kept thinking, ten minutes. Not two minutes, or three minutes, but it actually lasted for ten minutes. And that was only on one pill. Imagine if I'd taken two pills, maybe I would've gone on for twenty or thirty minutes.

I wanted to try and go another round with her. Shit, it was only another eighty dollars. It proved to me that this pill could do wonders for a young brotha like myself. I was no longer stressing my performance in the bedroom. Taking these pills, I could go all the rounds that I needed. This was only just the beginning of a whole new world for me. I felt that God had finally answered my prayers. There was no more short-term action for this fellow, it would be forever longevity, and I know the girls will finally give me the respect that I deserve, once I was able to prove myself sexually.

I felt like a man. I finally felt like a man.

SHANA
13

The night is young and my body is quivering. I stare up towards the ceiling. I close my eyes, and enjoy this moment with my man in our bedroom, as he devours me with his tongue.

The television is still on, but our attention is somewhere else, somewhere more important than watching an anchorperson broadcast over TV something we see everyday, crime, murder and corruption. I moan, as I clutch my hands around the back of his head, scratching and digging into his cornrow-braided hair.

"Oh, baby." I cried out.

His hands reaches its way up to my breasts, pinching and squeezing them. Ever since I've moved in, our nights have been nothing but sexual. We just couldn't get enough of each other. Naja continued to warn that I was making a big mistake moving in with my sweetheart Tyrone. She couldn't be anything but wrong. I'm a woman now, and I know what's right and what's not right in my life, and right now, Tyrone was feeling so damn right.

"Oh, baby, turn off the television." I faintly said, it was starting to bother me.

He reached around the bed for the remote and clicked off the television. The only light peeping through our bedroom was the light from the streetlights.

As I was about to tell him to enter me, his cell phone went off, and causing my man to be distracted. He jumped off the bed and retrieved it off the nightstand.

"Yo!" He answered.

I leaned over to my side and watched him. I can really see spending the rest of my life with him.

"Yo, Shana, I gotta bounce for a minute." Tyrone said, clicking off his cell.

"What? Go where?"

"That was my boy, some shit went down earlier, and I gotta go take care of it." He said, throwing on his clothes.

"I'm sayin' though, why they can't handle shit for once without you, Tyrone?".

"Cause this is business, Shana."

"I thought I was your business a few minutes ago?"

"Don't worry boo, when I get back, I'm gonna dig all up in that pussy for the next twenty-four hours, just me and you. He then gave me a kiss on my forehead, threw on his beige leather jacket and just left, leaving me alone, horny and naked. My vagina was throbbing sumthin' serious, it needed to be fed. When I heard the door to the apartment slam, I became angry, angry with myself, then with him. I should have fucked him earlier, and maybe I wouldn't be feeling like this, I thought

Before you knew it, the next morning came. I rolled over to an empty space in our bed, a space where Tyrone was supposed to lay, and snuggle up against me. But he hasn't arrived home yet, been out since he left me horny and out to dry last night.

I turned to the weather channel and the forecast was for snow. I cringed just thinking of the snow. I really hated the cold months. I love the warmth, because a woman like me was able to sport cute outfits. Jakim used to hate what I came to school in sometimes. He threatened to send me home and change, say I was embarrassing him because all of his friends were clocking me. He'd play himself out and scream on me like I was a four year old. *"Niggah, you're my boyfriend, not my daddy."* I would shout out back to him. Then we start to argue in front of everyone like two fools.

I covered myself in the sheets and blanket, only exposing my head out, because it was cold in the room, and being naked in bed didn't help matters much. It was 25 degrees out, a week after the New Year—2001. Tyrone and I celebrated the New Year lovely. He bought a few bottles of E&J and champagne and we stayed in enjoying each other's company. Ten minutes to midnight, we went out on the balcony of our apartment, peering over the Queens neighborhood on the 12th floor with a glass of Champagne in our hands. He held me tight in his arms, as the cold air gave us chills and shivers as we waited for midnight to come.

"5,4,3,2,1...*Happy New Year*!" we both shouted simultaneously, glasses raised in the air, hearing cars honking from below, people shouting from the streets below, *"Happy New year!"* to each other. Tyrone clutched me softly into his arms, giving me a gentle and very passionate New Year kiss. "I love you, Shana." He proclaimed.

"I love you too, baby." I repeated.

Afterwards, he carried me off into the bedroom, in the threshold position, lying me softly down. Then we stripped naked, and made love for the very first time in 2001. They say that the person you bring in the New Year with, is the person you're gonna spend your entire life with—I prayed so, because Tyrone was definitely the kind of man that I wanting to spend forever with.

That afternoon, I went to get my hair done up by my girl Sandra, and of course, she had the latest gossip on everyone around the way. "Girl, let me tell you about so, and so, and let me inform you on what'cha ma call it." She would run her lips and I would sit there laughing, listening and running my mouth along with her.

"Shana, let me tell you sumthin' about your friend, Sasha. Oh, sorry girl, I mean your ex-friend, Sasha. You know she still fuck with that bouncer from the club right?"

I was surprised. I thought she woulda fucked him, used him, and then dump him a long time ago.

"Well, they were arguing and fighting right here on the corner the other day." Sandra continued on. "I mean, she slapped him, spit in his face, then he yoked her up, and threw her down to the floor."

"For   real?"

"Someone had to call the cops on them two before it got worse out there. I don't even know why she's messing with him, he ain't cute."

"You telling me, but that's her man and her business."

And to believe that bitch dumped our friendship over some ugly, black and trifling brotha. Just to think it all started because she volunteered to suck his dick that night we went to the club.

She continued to talk and do my hair for the next hour. "Girl, I heard you moved in with Tyrone, damn, y'all together like that?" She asked.

"Yeah, girl."

"Um, um, that's a fine man." She said.

"Word, Sandra, that niggah knows how to handle his business in and out of the bedroom. Shit last night, he had my toes curling like pretzels that niggah tongue felt so good."

"Word, he be going downtown on you like that?"

"Yup, whenever he can, and I don't even ask him for it...that niggah just be like 'lay down on your back and spread your legs' and I don't complain or say shit about it, I just let him do his thang."

Sandra smiled. "Damn, girl, you are so lucky. I have to practically beg my man to eat my pussy ...but he ain't got shit to say when I be suckin' his dick."

"Then stop suckin' his dick." I uttered.

"Yeah, but that niggah shit be tasting good, I love it when he gets hard in my mouth."

"Nah, see, you're nasty bitch!"

"Shana, don't front, you know you be suckin' Tyrone off, too."

"Yeah, but it goes both ways between us, I don't keep doing him a favor and he's not returning it back to me…nah, it's fifty, fifty between us."

"Do he got a big dick too?" She bluntly asked.

"See, bitch, now you're asking too many personal questions."

"I'm sayin' though, I'm just curious… I know his fine ass gotta be packing sumthin' lovely below. So do he?"

"You see me smiling, right."

"See, I'm hating …but you go girl."

She remained quiet for a few minutes, as she focused on my hair. I gazed at myself through one of the many mirrors. As soon as I walk into this place, bitches in here, stare and start to hate on me, just because I don't need a weave. Bitches eyes be scoping me from head to toe, either impressed or envious of my style and my looks. But I don't give a fuck because it's only about me. I got what I want in life, a lovin man, a little money, beauty, my own place, and that good piece of dick that runs up into me almost every night.

"You'll be done in another thirty minutes." Sandra informs me, as she presses my hair out. "Have you heard from Jakim?."

I let out a huge sigh. "We're over, Sandra. It was time for me to move on."

"Yeah, with Tyrone. Jakim ain't beefing about that?"

"Yeah, but I ain't run into him to talk to him yet. I feel bad for him, but that's life, what you gonna do?"

"Girl, you just got better dick in your life, forget about him, and do you."

I smiled.

By two-thirty I was done, and lookin' finer than when I'd walked in. I paid Sandra, and tipped her my usual twenty.

I returned home around three via taxi. I was hoping that my baby was going to be home, because I wanted to really give him some. After he left me hot and out to dry last night, there was no way I was going to let him slip through my fingers today.

I walked into the apartment to find the place was completely quiet. The first thing I did, was turn up the heat. I came out of my coat, climbed outta my shoes, and plopped down on the couch, turning on the television. I had my hair done, my nails done, and a new outfit hanging in the closet. I wanted to go out tonight out with my baby. I felt that this was not the time for me to be sitting around this apartment wasting my beauty.

By four, the phone rang. It better be Tyrone.

"Hello." I answered.

"Baby, what's up, it's Ty'."

"Ty', where you at? You got me sitting here waiting and worrying about your ass." I chided over the phone.

"Yo, I'm up in the Bronx right now."

"The Bronx." I repeated.

"Yeah, I had to take care of some business that went down last night."

"I've called you, and you're not answering your cell. What's up?" I asked.

"Nah, ain't nuthin' wrong. I'll be home around eight tonight."

"Eight! Why so late?"

"C'mon, Shana, I don't need the stress right now, I've got too much shit to take care of tonight."

"I need taking care of too." I told him in my softest and sweetest voice.

"I know you do, Shana. That's why tonight, when I get home, I want you dressed in your finest and sexiest outfit, because I'm taking you out."

"For real, where?"

"It's a secret, boo…you know I'm gonna look out for my lady love, right."

"Yeah, I know. And I'm gonna look out for you too."

He chuckled over the line, causing me to do the same. I couldn't wait until eight to see my man. I looked at the wall clock over the television and it was five after four—four hours to go.

"Keep it warm for me, Shana, because it's fuckin' brick out here."

"Don't worry, Ty', it's staying warm until you get here and make it catch fire."

He laughed. "You a trip, Shana."

"I love you."

"I love you, too." He repeated, making my body temperature rise and causing my pussy to run rapidly, like Niagara Falls. I hung up, feeling like I was on cloud nine. I wanted it to stay that way forever.

Eight he said. What was I to do until eight? I love living in my new home, but it wasn't much fun staying in, without Tyrone being here to heat things up with me. You can watch so much television, and the radio wasn't playing nuthin' good. It was too cold out for me to go and drink and chill out on the balcony. And it was too cold for me to be going outside. I went through the hundreds or so collections of CDs we had. Tyrone had everything from Pop, Jazz, to rap, hip-hop, and R&B. I wanted to listen to something that was smooth, romantic—sexual. I wanted to listen to something that would get me in the mood until my man arrived. Something that would get and me hot and horny.

I put on a Miles Davis CD, and then I went into the bedroom with a glass of wine in my hands, and just sat on my comfortable sheets, wearing nuthin' but a sheer nightgown. The day was about to fall, as night was about to rise. It was winter, January, and nightfall came much earlier that in the summer. The apartment was steaming hot, as I set the thermostat to eighty.

I sat there listening to the words and the music of Miles Davis, thinking about my man. I wanted to feel his touch, his fingers exploring all of my body. I laid back on the comforter, spreading my legs, and placing my hand in between my thighs—touching myself, exotically. He told me to keep it warm, and I was going to fulfill his wishes.

I played CD to CD, from Miles Davis, Curtis Mayfield, R-Kelly,
Blackstreet, and Sade. I was so wet, so horny, and hot, that I needed to take a step out on the balcony for a little cool, cold air. The time went fast. I looked over at the clock on the nightstand, and it read 6:25. Damn, I thought. I wish my man would hurry up and get here. I didn't want to get too started without him.

I decided to take a bath and find some solitude. I had the small hand held radio in the bathroom on 98.7 fm, and a few candles lit around the tub.

A half an hour later, I stepped out of the tub, dripping wet, reaching for the towel. I gazed at myself in the full-length mirror placed on the bathroom door and blew myself a kiss. I lotion my skin, and put on my blue cotton robe. looked over at the bathroom clock, and it read, 7:15. I went back into the bedroom, opened my closet door and threw an outfit on the bed. Tyrone was going to love me in this tonight.

When he gets here, we both had plenty of time to do our thing, and then we would go out tonight. So, I searched through my closet for something sexy to be in when he arrived home. I spotted the right thing, my mink coat and some heels. I would be completely naked underneath. I knew he would love to come home to see me like this, no wasting precious time stripping me down. All he had to do was jump in it.

So for the remainder of the night, I walked around nude, with my mink coat placed neatly across the sofa. And my heels to the side. I was excited.

I sprawled out across our lush carpet and watched some cable TV. At 8:15, the doorbell sounded. Why would Tyrone ring the doorbell when he had his own key. But, being excited that I was, I rushed up from off the floor, threw on my mink, and slipped into my heels, and went to open the door. I didn't even ask who it was? I quickly opened the door, slinging back one side of my mink coat so Tyrone was able to catch a good view. I was stunned to see Jakim standing in front of my eyes. I quickly draped both sides of the mink together, clutching both ends tightly.

"Jakim, what are you doing here?"

"I'm here to see you." He replied, staring harshly at me.

I took a step back into the apartment, releasing the door. He had totally caught me by surprise. Jakim caught the door and wedged himself between the doorway and the foyer.

"What's up wit' that? You gotta cover yourself around me now?" He chided. "It ain't like I never saw it before."

"I was your woman then, I'm not now." I told him, standing just a few feet away, as he let the door shut, and stood in the foyer. I could see the hurt and pain in his face. His arms were down by his side and his hands clutched into a fist. He had on a black leather jacket, faded Guess jeans, and a wool Yankees hat.

"What's up wit' us, Shana?" He asked.

"What're you talking about?"

"I'm sayin', you and Tyrone being together…what's up wit' that?"

I remained quiet. I was actually scared. I looked into his eyes. I prayed that he didn't go crazy. I didn't want to end up on the eleven o clock news, with some reporter telling the city about a young girl being murdered in her apartment by her crazed and jealous ex- boyfriend.

I loved my life.

Everything was finally falling into play for me, everything was finally going right. "Jakim...I still love you. But I feel that it's time for us to move on." I softly said to him.

"What the fuck do you mean move on? I'm trying to be with you, Shana. I don't want anybody else."

"Well I do. And no matter how much it's gonna hurt you, you have to accept that I'm with Tyrone now. And we're in love."

"He don't love you. You ain't nuthin' but a showcase to him, Shana. I'm telling you, Tyrone ain't nuthin' but a dog...all he's gonna do is fuck you, front like he really care about you, then trash you like the rest of his hoes out there."

"Please, Jakim, you don't know what you're talking about. Then why he got me living in his crib? Why he bought me all of these things for Christmas?"

"Shana, you ain't nuthin' but some in house pussy to him!" He proclaimed. "You think you're the only female he bought things for? Yo, I'm telling you, I grew up with him, I know how he gets down...he don't love you, Shana...I do!"

"Jakim, please...I think you need to leave."

"Why you playing me out like that, Shana? You mean the world to me."

"Well you should have thought of that before you got wit them hoes around the way." I said.

"You gonna keep bringing that shit up! I'm telling you that I'm sorry. You just gonna throw what he had together out cold like that?." He said, coming closer to me. "I love you so damn much. I'm hurting being without you. I hate to see you with a guy like Tyrone, when I know what he's all about. You're my heart, Shana."

I swear I saw a tear run down his eyes as he said it. He stood directly in front of me, teary eyed, looking pitiful. I still clutched my mink tightly, staring at him. Nothing he was saying was getting through to me. All I kept thinking was that Jakim hurt me, and fucked up our relationship. He was at fault, not me. I felt that he was lying, willing to say anything negative about his friend just to break us apart. Since Tyrone and I'd been together, he treated me like his Royal Queen.

Jakim reached into his leather jacket, I took a quick step back, thinking that he was reaching for some kind of weapon, a gun maybe. I got scared. He came closer, and I took a few steps backwards away from him. I knew he saw the fear in my eyes—this was the first that I felt threatened by him.

"Why you backing up for?" He asked.

I searched the room for a weapon, but felt stupid when he pulled out a small black case, griping it in the palm of his hand. He got down on one knee. He slowly opens it, brandishing a diamond ring.

"Shana, I want you to become my wife...will you marry me?" He asked

The ring looked flawless, as I peered down on him and the ring. It was beautiful. Baffled! I was speechless. I eased the grip off my mink, exposing my nakedness. I no longer cared of him seeing me in the raw. I slowly placed my hands over my mouth. I gazed into his eyes, and saw that he was dead serious, he didn't blink or turn his head. He just kept his eyes fixated on me, waiting for an answer.

"Jakim..."

"Please, don't say no. I love you too much to hear a no from you." He interrupted. "I want to marry you, have kids, raise a family with you, Shana. I know I've made a mistake. But I promise you, if you become my wife, you will always be first in my life. I will always do right by you, Shana. I'm done with all the bullshit. Lets just put that behind us, and move on from here."

A tear evaded from my eye, flowing slowly down my cheek, I gazed down at him, as he was still on one knee, with the case still clutched in the palm of his hand. My heart pounded vigorously.

"Jakim...I can't." I told him.

He closed his eyes, opened them again and said. "Please, Shana, I've already made one huge mistake, I don't want you to make that same mistake by saying no, I know we'll work out together. I can feel us strongly in my heart. I know you feel it too."

"Jakim, this is too much for me to handle right now." I sighed.

"All I'm asking is for us to be together, for you to be my wife."

"I can't, Jakim. I'm in a relationship right now."

"But Shana, believe me, he ain't no good for you." He warned with tears in his eyes.

This was hard, but I already knew my answer. I had to say no. I couldn't hurt one man's feelings, by marrying one who'd already hurt mines. Yes, I still do love him. But I'm a woman. I make my own decisions.

Jakim stood back on his feet, he slowly closed the case, he couldn't even look me in the eye.

"I just can't right now." I repeated.

He didn't say a word. The silence between us felt a bit eerie. My ex-man just proposed to me. I wanted to run into the bedroom and put something decent on. It felt awkward standing here in my apartment in only a mink and some heels.

"Shana..." He spoke, then he paused.

"Oh, shit, what time is it?" I blurted out, just remembering that Tyrone was supposed to be home soon. I dashed to the living room, glancing at the clock over the television. It read: 8:25.

"Jakim, you have to get going." I said to him.

"You break my heart, now you gonna rush me out." He said.

"Tyrone's about to come home soon." I told him.

By the look on his face, I knew he wasn't too thrilled about hearing his name right now. But I had to warn him.

"Fuck him! I got a few words for him." He angrily said.

"Please, Jakim, just leave here in peace."

"Nah, you're my woman. How that niggah gonna disrespect me like that?"

I stopped myself from what I was about to tell him. I had to calm my nerves, because I just wanted him to leave here in peace. He was really beginning to upset me, talking this shit about I'm still his woman. He just couldn't the fact that it was over in his mind.

"Yo, Shana, just think about us…my proposal…"

I just looked at him. Didn't I already tell him no. "Jakim…"

"I'm not leaving here until you tell me that you'll at least think it over." He said very firmly.

Frustrated with him still being here, I shouted, "Okay, I'll think about it, now can you please just leave!"

Jakim proceeded to head towards the elevator, as I stood in the doorway, clutching my mink and watching him leave. He glanced back at my way, and cracked a halfway smile. The elevator doors opens, and my worst nightmare came through. There was Tyrone stepping off the elevator, seeing Jakim standing right there.

They just stared at each other.

He looked over at me, and saw me standing there clutching my mink coat tightly in some heels. Oh my god, I thought, why is this happening?

Jakim just glared at him, his eyes furiously fixated directly at him, not saying one damn word to him.

"So what's up wit' this?" Tyrone asked, "My girl's halfway naked in the doorway with you standing here."

"Your girl!" Jakim finally spoke.

"Yeah, my girl, niggah. She wit' me now."

"Fuck you, you fuckin' thief!" Jakim shouted.

"Yo, you don't even have to hate like that, Jakim. I ain't steal your bitch...niggah she came to me." Tyrone replied.

"Yo, I thought you was my boy. How you gonna diss me like that? You know how I feel about her."

"Feel about her. Niggah you cheated on her so many times I lost count. Besides, if you was fuckin' her right, then she wouldn't be coming to me."

"Oh, word, it's like that?"

"Yeah, niggah, it's like that" Tyrone shouted.

The both of them' were just arguing and shouting at each other like I wasn't even standing there listening. I just wanted this to stop. I shouted, "Tyrone, can you just please come inside and let it be."

"What? Shana, you gonna take his back...both of y'all just gonna stab me in the back like that?" Jakim exclaimed.

"Yo, just fuckin' bounce, so I can go inside and fuck my bitch right." Tyrone proclaimed.

That busted the bubble. Jakim just came up on Tyrone and snuffed him against his jaw causing Tyrone to stumble and fall back. I screamed, as they both started to fight in the hallway. They both grabbed each other by their clothing, flinging each other from side to side, then they both just collapsed to the floor, Tyrone falling on top of Jakim.

"Get off him." I screamed. "Stop it! Please, stop it!"

Tyrone was stronger, and quicker. He gave Jakim a staggering hit across his cheek.

"Get off me! Yo, get off me!" Jakim hollered, as Tyrone had him pinned down tightly, whipping his ass.

By this time, neighbors started to peek through their doors, some coming out to see what was all the commotion about.

"Cut it, with all that fighting." An elderly lady said in her red house robe.

I was embarrassed. Some gawked at me, like I was at fault. I was in tears. Two men were fighting over me in the hallway, some bitches woulda been proud about it, but I wasn't.

Jakim managed to get back on his feet, gripping Tyrone by his collar, his lip was bleeding, and his cheek bruised. Tyrone had put a serious hurting on him.

By this time, security had made its way up to our floor, stepping in between the two and breaking them apart. They had both of them on the opposite sides of the hall, Jakim screaming, and threatening Tyrone. It seemed that everyone from each apartment was out in the hallway catching a glimpse of the little excitement that was happening.

I had to run into my bedroom to throw on something decent. I caught a few eyes staring at me with excitement and lust. After all I was in the hallway half naked. I threw on a light blue over-sized T-shirt that came down to my thighs. When I made it back out to the doorway, they had Jakim subdued down on the floor. He just wouldn't calm down. He was still hollering and cursing. Tyrone was just standing there, looking pissed. He was holding his right jaw, massaging it with the tip of his fingers.

The police came also, it was total chaos. They asked who were the occupants of the apartment. I answered that it was Tyrone and I. They started to ask what happened. At first, no one said a word. We all just stood there. I could see it in the officer's face, that they were becoming upset.

"Nuthin' officer, just a little misunderstanding here." Tyrone finally spoke.

"Misunderstanding, it looked like y'all were ready to bash each other's heads in." One of the security guards said.

"Everything's cool." Tyrone said. He started to walk towards my way, still soothing his jaw.

"Sir, is this your place?" One of the officers asked. He was heavy set, pale, with short blond hair.

"Yeah, didn't my woman already tell you that."

"Do you want to press charges against this man?" He asked.

"Man, you don't even know what happened, and you already want me to press charges against a brotha. Fuck no, I ain't pressing no charges." Tyrone said.

The officers didn't look too pleased. They looked like they were about ready to take him in. They started to ask the neighbors that were standing around if they saw what happened. But all they could say was that they heard yelling and then saw fighting.

"Well, we're gonna escort him out of the building and off of the premises." A slim, young lookin' cop said.

"Fuckin bounce then." Tyrone uttered out. "And take that faggot niggah wit' you."

"Fuck you." Jakim replied back.

"It's on, dog."

"That's a threat?"

"That's a fuckin' promise." Tyrone shouted.

The hallway started to clear, as the cops and the security guards all made their way in the elevator, leaving a few neighbors still standing outside of their apartment doors. They peered over at Tyrone and I.

"What? Is there sumthin' wrong? All y'all need to mind y'all fuckin' business." Tyrone yelled at them.

Of course I knew it wasn't yet over between him and me. He had some words to say to me, as I had some explaining to tell him. For one, why was I butt naked in a mink and some heels, with my ex-man coming out of the apartment? I told him that Jakim just stopped by unannounced, and he caught me by surprise. We yelled at each other for a few minutes. I knew he was upset, and I couldn't blame him. Because if I came home and saw some butt naked bitch in my apartment, shit I would yell, curse, and scream too. So I give him that, he had a right to be upset.

I finally calmed my man down. I explained to him again everything that happened. I can't control Jakim from coming to see me here. He knew where we lived. Shit, he came here all the time when they were best friends. Tyrone understood that. The only thing that I didn't tell him was that he had proposed to me. I felt that he didn't need to know about that.

About an hour had passed. Despite everything that had happened, I still wanted to go out, and I still wanted some dick. I figured going out wasn't happening, but sex, well that was something different.

"I love you, baby." I whispered in his ear, sliding my hands down to his chest, as he sat down on the floor in between my legs, with his back propped up against the couch. "And you know I wouldn't give this away to anybody accept for you."

He smiled, looked up at me, and then gave me a kiss. "I'm sorry that I flipped out today, but you know you're my boo, Shana."

"Yeah, I know."

"So, it's definitely over between y'all two, right?"

"Now how you gonna ask me that. Of course it's over, I'm in love with you, Ty'" I told him, massaging his chest gently.

"Ayyite, cool."

I didn't like his tone.

"What you thinking, Ty'?" I asked.

"Nah, nuthin' Shana."

"You thinking sumthin'." I said. I hesitated before saying. "Tyrone, don't you do nuthin' to Jakim."

"Jakim, that pussy niggah ain't even on my thoughts right now." He said.

"Promise me that you won't do nuthin' to Jakim." I said.

"Why, y'all ain't together, so what do you care?"

"Tyrone, promise me. Y'all used to be boys."

"Used to be." He firmly said.

"Tyrone, if you touch him, I swear…"

"You swear what, Shana? Yo, I ain't gonna touch the niggah, so stop getting your panties stir crazy, that's my job."

"You promise?"

"I promise." He said. "Come here." He turned around, and climbed up on the couch in between my legs, pressing down on top of me. He began kissing me, parting my lips with his tongue.

"I'm not even sweating that niggah no more. It's forgotten." He assured me as he pulled off my panties. "I'm about to make up for last night." He said, stripping off his clothes, with me lying on my back, on the couch—waiting for some dick. I said it once, and I'm gonna say it again. He was nuthin' but right in my life.

There were too many haters out there trying to fuck up my shit.

Our Love is bliss!

SPANKY
15

Once again, I found myself back at that little underground strip club, between Anita's legs. This time I knew her name. She recognized me from the get go, smiled when she saw me come into the place, this time solo. I couldn't find any of my boys. So as horny as I was, and desperate to try these pills out one more time, I came back in search for her freaky and sexy ass. I paid for another VIP with her, and I was in this dingy, uncomfortable room humping and fuckin' her brains out. The pussy was even better my second time around.

Surprised, I lasted fifteen minutes in the room with her. I was elated. I felt like a fuckin' king. My soldier was definitely hanging in there for me. He was standing at attention for a much longer period of time. I felt proud, I wanted to award him a medal for achievement and accomplishment. He had come a long way.

I got up from between her legs, as she laid there, staring up at me.

"Damn Papi', you felt good up in me." She said, smiling, as I smiled back.

It felt good to be a man and finally able to take care of business in the bedroom. I felt like smoking a cigarette, some weed, sumthin'. I got dressed, tipped her a ten, and left the room, and the club all together. Anita told me to give her a call, said that she does house calls too. I was definitely keeping that in mind.

When I arrived home I went to my room, all I could think about was Carla, her beautiful smile, and her lovely brown skin. Yup, I had it bad for her. I was now more confident and ready to ask her out on a date. Shit, I might get lucky and show her the real deal and what I was working with. I don't know, maybe these pills weren't just having an affect on my sex life, they were also affecting my confidence in getting with women also. I wanted to try and Mack it to every female that I came across, like Limp and Tommy. They would talk to anything that moved in a skirt, and had some tits. And they got lucky in getting some most of the time. I wasn't in the ballpark figure yet. I hadn't slept with over a hundred women like my co-worker, Greg or met ten to twenty different ladies a month like Michael and Johnny. Nah, I was still wet behind the ears. I was still learning the fundamentals of the game. I knew I still had a long way to go, before I can ever call myself a playa. I wanted to be so bad to be part of the in crowd and tell my stories.

Friday night, we were all up in Clark's basement getting treed up and cracking jokes on each other as usual. I was on my second L, as we watched this old car movie on channel five. And of course, once again, Limp was bragging about how he fucked some bitch in the back seat of her Honda. Tommy tried to out do his story, by mentioning that he once fucked a mother, then her daughter all in one week. Then Peter had his story to tell, and Clarke added his two-cents in about fuckin' some bitch that was twice his age. It seemed that they all had their own story to tell, some freaky experience they had with a female. I was shit out of luck, with nothing really to tell. It was kind of embarrassing. I knew it was coming my way, and it did. Limp gazed over at me, then asked, "So what's up, Spanky, you ain't got no wild sex story to share among the fellows? I'm sayin' you sitting there all quiet and shit, keeping your thoughts to yourself, you and Mark."

I just sat there thinking hard of something to come up with, but my mind kept coming up blank. Mark was in his own little world, as he was for the entire night. He didn't even feel like smoking with the rest of us. Come to think of it, he's been like this for the past three or four weeks. I knew something had to be bothering him.

Limp pressured me to tell him something wild, bizarre, or freaky that I'd did with a bitch.

"C'mon dog, say sumthin', I know you ain't a virgin up in this room. Shit, I remember when we ran the train on that gullible freshman back in high school." Limp reminisced.

"Nah, dog, I can't right now, I'm too high, and too tired to think of one right now." I tried to play it off.

"Ah, man, you frontin, Spanky, that's probably the only panties you dug into." Clark said.

"Nah, man, I had pussy after that, believe me, dog...a niggah gotta keep feeding his shit to keep it going." I said, nervous as fuck, hoping niggahs didn't catch on to me trying to bullshit my way out of this conversation.

"Forget about that niggah." Limp said. "Yo, Mark, what's up wit' you? You've been lookin' spaced out for a while niggah, and you ain't even smoke wit' us."

Mark just ignored them, sitting on the couch, leaned to the side, resting against the arm of the couch looking like he had a lot on his mind. He did look spaced out. Limp called his name a few good times, but Mark just sat there, acting like he ain't even hear him call.

"Fuck him, yo pass that shit." Limp said.

I gazed over at Mark, sumthin' was up with him, and he wasn't saying what it was. He just kept that shit quiet, and to himself.

About an hour after, it was getting late, and niggahs were getting tired. There were no more trees to be smoked, and that whack car movie went off about a half-hour ago.

I've decided to call it a night, and retreated out the door, giving the fellows closed fist pounds and slapping fives. As I made my way towards the exit, Mark was right behind me. I guess he was getting tired too.

We were outside in this freezing cold weather. I zipped my coat up tight, pulled my ski hat down over my ears, and threw on my gloves. I was able see my breath escape from my mouth, looking like a small clear cloud, it was so cold out.

"Yo, hold up Spanky, I need to talk to you." Mark said, coming up right behind me.

"What up?"

He came right beside me, bundled up in his black-leather, and a Nautica ski hat. "Yo, don't even trip about that thing that happened with my sister." He said, referring to when I saw his sister naked while she was getting dressed.

"Nah, I ain't trippin' about that."

"Yo, she just be acting like a bitch, all uppity and shit. She's my sister and all, but I can't stand that bitch."

I chuckled, as we trotted along down the street, a few blocks away from my crib. There was silence between the two of us, as we passed three or four houses. We both walked, looking ahead. I wanted to ask what was bothering him so much, that it was making him look zoned out.

"Yo, dog, that bitch is pregnant." He suddenly uttered out.

"What?"

"Remember that bitch I met last year at that house party on Linden and Foch?"

"That short light skin bitch, with the phat ass?"

"Yeah, her."

"She pregnant?"

"Yeah."

Then it suddenly clicked in. "By you?" I asked.

"She claiming its mines, calling my crib at all times of the day, talking about I'm the father and shit. Got my moms bugging, cursing me out and shit. She talking about she ain't raising no grandkids."

"Damn, son…what you gonna do?"

"I don't know. I think that bitch's lying. I know she's a hoe. Then come to find out that she's only fifteen."

"Word?"

"Yeah, yo. Her moms trippin', talking about she gonna try and press charges, get me on some statutory rape shit, talking about I took advantage of her daughter."

"What?"

"Yeah, yo. She told me that she was seventeen. Her lying ass."

"Damn, Mark. I ain't even know that you were still messing with her."

"I was hitting that shit here and there. I know that baby ain't mines. I know that bitch is a hoe. I fucked her too quick for her not to be. Like in three days, I got into those panties."

"Yeah, yo, that bitch's lying. Don't even stress that. Have that bitch get a paternity test done, you know how it's gonna come out."

"Yo, Spanky, you don't understand, this bitch got me heated right now, she keep stressing me. I'm telling this bitch to stop calling my crib, yapping about that nonsense, but this fuzzy dust head hoe won't stop. My mom's thinking about changing our number, she's so sick of hearing this bitch voice over the phone everyday asking for me."

"Damn son, that's fucked up." I once again repeated. I was at a loss of words to say to him right now.

"Yo, Spanky, do me a favor."

"What up?"

"Don't tell Limp and Clark about this shit, don't even tell Tommy's ass, you know them niggahs don't take shit serious. Everything to them is a fuckin' joke. I don't need these niggahs clowning me right now on this shit."

"Ayyite yo, you got my word." I promised.

By the tone of his voice, I knew that he was taking this shit much more serious than it seemed to be. We continued to walk towards my home, chitchatting here and there. As we approached the front of my crib, I slapped him five, told him to keep his head up, and stepped my ass into the house, outta this cold weather.

I thought about Mark's situation for a minute. Damn, that was some fucked up shit to be in, with him only being twenty. Yo, that bitch moms was trippin, trying to put the blame on Mark because her daughter's a hoe. I asked myself, what was her daughter doing at a house party after midnight when she was that young anyway? She need to check up on that, instead of putting a good man behind bars because your daughter slipped up and gave up the pussy a few good times, too a few good men.

Around eleven, on a Friday night, I found myself dozing away watching TV in my room. This was pathetic; I was a grown man, without a girl, and without a sex life. I mean a pretty decent and sturdy one. A female I could count on to call and come over, or vise versa whenever I felt the need for some. I was getting tired of jerking off on the regular, shit I knew my right hand was getting sick of it. Everywhere I looked and turned, people were having sex, my parents, my co-workers, my friends, shit, even the fuckin' dogs and cats outside were getting a piece. Here I was, paying for some ass. Nah, this shit had to stop, and soon.

Monday morning, I was back at work, and feeling quite good about myself. It felt like a burst of positive energy just seeped into my pores.

I ran into Johnny, who was his usual pretty boy, wanna be black Mack daddy, boy. Of course, he had another bootie story that he had to inform me about. In this one he was with a sista from Brooklyn. He didn't sugarcoat the details. I stood there listening, slapping him five, playing it off, making his ego feel good. Reality, I stopped giving a shit.

After my little five, six-minute conversation with Johnny, here comes Michael, walking that "Yeah, I'm the shit" walk. He approached me, slapped me five with a cup of coffee in his hand. I stood there, waiting for him to spill out his wild and vulgar details that he had over the weekend. But surprisingly, he said nothing.

"You ain't go out and fuck like three or four hoes over the weekend, Mike?" I just had to ask.

"Nah, I just chilled, you know, getting my relax on." He said so cool.

"Damn, you all right, you ain't sick or nuthin'?"

"I'm cool, Jamal."

Finally, my dream girl walked into the office, sporting a cream skirt and a white and black blouse. Her eyebrows were perfectly done and she cut her hair short a few inches, it wasn't falling off her shoulders like it used to. She still looked good.

"Hi, fellahs." She greeted, with a warm smile and wave.

"What's up, Carla." Michael said.

"Hi, Carla." I said, gazing her down. "I see you've cut your hair and got your nails and eyebrows done." I added.

"Oh, you've noticed. How sweet."

I blushed. Yeah, only the man in love with you would notice something different about you, I thought. She went up to her desk, getting ready for today's work. I just stood there along with Michael, daydreaming about her.

"Let me get to work." Michael said, leaving my side.

I continued to watch her at her desk for the next five minutes. I wanted so bad to go over and ask her out on a date. My confidence level was up a few notches, why not, I thought. Anything can happen. But not right now, there were too many people around, I ain't want everyone all up in my business, so I would wait until it was the right time.

By lunch, I felt that I was ready. Her and some co-workers went out for lunch and came back with Chinese food in their hands. Michael went over to her and said a few words to her. He had her smiling, chuckling and all. She looked like putty in his hands, like every word that came out of his mouth, she believed. That wasn't good. I wondered if he still had that bet going on with Johnny. He said he canceled it, telling Johnny that the bet was off, but now the way he was over there, kicking it to her, I've could of sworn that he was back on the job again.

She looked like she was in a really good mood today, I mean everyday she's cheerful and friendly, telling everyone good morning when she arrives, and good night when she leaves. But today, she looked like she was in extra high spirits. That made me feel good, made me feel like I really have a chance to get with her.

As soon as Michael left, I walked up to her. "Hi, Carla." I said. She looked up at me.

"What's up, Jamal?" She asked, while filing through some papers on her desk.

"Carla, can I ask you something?"

"Of course, Jamal, ask me anything. What's on your on mind?"

"Um, I was thinking that maybe someday…"

"Day, get over here." My boss interrupted, standing in front of his office doorway, looking unhappy.

I sighed, glancing over at him, then looking back over at Carla. She shrugged her shoulders, looking up at me. "I'll be right back." I said, as I slowly walked over towards my boss, Mr. Price.

"Yes?" I answered

"Get me another cup of coffee." He said.

I took the coffee mug from him, feeling so fuckin' stupid as some people in the office looked over at us and chuckled in their seats.

"I don't want a lot of sugar this time. Oh and bring me back a bagel too." He said, handing me a five.

I walked through the office, retrieving my coat from the closet, and made my way to the outside deli across the street. I couldn't even look over at Carla after that. How could I? I just quickly headed towards the door, feeling like my chances of asking her out were over I felt to embarrassed with the way Mr. Price talked down to me.

By the end of the day, I was ready to go home. Mr. Price had me running back and forth all day completing different tasks in the office from morning to evening. I thought that maybe he had a personal grudge against me. All I wanted to do now, was go home and chill.

Everyone was starting to pack up and was getting ready to head out for the day, but not Carla, she just sat there still working hard at whatever she was doing, and so was Michael. He didn't budge from his desk in two hours.

I started to re-think my chances with Carla. I still wanted to ask her out, regardless of what happened just this morning. Yeah, I was a nobody in the office. I wasn't a real estate agent, or financed homes, or sold them. I was an office puppy. I did whatever Mr. Price or whoever was over me told me to do for the day. I was nothing but the office errand boy making less than all of my co-workers. It was embarrassing, but I had to do it. I needed a job after high school, and this was the only one available with my experience.

Ten after five, everyone had already left to go home. Only Carla, Michael, Mr. Price and I remained behind. I stayed because I wanted to try and ask Carla out on a date, and I felt that now was the perfect time, since all most everybody went home for the night. I had butterflies flowing around in my stomach. My nerves were shaking. I had the jitters, but I talked myself into still going through with it. I couldn't back out. Imagine if everything worked out between us, you never know what could happen. I walked up to her, as she was just about to pack up her belongings and go home.

"You still here?." She asked, shuffling some papers on her desk.

"Yeah, I'm still here." I replied, smiling.

"So, what is it that you wanted to ask me earlier?"

"Oh, um...see, I really like you... and I was thinking that maybe we can go out..."

"On a date?" She said, disrupting my sentence.

"Um, yeah, sumthin' like that."

She smiled, that warm friendly smile, looking at me, hypnotizing me with those beautiful black onyx eyes. I was so nervous that I couldn't move.

"I remembered when you told me that you weren't seeing anybody, so I thought that it wouldn't hurt to ask." I added.

She chuckled. "How sweet." She said. "But Jamal, I'm seeing somebody now."

"Hunh?"

"For about a month now."

I was in shock, more embarrassed. "When did this happen?"

"To be honest, Jamal, he's a co-worker." She informed.

"A co-worker. Who?"

It felt like my heart was being torn into two, ripped out of my chest and stomped on. And what made it even worse, was that she was seeing someone on the job. It coulda been anybody.

"At first, I had my doubts about him, but he turned out to be a pretty nice guy." She said. "If I tell you, can you promise me that you'll keep this a secret?"

I was quiet for a while and hurt. I tried to play it off, keeping my inner feelings confined. I didn't want to look like a bitch, and start crying in front of her.

Michael came up to us, in his leather jacket, ready to go home. He had his car keys in one hand, and a leather briefcase in the next.

"You ready to go, Carla?" He asked.

"In a minute, baby." She replied back.

"Baby?" I uttered out, sounding baffled.

Michael looked at me, and then he looked over at Carla. "You sure about this Carla?" He asked.

"Yes, I'm sure." She responded. "We can't keep our relationship a secret from everyone else for so long." Carla said.

Relationship? What the fuck? I was shock. What the hell was going on here? When did this happen? I glanced back and forth at the both of them. Suddenly, I felt like disappearing, vanishing like Night Crawler from the X-Men, poof, gone just like that.

"Jamal, I've been seeing Michael for about a month. I surprised myself, because usually, I don't date co-workers, but he turned out to be an exception." She told me, as she nestled up underneath Michael's arm.

"But how did this happen?" I asked.

"Well, one day, we both stayed late after work, catching up on some paperwork. And we started talking, so we went out, and we took it from there."

Jealousy is a mutha-fucka! I couldn't describe the hurt and pain I was feeling right now. I was so jealous of Michael and Carla's new relationship that I blurted out, "You gonna get with Michael after he done bet on you during your first day here."

"What?" She uttered out, as she cut her eyes at him, and broke away from him.

Michael angrily glanced at me, then back at Carla. Oops, I thought, but I didn't feel sorry that I said it.

"Carla, let me explain."

"Did you bet on me, Michael?" She asked with disbelief in her voice.

"Nah, it wasn't even like that. See what happened was..."

"Michael, did you bet on me?" She repeated herself, as I just stood there quiet.

"Yes." He admitted, "But..."

Slap! He caught a hard right hand across his face.

"Fuck you! Fuck you!" She repeated, following with another hard right across his face. Her actions caught me off guard, because I've never seen her angry. She was always nice and friendly.

"Carla, c'mon...it was a mistake, I'm falling in love with you." He begged.

"You played yourself, Michael. You really played yourself, and here I was thinking that you were different, thinking here's a man I can trust, and then come to find out that I was nothing but a little wager to you. What Michael? Did you and your friends bet who can get into my panties first? Hunh? This is why I don't go out with people I work with, it's always a fuckin' mistake."

"But, Carla. It was a mistake. I deaded the bet with Johnny." He said, trying to comfort her.

"Oh, Johnny was in this too, wait until I see his white ass tomorrow." She rebuked, while pushing Michael away from her.

"I didn't mean for this to happen, I really like you, that's why I called off the bet, Carla, believe me."

"Fuck you, Michael. I don't believe a damn word you say anymore, stay away from, just stay the fuck out of my life." She yelled. "Yo, too, Jamal. You knew about this little bet that was going on around this office, and here you come smiling in my face, and don't even tell me about it...you can stay the fuck away from me. I don't want to see you, Michael, or Johnny around me ever again. All y'all trifling brothas can kiss my black ass."

"But..." I tried to say.

"And Michael, you thought you almost had a piece of this pussy? Niggah, you weren't even close. It takes more that charm and looks for a niggah to get up in me." She said, before storming off out of the office.

"Yo, Jamal, man, that's some fucked up shit." He screamed, coming up in my face. "How you gonna tell her some shit like that."

"This ain't my fault."

"It ain't your fault! It ain't your fault. Niggah, I should fuck your ass up right here in this mutha-fuckin' office." His eyes were beaded and red. You could see his veins popping out of his skin.

"Yo, you need to chill, Michael." I said, taking a step back.

"I need to chill, niggah, you think you got some balls now? You gonna fuck up my relationship with my woman, and think I'm gonna let you step off that easy. Nah, it ain't happening, partner!"

He took off his jacket and threw it on the floor. Then he took off his tie, and folded up his sleeves.

"I ain't gonna fight you, Michael." I told him.

"Well, I'm just gonna whip that ass...pussy mutha-fucka!"

He swung, hitting me in my jaw, nearly knocking me down. The second punch put me down on the floor. I was dazed.

"Get up, bitch!" He said, standing over me.

"Nah, chill out son."

"It ain't no chill. You disrespected me in front of Carla, and I really liked her. She was the one, Jamal. I was feeling her, and you fucked that up for me."

"I ain't fucked up shit. You shouldn't have betted on her." I yelled, trying to stand on my feet.

"That was a mistake, I told you. And you ain't even give me a fuckin' chance to prove myself to her." He said, kicking me back down to the floor. I landed on my hands. "You know what, fuck this shit." He said, picking up his jacket. "I'm out. I don't need this. Nothing I do now is gonna change things."

He walked out of the office, leaving me lying on my back looking up at the ceiling. Damn, maybe he really was changing his ways for that girl and I screwed everything up for him because I was jealous. But just seeing her with him, I thought he didn't deserve her. All I thought about was him just getting some skins from her, then later dogging her out, like he usually does to all of his women. But he was right. Who was I to interfere with his business, when I was too scared to even make a move on her.

As I straightened myself out, I heard Mr. Price's voice coming from the bathroom. "What's all that yelling out there?"

Feeling pitiful, and sorry for myself, I collected my things and left. I should have kept my mouth close, but jealously got the best of me. He said he really liked her, that 'she was the one.' That was the first time I ever heard Michael mention about any female being the one for him. Usually she was the one to please him for the night. I guess he was really falling in love with her. And I couldn't blame him, from the first day I saw her, I knew that there was something different and special about her. I guess that I wasn't the only one to see it too.

I kept my tears in, and cupped my hand over my jaw as I walked out to the street. I didn't mean to hurt Carla's feelings, but for the quick minute, I felt that she'd betrayed me. I never felt so wrong in my life. I never meant to hurt her, and I did. Now she hated Michael and me.

I took a look back at the real estate office, and said to myself, "I quit!"

SHANA
16

Pregnant, I can't be pregnant, I screamed to myself, as I was in the bathroom giving myself a home pregnancy test. I tested myself twice, and both tests came out the same way, positive. For the past few days, I've been feeling nauseous, my breasts were feeling heavier, and I was constantly using the bathroom. My mother was pregnant, this shit couldn't be happening to me. I couldn't deal with having kids. But then again, I thought about Tyrone and me being a family. I knew it had to be his child. He was the only one running up in me for the past few weeks now.

I sighed and threw everything in the trash. I needed to be really sure of myself, so I set up an appointment with a doctor.

I found myself sitting in the doctor's office waiting for my results. She came out ten minutes

"Ms. Banks, you're definitely pregnant." She informed, looking over at my charts.

I bowed my head and let out a huge stressful sigh. "How far along am I?" I asked, with serious concern in my voice. "Three, four weeks?"

She looked up at me, looking baffled. "Ms. Banks, you're eight weeks pregnant."

"What? You got to be shitting me." I shouted, startling her. "Are you sure that test reads right?"

"Yes."

I wanted to pass out. This couldn't be happening to me. That means if I'm eight weeks pregnant, then I would to have gotten pregnant sometime around November. That was not good, because that meant one out of three men could possibly be the father, Danny, Jakim, or Tyrone.

"Ms. Banks, when was the last time you had your monthly period?" She asked.

I thought about it—it was in November. But I didn't stress missing my period in December, because my Aunt missed hers, due to stress, and she wasn't pregnant. So I figured that was the same problem with me. I was dealing with a lot of stress during the time.

The doctor took my hand across the table, trying to comfort me, as I was bugging out. "Look, there are options you know, like adoption, abortion...I suggest you think about it, give yourself time."

I felt my eyes watering up.   This couldn't be happening. I was definitely pregnant, now the only question was, by who?

I went home and took me a nice long hot bath. As I sat in the tub, a lot of shit roamed through my head, like what if the baby turned out to be Jakim's or even worse, Danny's, how can I deal with that? Having me and my mother being pregnant by the same guy, just the thought of it made me run out the tub and throw up in the toilet. Then I thought, what if it turned out to be Tyrone's, I wondered how he would accept it? Or would he leave me if it turned out to be Jakim's? No matter which way, or how I looked at it, I was still in a fucked up predicament. I soaked in the tub for about an hour, dried myself off and went to bed crying for the night.

I woke up alone again for the third straight day. There was no Tyrone in bed with me. Frustrated, I called his cell-phone, there was no answer, then I paged him twice, he didn't call back. For the first time in weeks, I was starting to have doubts about my relationship with him. Maybe Naja and Jakim were really right about him. His actions towards me for the past two weeks had me thinking something else about him. When he was home, all he wanna do is fuck me. He didn't want to go out anymore, at least with me. He didn't talk to me, and he was forever on the phone talking secretly to someone late at night, when he thought I was asleep. What made me really upset, was when he would stay out for nights at a time, not even giving me a courtesy phone call to inform me that he was all right, or to check and see if everything was okay with me. Now here I was pregnant, and I wasn't even sure if it was his.

And here I thought that things couldn't get any worse, but I was wrong. I was starting to get threatening calls from Chinky. She wasn't trying to let bygones be bygones. She would call me at all times of the hour, whether it being three in the morning, or it being three in the afternoon. She would ring my phone and say things like, "It's still on bitch!" "I'm gonna fuck your ass up!" "Tyrone's my fuckin' man, you ain't nuthin' but some cheap in house pussy!"

Arguing with her was pointless, so I would just hang up the phone on her, and minutes later, she would try and call here again. I was starting to see that I was going to have to go to war with this bitch!

The fourth night when Tyrone didn't bring his ass home, I'd decided to go and spend the weekend over at my mother's. I needed some company around me, caring not who it be. Besides, I had to tell her the news of me being pregnant. I would just leave out the news of the baby having three possible fathers, including her own, Danny.

I caught a cab to my mother's house. I lugged my suitcase up the front steps, when I spotted Danny's jeep parked out front. The first thing that came to my mind, was that him and my mother had made up. Then I started to feel nauseous when I thought about the possibilities of me carrying his child, along with my mother. I paused half way up the steps, trying to get my head and my emotions straight. I wanted to look strong. I haven't seen my mother and my Aunt in weeks. I had to walk up in there and let them know that I was doing well for myself, no matter how fucked up things were looking for me.

I enter through the front door, dropping my suitcase to the side. The place still looked the same, even though I wasn't gone for that long. It was quiet inside. I assumed that they were fuckin' in her bedroom, making up for lost time being apart. When I walked past her bedroom, my mother's door was open, and there wasn't anyone inside. Then I started to hear noises coming from out of my Aunt's bedroom. Curious, I headed towards her door, thinking, Nah, she isn't.

Her door was cracked open, and the closer I walked to my Aunt's door, the louder the sounds of ecstasy came out her room. I peered inside, and couldn't believe my eyes, there was my Aunt with her back turned to me, riding Danny like there was no fuckin' tomorrow.

Stunned, I cupped my hand over my mouth. No this niggah didn't, I violently screamed to myself. No this bitch didn't!

"Oh, hells no!" I screamed, startling them as I flung open her bedroom door, making my way into her room.

"Shana!" My Aunt blurted out, jumping off the dick, as Danny quickly planted both of his feet to the floor, standing there naked.

"Yo, what's up wit' this?" He said, gazing at me.

"What the fuck is the matter with you? You got my mother pregnant, and now you fuckin' my Aunt." I yelled.

"Shana, I can explain." My Aunt said, with the sheets clutched to her chest.

"You're wrong, Aunt Tina." I said to her, shaking my head in disbelief.

"Bitch, you got some nerves trying to criticize me, when you was riding this same dick a few weeks ago, don't be acting like it wasn't good to you." Danny said, blowing up my spot in front of my Aunt.

"What the fuck is he talking about?" My Aunt asked.

"I fucked your niece, too, that's what I'm talking about." He said vulgarly, his words sending chills down my back.

"Oh, you nasty bitch." My Aunt proclaimed.

"Nasty! You're the one busted Aunt Tina." I replied back.

Danny just stood there with this fuckin' smirk on his face, like he was mocking us. Proud! Yeah, he ran up in all three ladies of the family, and we were the gullible ones to give it up to him. He played all of us. I just wanted to run over there and fuck his ass up.

"Look, I'm out." Danny said, pulling up his pants.

"Niggah, you think you just gonna come up here and fuck everyone and be ghost like that." I shouted, running up in his face.

"Y'all bitches need help." He said.

"What? Niggah you're the bitch—you ain't shit, Danny." My Aunt yelled, trying to play it like she was on my side.

"Whatever! I did y'all a favor."

"Fuck you, mutha-fucka, fuck you!" I shouted at him, slapping him across his face so hard, that my hand was stinging. I wasn't just mad at him, but mad at life period. Tyrone was acting up, I thought we had something special, but he recently started to show his ass. Then there was Jakim, he been showed his ass off when he cheated on me, now he wants me to marry him. He thought I was being hard on him, but he didn't' understand that this shit was hard on me too. Now this mutha-fucka Danny, he wasn't any good in the first place. I now saw that all he ever cared about was a piece of pussy. He didn't give a fuck about my mother and her feelings towards him. I also saw that I had no regards for my mother's personal feeling, because if I did, then I wouldn't have fucked her man, and now I'm worrying if I'm carrying his baby or not. That's where that slap came from. I was pregnant, and I was thinking to myself that life wasn't fair.

"Bitch, are you crazy? Don't you ever put your mutha-fuckin' hands on me." Danny shouted, as he came across my face returning the hit, pimp slapping me, and knocking me down to the floor.

My Aunt went hysterical, she jumped on his back, scratching and digging into his face. He knocked her back down to the bed. I just sat there on the floor, crying my eyes out. Why was this happening? I asked myself. I was more mentally hurt, than physically.

"I'm out on all y'all crazy bitches." He uttered out, fastening his jeans, and throwing on his shirt. "Y'all some fuckin' hoes anyway."

"What about my mother? You just gonna walk out on her too? She's carrying your baby, and you just going to walk out on her like that?" I shouted, still cradled to the floor looking up at him with tears in my eyes.

"Fuck that hoe, too. She's the stupid one that got herself pregnant. Tell that stupid bitch to get an abortion, because I ain't taken care of no goddamn babies." He said before exiting the room.

I was breathing heavily, feeling like I was about to have a panic attack. My Aunt kneeled beside me, cradling me in her arms. "It's all right Shana, fuck him! Fuck him! That mutha-fucka is definitely going to get his, I promise that shit." My Aunt assured.

"We ain't right, Aunt Tina. We ain't right." I painfully said.

"It's going to be okay, Shana. It's going to be okay." She tried to comfort me, despite everything that had happened.

"No its not, Aunt Tina." I uttered out, "I'm fuckin' pregnant! And I don't even know who the father is."

"What?" My Aunt inquired.

"I'm pregnant Aunt Tina." I repeated, sobbing my eyes out.

"Oh, god, Shana...by who?"

"I told you, I don' know by who."

She gazed at me, and then my Aunt read the signs of my pain. She wasn't stupid when it comes to situation like these. She quickly uttered out, "You think Danny is one of the possible fathers?"

I didn't answer her. I just cried, diverting my eyes toward the floor.

"Oh, Shana." She said, then pausing her words. "How could you be so careless?" She exclaimed. And this coming from a woman who just got caught fuckin' the same guy. She helped me to my feet. "What are you planning to do, Shana?" My Aunt asked, as she got dressed.

"I don't fuckin' know Aunt Tina. What am I supposed to do?"

"Do you plan on telling your mother?"

"That's why I came."

"Shit!" She mumbled to herself.

A few minutes later, we heard the front door shut, it had to be my mother. I agreed with my Aunt to keep her and Danny a secret, this family was already going through enough shit, for us to be piling anymore on. But I had to tell her about my pregnancy. My mother was already three months into her pregnancy, and I was two months. I thought, how would she react to the news?

I dried my tears, and went into the living room to greet my mother. She had the days mail in her hand, sorting through it.

"Hey, ma." I greeted with a phony smile plastered across my face.

She looked up, smiling. "Shana, it's about time you came by, girl, it's been weeks. So how are things between you and Tyrone?"

"They're cool." I lied; things were starting to look like shit.

"Is he treating you right?"

"I'm pregnant!" I quickly uttered out.

She just gave me a simple look, like "What?"

"I'm pregnant, ma." I repeated.

"I see, by Tyrone, I hope?" She asked.

I nodded my head, yes. I couldn't tell her the real truth.

My mother was fifteen when she had me, much younger than I am now, so she couldn't bitch about me being too young. I was born, two days after my mother's fifteen birthday, so that means she got pregnant when she was fourteen.

My Aunt Tina was undeniably no saint either, she already had two abortions, and from what my mother tells me, she had a miscarriage when she was only sixteen. So they weren't in any position to criticize me. This was my first pregnancy.

I had a long talk with my mother. She asked if I planned on keeping it, I told her that I wasn't sure, but there was a good possibility that I just might. She made me a cup of hot chocolate. Deep down inside, I really wanted to tell her the absolute truth, that Danny could also be this baby's father, and also Jakim. That I was a slut, and fucked her man behind her back many of times, but I held my tongue. I did tell her of the problems that I was starting to have with Tyrone, him not being home half the time, the proposal from Jakim, and the fight that broke out between the two in the hallway. She soothed me, and told me that I could always move back home.

It's been two-weeks since that talk with my mother and the problems with Tyrone didn't stop. We were arguing and bickering with each other almost every other day, moving in with this mutha-fucka was a bad idea, I would say to myself everyday. He would call home, and tell me to clean up the apartment, because some of his boys were coming over for the night to watch TV and chill. The phone would ring, or his cell phone would go off in the middle of the night, and he would quickly answer it, then ten minutes later, he'd be out the door.

Chinky wasn't making things any better for me. She was constantly calling here, harassing and trying to curse me out. I begged for Tyrone to change the number, but he told me no, told me to just stop answering the fuckin' phone. I had a very strong feeling that he was fuckin' some other bitch out there. Besides Chinky calling, some other hoe would ring here, and when I answer the phone, there was nothing but direct silence, and then she would hang up. I knew it was a woman, because all of his boys always called him on his cell.

I was procrastinating on telling him that I was pregnant, because once again, I wasn't even sure if it was his baby. And by the way he was acting up, I wasn't sure I wanted this baby to be his anyway. We rarely saw each other, and when we did see each other, we were either arguing or fucking.

I was starting to feel what Jakim, and the others said to me were true, "That I was nothing but some in house pussy."

It was Friday night, and I was in my apartment, but I wasn't alone tonight. I was spending some time with the girls, Naja and Latish. Even Sandra came by to check me out. We ordered Chinese food, and rented a few flicks for the night. It felt good having my girlfriends around, even Latish, in spite of that nasty stunt she pulled with my Uncles on Thanksgiving. At first I thought I should whip this bitch's ass, but I let it go, because I had bigger problems to deal with.

I didn't tell anyone of them about my pregnancy. I would tonight.

Naja put in one of the movies that they rented and we all started digging into our Chinese food. I myself couldn't eat or enjoy the movie. I had too much worries on my mind. I haven't seen or heard from Tyrone in three days, and it was pissing me off. Then I'm starting to hear rumors about Jakim being with another woman, I know that it shouldn't bother me, but it did big time. I couldn't blame him for getting on with his life, he needed to. I just never thought it would be so soon.

Naja looked up at me, and asked, "What's wrong girl?"

"Nothing, I'm cool."

But this girl knew me since elementary school, she knew how to read me, knowing when I was upset about something. So she pressured me, by asking, "How's everything going with you and Tyrone?"

I let out a sigh, knowing that I had to be honest. Maybe she knew some things that I didn't?

"Fuck Tyrone!" I uttered out, feeling a painful tear coming to my eye.

"Damn girl, it's that bad between y'all two?" Sandra asked.

"What's wrong Shana, talk to us." Naja said, sounding concern.

"I haven't seen or heard from his trifling ass in three days. He don't call, he don't come by the place to see if I'm alright, and now this bitch Chinky is calling here, harassing me, trying to threaten me and shit. I wouldn't be surprised if he was still fuckin' that bitch." I said in one breath.

By the way Latish and Sandra gazed at each other, I knew something was up. I was waiting to hear Naja say, "I told you so." But she kept her mouth quiet.

"Look, Shana. I'm your friend and I ain't trying to be all in your personal business." Sandra spoke, "But I know a girl who live out in the forty projects, and she told me that she be seeing that niggah Tyrone's BMW parked there almost every night for the past few weeks now, right in front of that bitches building. She said he be spending the night there, because that mutha-fucka don't be leaving there until nine, ten, sometimes eleven the next morning."

What Sandra said, hurt me more than a slap across the face. Tyrone told me that it was definitely over between them two, told me that, that bitch was lying. He even said that wasn't his seed she was carrying! I was devastated and distraught that tears started to build up in my eyes. Naja came and sat next to me, placing her arm around me, she tried to talk words of comfort in my ear. "Fuck him, Shana, he ain't no good for you anyway." She said.

I knew what Sandra told me was so true, why would she lie?

"Why don't you just leave his bitch ass." Latish said.

"If I were you, girl, I would just pack my bags and leave. You don't need to be taking this shit from him. And what I'm hearing, Chinky ain't the only hoe he's fucking. I heard that niggah got two kids in Jersey, and he got one more on the way from some hoe out in North Carolina." Sandra said with attitude in her voice, causing me more pain hearing this than I already was in.

"That niggah can't keep his dick in his pants. You better leave that niggah before he gives you something." Latish warned—look who's talking, can't keep her legs closed.

"Or worse, before he gets you pregnant, then you'll be carrying his seed like all these other hoes he done already knocked up." Sandra said.

I cut my eyes over at Sandra. The truth was, I already was pregnant.

"Shana, are you sure you're okay?" Naja asked.

I took a deep breath and blurted out, "I'm pregnant."

Everyone gasped and stared at me like I'd just told them that the world was ending.

"What girl, you're kidding?" Sandra asked.

"No, Sandra, I'm so for real." I dragged out.

"By who?" Latish asked

I didn't answer her, just stared over at her trying to get my thoughts together.

"It's Tyrone's, right?" Naja asked.

"I'm not sure." I told her, diverting my eyes from her, feeling ashamed.

"Don't tell me it's Jakim's baby." Latish said with her ignorant self.

"Look, it could be his too, or it could be..." I paused with the last name of the possible father stuck in my throat. They all looked at me like I was about to tell them the key to life.

"It could also be Danny's baby." I quickly said.

"What? You slut!"

"You fucked your mother's man?" Naja was stunned.

"It just happened." I defensively said.

"Yeah, he slipped and his dick just happened to fall into you, right." Naja sarcastically said. "What the hell were you thinking Shana?"

"Damn, girl...you ain't been using no protection with any of these guys?" Sandra asked.

"Does any of them know yet?" Naja asked

"No, I didn't tell them yet."

"Don't you think you need to tell at least one of them." Naja said.

"I'm scared. What if I tell Tyrone, and it turns out not to be his."

"What about Danny?" Latish asked.

"Does your mother know about you and Danny?" Sandra asked.

"Shit, does your mother know that you're pregnant?" Naja asked.

"Would y'all shut the FUCK UP, PLEASE!" I shouted, getting tired of being bombarded with questions.

They all gazed at me with screwed up faces. "Damn bitch, you ain't gotta curse a sista out." Latish said, "we just trying to look out for you and shit. It ain't my fault you can't keep your fuckin' legs closed."

"What, bitch?" I shouted. She had some nerves trying to play me out like that—like I was the hoe sitting up in here, where she'd fucked more niggahs than Heather Hunter.

"Latish, chill." Naja said.

"Shit, don't be getting upset with me, I ain't the one pregnant with three possible fathers, that bitch needs to get an abortion or something." Her stank ass said.

I raised up out of my seat feeling that now was the time to give this bitch a proper ass whooping. She stood up too. I stepped to her, as Sandra and Naja came between us.

"Bitch, you don't come up in my mutha-fuckin' house disrespecting me like that. I'll scratch that fuckin' weave out your mutha-fuckin' bald head ass!" I yelled.

"Do it then, bitch!" She warned. "Pregnant or not. I'll fuck your ass up."

I lunged toward her, but Sandra held me back. I was sick of this bitch. She comes smiling up in my face, trying to be my friend and shit, when I know she done fucked my ex man, Jakim. Then she had the **"NERVES"** to try and fuck my Uncles in my fuckin' room. And now she gonna sit here in my place and try to criticize me, calling me a slut, when she done fucked` twice as many niggahs than anyone of us sitting in this room. Ooh, I was about to kill the fuckin' bitch, whether I was pregnant or not!

"This bitch thinks she's too pretty to get hurt, I'm sick of her trifling ass." Latish chided.

"Then leave!" Naja spoke, pointing to the door.

She gave me a wicked stare. "Fuck all y'all. No wonder Sasha fucked her ass up, stupid cunt!"

After she left, things settled down a little. Naja and Sandra were both trying to give me advice on what to do about my situation.

Naja said I needed to tell all three of them about me being pregnant, she said to be straight up with them. I didn't know if I could. I already knew that if it was Danny's, he wasn't going to take care of it. He dissed my mother, so why should I be any different. If it was Jakim's, I thought of him being so hurt by me, that he would probably neglect his own child just to get back at me. And Tyrone, he was another headache all together. If he had all these children by different women like I'm hearing, then I wouldn't be nothing special to him, just another one of his baby mothers.

Sandra told me to don't even bother with the headache of carrying this baby, and worrying myself on whose the baby's father. She straight up told me to get an abortion, since I was still early in the pregnancy. She said all three men ain't worth shit, so why carry their baby around for nine months, when you know none of them ain't gonna be around to help you take care of it.

All night we talked. They cheered me up a little. We reminisced over the good times, and also talked about the bad ones. We finished up the Chinese food, and continued to watch the movie. I wasn't even thinking about my pregnancy no more, or stressing over that stupid bitch, Latish.

My home girls put me in a good mood for now.

When Tyrone finally bought his ass home, two days later, me and him had it out. I confronted him about Chinky. He argued with me denying that it wasn't true. I told him that one of my girlfriends saw him with her a few times, and he called her a "Lying bitch!" I was so fed up with his bullshit that I almost went to blows with him. We argued for hours, shit, we were so loud, that our neighbors had to bang on their walls, shouting for us to shut up, or they'll call the cops.

I was so hysterical and out of control, that I told him I would commit suicide by jumping from off the terrace with his baby inside me. That's how he found out that I was pregnant, by threatening to kill myself with his seed in me.

He went mad, cursing, and calling me a "Crazy ass bitch!" For that moment, I actually thought that I was mad and crazy, and felt that I was really going to kill myself. This shit was too much for me to handle.

When I started walking towards the terrace, he yoked me up from behind, throwing me down to the floor, threatening me, saying that if I keep acting up, he would kill me his damn self. He didn't even acknowledge me being pregnant. It was like he didn't care, probably because he had so many damn kids already. Afterwards, he just left, slamming the door so hard that a few pictures fell from off the wall and shattered. I remained on the apartment floor crying my eyes out, thinking about nothing but suicide. Life was hard, I can't take this shit any more, I kept thinking.

When it starts to rain, sometimes a storm is soon to follow. After the blowup with Tyrone, things eased up a little between the two of us and he apologized for his actions, and of course I forgave him. He charmed me with that gift of gab, and worked his sweet way through my panties. He gassed me up, telling me that our baby was going to be special, smart, because it has his genes. He even promised that he would take care of us. When I bought up Chinky, he warned me not to go there. He told me that he didn't want to hear that bitch's name in this house. He said he was going to be home more now, no more staying gone for days at a time. I wanted to believe him. I felt that I had to believe him, for my baby's sake.

So for the next few days, I endured nothing but his sweet-talking, and his wicked lovemaking. He said if the baby's a boy, he wanted to name him Tyrone Junior, which I thought was sweet. Then the thought came up again, what if it ain't his baby. And that put me in a more depressing mood. I felt that I couldn't afford to have this baby be anyone else's.

Just as quick, it seemed like things were turning to shit again. Tyrone disappeared for three days, not a phone call or nothing from him. I was four months pregnant. My mother would come by sometimes, and she would stay the day with me, and the both of us being pregnant together we would sooth each other. She was due the 4th of August, and I was due on August 24th. It was ironic, my mother and me giving birth in the same month and if things could get even more fucked for me, probably by the same guy.

Sandra and Naja were stopping to check up on me on the regular too. Sandra would inform me on what's going on around the way, while I was being cooped up in this apartment. I was getting fat, and felt my beautiful shape disappearing from me everyday. My self-confidence was dropping to a low. Don't no body wanna see or hang out with pregnant Shana, I would say to myself. I gained twenty pounds in the last four months and that was twenty pounds too much for me. I went from being 125, to 145.

On March 20th my day came crashing down on me. I was in the shower when I heard a hard knock at the door, more like someone was banging on it, trying to knock it down. I hurriedly turned off the shower and wrapped myself in a towel, stepping out of the bathroom still dripping wet so I could answer the door.

"I'm coming, wait the fuck up!" I shouted getting annoyed.

"Tyrone Sorbs, this is the DEA, we have a search warrant for your apartment." A guy announced through the door.

"What?" I mumbled, as I quickly unlocked the door, as about eight to ten officers in flight vests, plain clothes, and some in uniforms stormed passed me rushing their way into my apartment.

I stood by the door clutching my towel tightly, soaking wet leaving a small puddle of water on the floor.

"What's going on, do y'all have a warrant?" I angrily asked.

"Yes we do." A tall slender man said, as he showed me proof of his warrant to come and ransack through my entire apartment.

"I'm agent Childs, we believe your boyfriend is concealing controlled substances in this apartment." He informed, while the others went through everything making a mess everywhere.

"Do you have any knowledge of his whereabouts?" He asked.

Getting emotional, I answered, "No. I have no idea where he is. That niggah comes home whenever he feels like it."

I heard them rummaging through my bedroom, bathroom, the kitchen, hearing pots and pans being tossed from the cabinets on to the floor. They were tearing my apartment apart.

"Would you like to have a seat?" Agent Childs suggested.

"I would like for y'all to fuckin' leave so I can get dressed." I scolded.

"That's not happening, your boyfriend's a wanted man." He said.

For the next forty or so minutes, they went through everything, room to room, draw to draw, from floor to floor. They even violated me and went searching through some of my personal belongings, like my panties, bra, lingerie, even my tampons. It was a mess.

I sat on the living room couch, still in my towel, as agents tried to find something, but they came up with nothing. Tyrone wasn't stupid. He's been hustling for years, so he knew the ropes, the tricks and trades of the game.

Frustrated, Agent Childs yelled out, "Find anything?"

"This place is clean." Someone answered.

He turned to me and said, "We would like for you to come down to the station and answer a few questions."

"What? Mutha-fucka, don't you see I'm four months pregnant."

"We're not asking, we're telling you." He responded nonchalantly. "We'll give you ten minutes to get dressed."

I couldn't believe this shit. These mutha-fuckas ain't got shit on us, or should I say Ty's ass, and yet they persisted on taking someone in. I got dressed anyway, throwing on whatever I could put together, seeing that my bedroom was in a complete disarray, clothes tossed out of my closet and dresser drawers, my mattress turned over, the television laying on it's side on the floor, these mutha-fuckas ain't got no respect for people's personal shit.

I put on a pair of blue jeans, a sweater, and a pair of white Nikes, and threw my hair into a ponytail. The agents escorted me out of my apartment. It was embarrassing, everyone stepping out of their apartments to see what was going on.

It was the same way outside, a small crowd had gathered around, as I was led to one of the cars. It looked like a crime scene outside of the building, with flashing red and blue lights from a fleet of squad cars.

Down at the precinct I was questioned and informed about some disturbing details. Come to find out they raided Chinky's apartment two-weeks ago, and they came up with a shit load of drugs. She was taken into custody, but Tyrone wasn't anywhere to be found. They want her to testify against him, but she's willing to take the rap for him. The shit they found in her place, 4 kilos of cocaine, three pounds of marijuana, and $20,000 cash money, would have her looking at a mandatory 15 years. They bought me here hoping that I would squeal him out, and inform them on anything that I knew that they didn't—but I knew nothing.

They had surveillance on Tyrone for months now, but they didn't have any real evidence to put him away for the number of years they wanted to. The charges they had pending against him, the judge could only sentence him to three, maybe five years, and the prosecutors wanted more time than that. With Chinky not cooperating, their case looked more bogus everyday. I asked myself, what the fuck is wrong with that bitch? If I got caught with the amount of shit they busted her with, I would be telling it all. I'm not doing any time for any man, especially 15 years in prison—I don't love a mutha-fucka that much. I know he doesn't love her, shit, if he did, then Chinky wouldn't be in the position she's in now.

After spending hours in the precinct, I just wanted to go home to my mothers and forget that any of this was happening. My life was really turning into shit. As I stood up from my seat, a familiar face entered the room, Detective Rice came to greet me. "How you doing, Shana?" He asked. He had on a leather bomber, and black Jeans.

I sighed. "What the fuck do you want?"

"Look, leave the hostility somewhere else. This is a personal greeting, nothing to do with law enforcement."

I knew he liked me, but I got this thing with cops, I just don't date them or fuck em.

"I gotta go." I said, passing by him.

He grabbed me by my arm. "Shana!"

I turned around, lifting up my sweater exposing my protruding stomach. "I'm fuckin' pregnant, so just fuck off!" I chided.

He let go of my arm, as I stormed out of the room, crying.

I caught a cab outside of the precinct, but couldn't think of where to go. There was no way I was going back to that apartment after what the cops did to that place. I wasn't trying to go to my mother's in the condition that I was in. So I thought real hard of an alternative destination. Who could I see and spend time at a time like this? I thought about it, and I thought about it, then his name came up, Jakim.

It was funny, because after all we done been through, I somehow knew that he would still accept me in his life, that he would still be there for me no matter what. He was always a caring boyfriend and he was the only one that I felt I could really seek comfort in. I took a deep breath, dried my tears, and told the cabbie of Jakim's address.

I felt that deep down in that he still loves me. At least I prayed that he did.

●

SPANKY
17

It's been a week since I quit my job. I stayed up in my room during the time sulking, and feeling sorry for myself. The one girl that I truly loved and had feelings for told me to stay the fuck away from her. And Michael hated me, nearly beat me down because he felt that I fucked up his relationship with Carla. It makes you say and do things that sometimes you may regret in the future. I was envious of everyone.

Me, I was stuck with some pills, hormones, and bitterness. I was paying for it, trying to get some by any means necessary. I can't front, I was living for sex, but how can one be living for sex, when one wasn't getting that much of it to be living for in the first place? It was constantly on my mind twenty four seven, from when I woke up in the mornings, until when I went to bed at night.

I didn't want to tell my parents that I'd quit my job, so I tried to avoid them the best that I could. My mother told me that I had two options after high school, going to college, or getting myself a job. Now that I was unemployed, and wasn't going to college, I wondered what would they say or do to me.

Well one evening they found out that I had quit my job. My former boss called up my stepfather and told him that I haven't been to work in the past few days. My mother came storming into my bedroom, upset, yelling, asking, "Why did you quit your job?" I couldn't answer her, or at least tell her the real reason.

She yelled, "I told you after high school, I want you either in school, or working. Now you pull this shit with me Jamal. Leroy went out his way to get you that job down at that real estate office, and you just throw it all away that easy."

For the next ten minutes, I heard nothing but her mouth, lecturing me, telling me that I had to find another job, ASAP. She kept telling me that I have it too good here, living under her roof, rent-free, not worrying about bills, mortgages, and food. That she didn't understand.

After about fifteen minutes of shouting and reprimanding me, Leroy walked into my bedroom, with this nonchalant look on his face. He went over to my mother, and told her to take a walk outside. He wanted to have a talk with me, man to man.

After she left my room, he slowly closed the door behind her, and then took a seat in a small-woodened chair next to my bed. He peered at me, not that he looked like he was angry with me, but more like he was concerned. He remained silent for a few minutes, like he was gathering his thoughts together. Then he looked up at me, and asked, "It's a woman, right?"

I was stunned. I told no one why I quit, and some how he figured it out. I glanced at him and asked, "What makes you think I quit my job because of a woman?"

"Because, only a woman can make a man make such a foolish choice in his life."

I didn't respond to his comment, just sat there sulking looking like a fool.

"Talk to me, Jamal." He continued, "What's bothering you, I know it's just not about work."

I wanted to open up, but I felt too embarrassed to do so. Everything was bothering me, not just work, and Carla, but my entire life. I was becoming envious of others. I was attending these underground strip clubs on a regular and paying females for some ass. I was constantly watching porno movies and masturbating on a regular. I didn't have game like the majority of my friends, sometimes I would get all tongue tied, and wouldn't know the first things to say to a female if I had the opportunity. And to top it off, I was taking these pills trying to keep my dick hard longer than five minutes. I felt that everything was wrong with me.

"Jamal, I may not be your biological father, but I love you like my own son, and remember that you can come and talk to me about anything. Don't forget that I was once your age, so I can relate to some of the things that you're dealing with."

I felt myself about to breakdown and cry in front of my stepfather. I wanted to tell it all. I started choking up, felt my eyes tearing up. But I felt that it wasn't right to cry in front of another man. I tried to hold my pain in, but my emotions soon got the best of me. I felt a tear trickling down my cheek, and both my eyes started to watered up. No wonder I ain't getting no pussy, because I am pussy, I thought to myself. He sat there and waited for me to pull myself together and dry my tears. He didn't say a word.

"It ain't right." I muttered out.

"What?" He asked.

"My life."

I peered up at the ceiling, crying, choking on tears. It was definitely hurting me inside, and I kept my weakness bottled in for too long.

"I can't do nothing right, Leroy." I continued. "I feel like a pussy, sitting here, crying to you like some woman."

"No, Jamal. It's good for a man to let out his emotions sometimes, instead of keeping them bottled in. Shit women do it, so why can't men." He paused for a bit, then asked, "You're not in some sort of trouble?"

I shook my head no.

"Then talk to me Jamal. Why did you quit your job?"

"I got into a fight." I answered.

He sighed.

"I was jealous of one of my co-workers." I continued. "It was over a woman he was dating, so I said some things to her about him that I shouldn't have said. She got mad at the both of us, and then he got mad at me and tried to fight me.

"I thought I was in love with her, but I was too scared to ask her out on a date. So this guy Michael started dating her, but he betted on her, him and another guy to see who could have sex with her first. So I blew up his spot in front of her, and that's how the fight started."

"It's natural sometimes to be nervous when you're approaching a woman that you like. God knows it happened to me plenty of times. I remember when I first met your mother, she was so beautiful, and she still is until this day. But I went up to her and started a decent conversation with her, then one thing led to another, and now we're here happily married and in love. Jamal, you just have to be yourself when it comes to dealing with women."

"But I'm twenty one, I should be a pro at playing the game right now."

"Playing the game?" He repeated.

"Yeah. I mean, I look at Limp, Tommy, and some of my co-workers, they got their shit down pat. I see them with different women all the time, always bragging, and then I look at me, a guy who never even had a girlfriend before."

"Jamal, let me tell you something about your friends and guys just like them'. The game you say they're playing, that's a dangerous game. Jumping from different women here and there could cause a man a very short life. There are too many diseases and too many jealous lovers out there for a guy to be playing a game. Your friends are going down the wrong direction. I'm not going to tell you to stop hanging around them, you're an adult, and you make your own decision. But I will tell you this, don't try to follow in their footsteps because they're headed for nothing but trouble. You may think that it's fun now, but someday that lifestyle is going to catch up to you and hit you when you least expect it.

"Jamal, you don't need to rush sex, it will happen with the right woman, at the right time. I didn't loose my virginity until I was at least nineteen, twenty. And just like you, all of my friends were out there pimping it, sleeping around with many different women here and there, and thinking that it was hip and fun. And yeah, they made fun of me because I was still a virgin, I didn't hide it but I was proud to be one, it made me unique from the rest of my friends. I was holding on to something that they lost years ago. But in the long run, their promiscuous ways caught up to them. My friend Jimmy is forty-two now with six kids from so many women. He can't live a good life because child-support is kicking his ass. They take so much out of his check every week that he had to go and live back in his mama's house. And another friend of mines, Jack, he's sitting in a wheelchair for the rest of his life, because he decided that it was fun to mess around with a married woman, well her husband didn't find it to be any fun, he put three bullets in his back, paralyzing him from the waist down.

"Jamal, like I always tell you, I love you, and your mother. And I would hate to see anything happen to you, so I'm not telling you any stories. There's more to life than just sex. Think with your brain, instead of your dick. And if you do have sex, please use protection."

I sat there absorbing in every word he said to me. Damn, he was still a virgin until he was twenty, I thought. It musta been hard for him to go that long not knowing what a piece of pussy felt like. I would like to say that his words did me some good, but it didn't, I was still feeling kind of bent out. I mean I have other problems too, like stamina, hormones, etc. I wanted to ask him questions but didn't, I felt too embarrassed to.

He talked to me for about an hour, coaching me about women and life. Telling me how it was like growing up in the sixties and seventies, explaining how times had changed so much.

He was preaching to me about being faithful to one love, telling me shit like a relationship is fifty-fifty between a man and a woman. You share everything you have between each other, sometimes even closet secrets. So I asked him, "Are you faithful to my mother?"

He smiled, and said, "More faithful than a wino is to his liquor. I love your mother very much. If I didn't, then I wouldn't have married her. I believe marriage should only happen once, because I don't believe in divorces. That's what's wrong with this country today, too many people rushing into marriage thinking they're in love, when majority of marriages end in divorce. I dated your mother for two years before I asked her to be my wife. And during those two years I got to know her, and see that she was a really good woman. A woman like your mother, Jamal, you hold on to, because they come once so every often. So, yes I'm going to be faithful to your mother, and my wife, because I love her, and I won't do anything to jeopardize our relationship—because let me tell you something; it takes a stronger man to be faithful to his woman, than a weaker man who's faithful to his dick."

Damn, that was deep. He got up out of his seat, then spotted my pills on the bed. "Anything else you need to tell me."

Embarrassed, I tried to hide them. He smiled, shook his head, and walked out of my room. I lay back down on my bed, thinking about some of the words he told me. Leroy's a good guy, I saw what my mother saw in him. He's a good father and a husband. I think she struck gold when she met him.

The next morning I promised my mother and my stepfather that I would go and try to get my old job back. Leroy talked to Mr. Price, and he said that he was willing to accept me back to work. But how could I look Carla in her face knowing that she hated me. And seeing Michael, wondering was he still upset with me. But I had to set aside my pride, and do what I had to do.

Around eleven that morning, I went strolling back into work, nervous. It's been a week since I quit. I walked through the office and all eyes were on me. I tried not to, but my eyes were searching around for Carla and Michael. I wanted to apologize to the both of them. I was hoping that they could forgive me.

I ran into Mr. Price. He was standing there gawking at me as I came walking towards him.

"Good to see you back." He said.

I stepped into his office, and he had a little talk with me for about a half-hour. He warned me that if I ever quit again, that there was no coming back. I had a second chance with him. I listened to his bullshit, then he told my ass to get back to work and get him a cup of coffee.

As I stepped out of his office, I bumped into Carla. She was carrying a bunch of folders in her arms. I gazed at her, as my heart beat rapidly. I was speechless. Was she still mad at me? I thought. We both were quiet, just looking at each other.

"Hi." I uttered out. It was the only thing I could think of saying right now. I didn't know if she was going to react violently or forgive me.

"Listen, I'm sorry about the other night." She softly apologized.

"No, Carla, I'm sorry. It wasn't my business to interfere between you and Michael. I was just jealous because I really like you. I couldn't even ask you out. I was scared to." I finally admitted to her.

She let out a peaceful smile. Does this mean everything's forgiven? "I don't bite." She playfully said.

I guess that meant that everything was forgiven. I couldn't take her being still pissed off at me.

"Do I intimidate you that much?" She asked.

"No, it's just that I'm not good with women period. I sometimes get tongue-tied. I'm not what you would call a ladies man."

"But you're a sweetheart, Jamal. One day a lady out there is going to be very lucky to have you in her life."

"I hope so, that day is taking forever."

She giggled, and then asked, "So, are you back to work?"

"Yeah, Mr. Price gave me another chance."

"That's good. I'm glad to see you back."

And once again, there was silence between us. I wanted to ask her about Michael, curious to find out if she forgave him too? But I said to myself that it wasn't any of your business.

"You're wondering about Michael?" She guessed.

"Nah, see…"

"It's okay, Jamal. I guess I should be the one to tell you the news."

"News, what news?"

"We're getting married." She announced.

"Married!" I repeated, stunned by her news.

"Yes, we're getting married."

I guess she really forgave him, in a way that was good to hear. But I couldn't help to feel a bit of jealousy in me. I always pictured her as my bride to be, since I first saw her. Now she was getting married to Michael, one of the biggest playboys in the office. I guess what they say is true, *"good guys always finish last."*

"What brought this on?" I just had to ask.

"That night I was upset with the both of y'all, he came banging on my door two-o clock in the morning, apologizing, crying, telling me that he was sorry. I didn't answer the door at first, I was still furious with him. But he stayed out there and just kept banging and banging on my door, asking for me to let him in, he wanted to talk to me. So I gave up and let him in, he apologized, said that I was the best thing to ever happened to him, and we talked all night until sunrise. Then that morning, he proposed to me.

"I knew he meant every word he said, you just get that feeling inside of you. I knew he was truly sorry. I mean for him to come crying, banging down my door at two in the morning, there had to be something special about that. He said he was going to propose after work, during dinner, but you know, that little incident happened. He deserves a second chance, Jamal, don't you think?"

Damn, Michael getting married, how ironic was that? I thought to myself. This was the same man who two months ago was bragging about how marriage was for suckers, talking about how his dick might get bored fucking the same pussy every night. Now this playboy was getting married to a woman he knew less than two months. I guess love and life is funny like that.

"You got a good man there, Carla. Y'all are gonna make a lovely couple." I told her. In some twisted way, I was happy for them, hoping that it works out for the best.

"Thank you." She said, giving me a hug and kiss on my cheek.

"Day, you been back five minutes, and you're already fucking up, where's my cup of coffee?" Mr. Price hollered out of his office door, interrupting my intimate moment with Carla.

In a fucked up a way, it felt good to be back.

Retrieving my boss's cup of coffee, I ran into Michael.

"Congratulations, I heard the good news." I meekly said, trying to break what looked like some tension between us.

"Yo, dog, it ain't nuthin', you're still cool with me. I guess we both fucked up. It was my mistake, and I took it out on you." He came up to me and gave me dap.

I let out a sigh of relief. Our little friendship has been mended. I couldn't feel any better. He asked for me to be one of his groomsmen at the wedding. I agreed.

Sometimes things don't work out how you expect them to. I guess Carla and I weren't meant to be, and I finally accepted that, life would go on, maybe for the better or for the worst.

My mother would always say to me, if you don't learn from your mistakes, then learn from others. Be observant of those around you and watch their actions and their downfalls in life.

A few days later, I received a fucked up call from Clarke, who informed me that Mark had got locked up last night. I jumped out the bed, stunned by the news. I asked him over a dozen questions, but he couldn't answer any, he was clueless to why.

I got out of bed, showered and dressed, then dashed out the door. I must have banged on his door over fifty times in one minute. He let me in, and I was greeted by Limp and Abney who were already sitting in his basement.

"What happened?" I asked, out of breath.

Limp shook his head, "That niggah went crazy, Spanky. He fucked up some bitch that was standing in front of his crib waiting for him." He explained.

"What?"

"Yeah, dog, neighbors called the cops, and they arrested him with the quickness."

"Ah, man, what the fuck was this niggah thinking?" I screamed out.

We all piled in my hooptie and trooped in down to the precinct to see Mark, but he was already escorted down to Central Booking on Queens Blvd. His hearing was coming up sometime this afternoon. Ah, man, it had to be serious for him to be locked up in Central Booking, I thought to myself. So all four of us, Limp, Abney, Clark and I made it down to Central Booking in search for Mark's case. It was hell trying to find him, until we ran into his mother. She was cursing, and running a muck, angry with her son, and with the cops the same time. She even screamed on us, she was so frustrated.

It was around four, when Mark's case was finally called. We had to be waiting for over three hours. We all sat together on one hard brown wooden bench, in a crowded courtroom.

Mark stepped out into the courtroom escorted by court officers, he glanced over at us, I waved my hand in the air for him to notice that we were here for him, but he didn't acknowledge us, not even giving us a smile.

He stood in front of a judge, a silver haired man, who looked meaner than a junkyard dog. He asked Mark how did he plead, and he answered guilty. I was dumbfounded. His mother sat next to us looking unemotional. She just stared straight ahead at her son being incarcerated.

The judge posted bail at $10, 000.

"What? Ten thousand is he fuckin' crazy!" Limp shouted, interrupting everything.

The court officer had asked Limp to please leave the room, shit we all asked him to leave. I wasn't trying to be jailed next to Mark over Limp's foolishness. I glanced at his Mother, and she remained seated, being unaffected by his high bail.

After Mark was escorted back to lock up, we lifted out of our seats, and headed to the hallways. The court attorney that was represented Mark wasn't worth shit. How he gonna have him plead guilty and allow the judge to post such a high bail?

"Let that mutha-fucka get what he deserves." Mark's mother shouted. "He wanna be sexing and beating up fifteen year old pregnant girls…I hope they throw the book at his ass!" She stormed off, not giving a fuck about her son.

We were going to be here for him, at least I thought.

Come to find out that Mark pleaded guilty to assault on a minor, who he beat up so bad, that she's in the hospital slipping in and out of consciousness, suffering from bruises to her head, a fracture pelvis and a broken arm not to include her still being pregnant with her unborn child who doctors think that it won't survive. Now he may be looking at murder charges if the baby dies.

I asked myself, what the fuck was he thinking? Is this mutha-fucka crazy or what? I knew she was stressing him about her pregnancy, but there are other ways to resolve his problem, don't beat the shit out of her.

Now I see why his mother was so ticked off.

We realized that there wasn't much we could do for Mark, but pray that his situation comes out for the best. A weak after his hearing, the fellows were just going on with their lives, forgetting, or probably not even caring that Mark was incarcerated. I heard that he was looking at some serious time, like ten years max!

Mark was being held over at Riker's island until his sentencing date, which was scheduled for sometime in May. I felt sorry for him, but what more can I do, he bought that shit down on himself. My mother kept asking how was he holding up, but I couldn't answer her, because I haven't heard from him in weeks. He called me collect once, and asked for me to come visit him. I promised him I would, but haven't been up to see him yet. And I wasn't the only one; Limp, Tommy, and the rest of the fellows didn't take the initiative to check him either.

I couldn't stress Mark's situation too much, because I had to live my life. And I have my own worries. Come to find out, my mother arranged for me to take Adina to her church's *Cotillion*, without asking me first. I thought she had to be fuckin' crazy. She went on babbling about how Adina was a sweet and nice girl. That she didn't have anyone to take her so she volunteered my assistances. I argued with her, telling her that I wasn't going, but she nagged and nagged until finally I gave in. She definitely owes me one.

My mother went on and said, "Jamal, you never know, one day she might surprise you."

"Yeah, that'll be the day when Halle berry comes knocking on my door." I responded.

I just knew I was going to regret this day for the rest of my life.

It was Saturday evening around six, I was dressed sharp in a black & white tuxedo, with a bow tie. I had a fresh haircut, with the thin trimmed side burns, and was sporting a pair of shinny black loafers. Even though I was taking a beast out, there wasn't any need for me to be looking busted. I mean there were going to be females there, so you never know who you might meet. I just hoped that Adina didn't cramp my style too much, scaring the ladies away.

My mother had her camera out taking pictures of me like it was prom night. "You look so handsome." She proclaimed, smiling taking snap shots of me.

I posed for a few of her shots, masquerading around the living room acting like I was posing for the cover of G.Q. Interrupting my little star struck moment was the doorbell.

"That must be Adina." My mother said, rushing to go answer the door. I darted upstairs. I wasn't ready for this. Why did I agree to such a horrendous thing? I stayed up in my room for about ten minutes, thinking about calling the whole thing off.

"Jamal, hurry down, Adina is waiting." My mother called out.

I didn't answer her. Maybe they'll both get the hint.

"Jamal." My mother called out again, this time I could hear her coming up the steps, knowing that she was heading towards my room.

"Jamal." She said, opening my bedroom door to find me lying face down on my bed still in my tux's. "You have a beautiful young lady waiting downstairs for you, now go give her the time of her life."

"Are you kidding?"

"Jamal, a promise is a promise. Now you get your ass off that bed, and go downstairs to your lovely date."

I let out an agonizing sigh, as I slowly got off the bed, and walked out of my room slower than a slug. My mother followed right behind. I took it one step at a time, as I made my way down to the living room, where I knew Adina was waiting. I really didn't want to go through with this.

Wow, Damn! My eyes or my mind had to be playing tricks on me, because standing in my living room was not the same Adina. Nah, this girl standing here in front of me was looking good.

"Adina?" I inquired.

She nodded her head, smiling. I was left utterly speechless. My mother stood behind me cheesing. She had on this long black and sexy halter tuxedo dress, showing that she had womanly curves. Her hair was done in a French roll, with little strands of hair falling exquisitely down to the side of her face. And she actually had on make-up, not a lot, but just the right amount. She had on a pair of lovely leather ankle wrap sandals, as she stood there looking like she can be on the cover of Vibe.

"What happen?" I asked.

She chuckled.

"She looks good, don't she, Jamal." My mother said, stepping in between us. "C'mon, the both of y'all come closer together so I can take a picture of the two of you."

I stepped up to her, placing my arm gently around her shoulder, pulling her closer to me. She actually looks like a woman, a very attractive woman. My mother snapped three shots of us together. Afterwards, I pulled myself away from her and peered at her one more time.

"When did the fairy God mother paid you a visit?" I asked, gazing at her from head to toe.

She chuckled again. She was still that shy Adina.

"Me and Adina here went on a little shopping spree." My mother said. "We went and got a complete make-over, bought new outfits, even visited the spa pampering ourselves."

"Well, you look absolutely gorgeous." I told her, taking her by the hand.

"You two have fun now." My mother said, as we walked to the door. She even gave me the keys to her 99 Nissan, which was something that she rarely did.

I was a complete gentleman. I even opened all doors for her. We made a grand entrance at her church's *Cotillion*. She had the fellows turning heads, checking her out. I was so glad to be her date. It felt like I was in the twilight zone, or a dream, waiting to wake up and catch the real Adina waiting for me downstairs in my living room. But this was no dream, I'd pinched myself three or four times tonight to make sure of that.

I, or should I say, we had a wonderful time. After the *Cotillion* was over, we went and got something to eat at an all night Diner. We talked, laughed, and reminisced over the old times. I kept complimenting her on how beautiful she turned out to be. She would smile, giggled, and say thank you.

I also apologized for my behavior towards her during these past years. I was just following the crowd, by being a Judas, and started dissin' and joking on her all the time. But now the joke's on me, because tonight, her true beauty emerged, not just from the outside, but also from her inside.

She accepted my apology.

SHANA
18

I arrived at Jakim's house and contemplated if I should ring his doorbell. My heart was vigorously pounding against my chest. I took a deep breath, and then exhaled. I felt my emotions escalating as I wondered if he had company. I was starting to have visions of Jakim loving somebody else. I mean he had the right to. I can't blame him if he curses me out, and slams the door in my face, shutting me completely out of his life.

It would hurt a lot, but right now, I just wanted him to hold me and comfort me. I wanted him to accept me back into his life.

I was trying to be strong, trying not to break down in front of him. I wanted to apologize, tell him that I still love him, and say that he was right about all of the things he said about Tyrone.

I took another deep breath, calming my nerves, and then slowly walked up to his door. I rang the bell, and waited. I heard the door being unlocked. It seem like everything was going in slow motion, feeling like my life was at a standstill. I diverted my eyes down. I started to slowly open them up and saw Jakim standing in the middle of his doorway. Neither he nor I said a word .

Then suddenly all of the pain and agony I'd suffered throughout the past weeks started to build up in me. My eyes started to dampen. I felt cold, and started to tremble. I wanted to scream, but felt this lump stuck in my throat. A tear escaped from my eye and trickled down the side of my face.

"Jakim, hold me, please." I begged..

I wanted him to drape his arms around me. I realized that my love was here, still with him. I'd tapered off from him for a minute, far too long, doing the wrong things with the wrong guys. Now I was pregnant, scared, and hurt.

By now, I was in tears, crying so hard that I wanted to pass out. "I'm so sorry, Jakim. I'm sorry." I kept apologizing and apologizing.

He came up to me and started to comfort me. He embraced me into his arms, nestling my head against his chest.

"It's okay, Shana, everything's going to be cool."

He held me in his arms, I felt his forgiveness, and his love. We stood there nestled together. We strayed away from each other for far too long, and now that I was here, I was planning to be here for a while. This was true love, forgiveness and being there.

Two months later.

Jakim and I were back together officially. I was six months pregnant, and was starting to look like a fuckin' mountain. I gained twenty-five pounds, my face was fat, and my ankles and feet were so swollen that I couldn't fit into none of my old shoes. I had three sonograms taken, and the doctor assured me that I was having a boy. I was bringing into this world a little boy.

Not knowing who my baby's father was, was still haunting me. Jakim knew that Tyrone could possibly be the father. I didn't tell him about Danny. I didn't have the courage. He said that he would still be there for me no matter whose child it turns out to be.

I was praying every night that this baby was his. Jakim says that it doesn't matter, but I know that deep down inside of him, it does. I mean it wouldn't look right for him to be raising Tyrone's child, when they were now enemies. They can't even walk down the same block without an argument, or some kind of fight escalating between the two.

Tyrone's was in between cases; he was out on $10,000 bail and living life like he wasn't seeing serious time. Chinky was still being held in Riker's, with a $25,000 bail lingering over her head. Tyrone wasn't even man enough to go and try to bail her out, and it was sickening me to see that I actually thought that I was in love with this man. I now saw that he does nothing but uses and abuses the women in his life. And when the thought came up that I might be pregnant with his baby, I would cry so hard that I would start to get headaches.

I felt like I was about to have a serious breakdown. Jakim was trying to keep my head up, trying to keep me positive. I tried and tried, but until I find out who the father of my child is, I would never be at ease. If it wasn't for Jakim sticking with me from day to day, I felt that I wouldn't have survived this far. He was truly being there for me, mentally and physically. We were even attending Lamaze classes together.

But you know in my life, in my neighborhood, in this time and age, when something positive and good finally starts to happen in your life, or with your life, there is always some fool out there crashing your walls down on you, or at least trying to.

It was the first week in June, and temperatures hit a high of 98 degrees. I had two burdens hammering on my back, one it was the summer, and very hot, and the second, I was seven months pregnant.

I'd moved back in with my mother, and we were pregnant, moody, gassy, and fat living under the same roof. My Aunt Tina finally moved out a few weeks ago. She shacked up with some old boyfriend of hers who was out of prison and hustling again.

I was shackled up in this house for the past two-weeks, and couldn't wait for my night out with Jakim tonight. He'd promised to take me out to a movie and dinner at this new restaurant in Valley Stream called *Goodbyes.* He was still at work, working for FedEx, which he started a month ago.

I was in my room with the stereo blasting WBLS, soothing my belly, and trying to keep my thoughts positive and my head up high. It took me a minute to realize that my phone was ringing. I quickly rushed over to answer it, thinking that it was Jakim calling.

"Hello." I answered.

"What's up, Shana." He spoke. I'd recognize his voice instantly.

"What do you want, Tyrone?" I unkindly asked him.

"What, you don't call no more. You out there carrying my child, and don't even check me."

I was silent; the thought of him mentioning that this was his seed was starting to stir up emotions in me.

"I'm hearing stories that you're back together with Jakim. What you think that you just gonna easily leave me for him...Bitch, you owe me." He said.

"Owe you...fuck you, after the shit you done put me through...fuck you!"

"Oh, so it's like that? After I done looked out for you, had you staying up in my crib, and bought you tons of shit, you think you just gonna play me like that."

"You looked out for me." I angrily repeated. "I'm sorry that I ever got with your trifling ass. You were nothing but trouble from the day I met you."

"Bitch, you sorry. You ain't nuthin' but a hoe! I'm gonna see that ass soon, you and that punk niggah, Jakim."

I got scared, knowing of the things he was capable of doing. I shouted over the line, "Tyrone, why don't you just let us be."

"Nah, that's my seed you're carrying. I told you that we were forever. What, you thought I was gonna get locked up cause cops raided my crib? Bitch, I'm gonna check you soon, you best to believe that." He hollered, and hung up.

I held the phone receiver to my ear, feeling that I was about to break down into tears. I was frightened. I didn't know what to do. I slammed the receiver down, then dropped to my knees.

What was I to do?

Later that evening Jakim proposed to me for the second time. I felt like I was the luckiest woman on earth. He didn't take my earlier rejection to heart. He felt that everyone deserves a second chance. Then he hit me with the most wonderful news, he said, "Let's leave here."

I thought he meant leave here as in just leaving Queens, but he wanted to leave this city for good. His cousin had a two-bedroom apartment in South Carolina that we could rent out for dirt-cheap. He also had employment lined for him paying up to $15 an hour. He wanted to move me and the baby down South. I was all for it. I told him that we should go for it; it was definitely a good idea.

Sometimes I wonder why certain things happen to certain people. Like why some people are blessed with good looks and charm, and some are just cursed with disfiguration and ugliness? Why some folks are born wealthy, and some are born so poor, living in the most dilapidated places, growing up in neighborhoods where some folks inquire how can they call this their home? Why do some women find Mr. Right, and some women are cursed with being abused and mistreated their entire lives. Why some men are blessed with bigger dickes and some of the unfortunate ones can't keep it up any longer than five minutes? Why are some children growing up in this world today without a mother or father to shield them from so much harshness, hate, and bitterness.

My million-dollar question is why can't something good for once happen to me without pain and suffering to follow?

It was Thursday night, Naja called me that night, as I was rested in my bed. By the somber in her voice, I knew that I wasn't ready for what she was about to tell me.

"Shana...Jakim's been shot."

I swear my heart stopped, as I stood there, with the phone clutched tightly to my ear. I started breathing hard, and then it felt like I was gasping for air. No, this isn't anything but a bad dream, I tried to say to myself. "THIS IS NOT HAPPEEENIIIING!" I screamed from the top of my lungs, and that's all I remember from that night. I had passed out and went into early labor.

SPANKY
19

I glanced at my watch for the fifth time, as I waited in the visitor's room in Riker's island. I was here alone, observing those around me. It had to be nothing but baby mothers, and girlfriends coming up here to visit their incarcerated boyfriends or baby fathers. I was nervous. I haven't seen Mark since the day of his hearing.

It was sad that I was here visiting him alone. When I asked, everyone soon became too busy. I decided to troop it up here solo.

After about fifteen minutes of waiting, I saw Mark coming out of a doorway walking in a single line with about six other inmates. They were all wearing gray jumpsuits, with **D.O.C** imprinted in the back in bold black letters. It was scary seeing him in jail. He looked different. Mark used to stay with a fresh cut, now he looked bugged out, with his hair looking rugged and uncut.

I saw him, but he didn't notice me yet. I wanted to wave, but that would have been foolish, in that kind of environment. I didn't want to look like a damn faggot. He glanced around the room searching for me, so I stood up. He saw me and started to come my way.

"What up, Spanky." He gave me dap.

"What up Mark."

I took a seat across from him, where a long gray wooden table separated us. The room was crowded with inmates and guests, as chatter and crying children echoed throughout the room, fathers hugging children, mothers missing husbands, and inmates showing emotions.

We both were silent for a few seconds. I didn't want to come off and say the wrong thing to him. So I blurted out the first thing that popped in my head. "How are they treating you up in here?" I asked.

"Shit is crazy, Spanky, you know I'm not used to no shit like this. I need to get up out of here."

I hoped he hasn't become anyone's bitch yet. Mark's not a big dude, 5'6, 135 pounds. He doesn't have that roughneck attitude. He wasn't born on the streets. But the way he beat that bitch down, it made me think twice as to what he was capable of.

"So what's going on with the fellows?" He asked.

"That's something I couldn't tell you, I haven't been hanging around them that much lately."

"Word?"

"Yeah. I found someone better to occupy my time." I explained.

"Spanky, you got a girlfriend now?"

"Nah, she's not really my girl yet, but we're just chilling...she's mad cool!"

"Who?"

I smiled, averting my eyes from him, then said, "You'll never guess in a million years."

"C'mon dog, who?"

"Adina." I revealed.

He jerked his head back, looking all surprised and shit. "Niggah stop playing...that ugly bitch."

"Nah, Mark, not any more. She's changed, dog. I'm telling you for the better."

"Damn, Spanky, I knew you were desperate, but damn, hooking up with Adina."

I pulled out a recent picture of her from my back pocket. It was the one my mother took of us the night of her *Cotillion.* I passed it over to him, and he took a good look at her picture jerking his head back being in shock.

"Damn, nah, this gotta be her twin sister or sumthin'."

"Nah, dog, it's her."

"Shit, talking about having a drastic make-over. You do your thing then, Spanky. Fuck them other niggahs, you do you. I've been in here four months now, and you're the first person to come visit me...fucked up isn't it...even my moms and my sister haven't paid me not one visit."

"They're probably just too busy." I tried to lie.

"You ain't gotta cover for anybody, Spanky, you're definitely a true friend. That's why I'm not hating on you and Adina, she's looking good now, so you do you." He paused for a few minutes glancing around the room at other inmates.

"Yo, I wasn't ready to be a father." He continued. "That bitch just wouldn't stop; she just kept on stressing her situation, harassing me, and harassing me, and when I came home and saw her standing in front of my crib, shit...I just flipped out. I don't even know what came over me."

"Well, I heard that the baby's okay." I said.

"Yeah, but I'm still gonna see some time up in this bitch. I nearly beat the bitch into a coma. Damn, the shit bitches can get a niggah in. I'm seeing at least five maybe six years up in this mutha, Spanky."

"You'll hold out, you might not even see that much time. They might be lenient."

"You really think so, hunh. Don't gas me, Spanky...I'm in here for a minute."

"Don't worry dog, I'll stay in touch." I tried to comfort.

"You're a good guy, Spanky...let me tell you something useful, don't ever let pussy run your life, because if you do, then you're going to start finding yourself in some really fucked up situations. If you and Adina get tight like that, stay with her dog...because this shit ain't worth it. I ain't gonna front, I'm fuckin' scared. My first night in this joint had me petrified. I nearly broke down into tears. They say that you get used to it, I just can't see that happening...ever! I'm hurting, Spanky, shit, I'm really hurting."

I saw the emotion on his face as he spoke. He looked like he was trying to stop himself from tearing up. He had both elbows resting against the table, as he averted his eyes away from me.

"Spanky, live your life, that's all I got to say. Fuck Limp, Tommy, and the rest of those fools. Them niggahs ain't here for me, and they never were."

He looked like he needed a hug.

"I wasn't ready to be a father." He repeated, it was more like he was talking to himself, than he was to me.

He stared down at the table, his hands clasped together. He glanced right then left, then stared up at me. I remained silent. I felt sorry for him. He's not supposed to be here. But because of one stupid mistake, he was paying for it. I knew that if he could rewind time, he would have done it in an instant. I couldn't do much for him, maybe write and come visit him sometimes. He's my friend, and the one thing that I will not do, is walk out on a friend.

It was time for me to go. I slowly rose up out of my seat. Mark did the same. It was sad, watching him head back into incarceration, instead of walking out back into the streets with me where he belongs. I gave him a quick hug, and told him to stay strong. I knew he could get through this.

"Spanky, keep your head up." He said, smiling, then being escorted back into lock up.

I watched him leave. It was like watching a fallen angel. Mark was the last person I'd ever suspected to be behind bars, now Limp or Tommy, that's a different story.

For some strange reason, seeing Mark in jail made me want to change my life, not that I was living in corruption. But I saw that there was more to life than just sex, and trying to get some sex. I had to change my frame of thought. I thought that being a pimp, a playa, or a ladies man was the way to live. Like I said before, my mother always told me, learn from your mistakes, and if not yours, then learn from the ones around you. And I saw that a lot of men were changing their way of life, like Michael who decided to get married, and my next co-worker, Gregg, who claimed he had sex with over a hundred women, and now he's settling down. Shit had me thinking, I've been lucky, and maybe I've been lucky for a reason. There were too many flaws in living a fast life with fast women. My stepfather warned me of the consequences, and I was now starting to see the picture.

It was all about sex, stamina, and pleasing the ladies. Why put so much effort into pleasing so many ladies, when you can take that same energy and just please the right one. My stepfather said, "That's what being a man is all about, showing strength, love, and respect to your woman, by not falling into these pits that most men fall victim too."

I was learning.

My mother said, that her body was her temple, and who she gives herself to is the most important thing to her. She respected herself so much, that after she left my abusive biological father, she became a born again virgin. She made a vow not to ever go through that again. She told me that first, a man had to win over her heart, and once that happens, when there is trust, love, and respect, then a man was able to enter her temple. It so happened, that my stepfather came along. He had the right keys to enter her temple and he was the best thing that ever happened to my mother and me. Seeing their happiness, and respect for each other, I knew life wasn't just about sex.

I called Adina the next morning.

I was planning to start up a new and better chapter in my life.

EPILOGUE

I gave birth to a premature four pound, two ounce baby boy. I named him Jakim Jr. He's my world. The doctor assured me that he was going to be fine, though.

My mother paid me recent visits, along with my Aunt and some of my friends, like Naja, and Sandra. They brought me flowers, balloons, and cards. But nothing could cheer me up after Jakim's death.

He was gunned down.

was taking his death real hard. I tried to imagine him being by my side when I was giving birth, but it made it much more harder for me to get through the delivery. After I pushed my son out, I'd cried for hours and hours. The nurses tried to cheer me up, they bought me gifts, made me visit my son from time to time, and they broke hospital rules by sometimes letting visitors in after hours.

Seeing Jakim Jr. sometimes faded the pain of Jakim's death. I would hold his tiny little frail body into my arms, and comfort him, and talk to him. I'd convinced myself it was Jakim's. I tried to look for similarities in his features, but he was really too young to tell.

They arrested two guys in connection to Jakim's murder. Naja somberly explained to me the details on what happened the night he was killed.

She said that they were at a club having a good time, and Jakim was buying them drinks from the bar. She then said Tyrone walked in with his entourage of thugs, and a confrontation took place, they all tried to jump on Jakim. But the fight was quickly broken up, and Tyrone and his crew were all thrown out.

Jakim was really upset, and Naja suggested that they leave. So they left the club. Tyrone and his crew didn't leave the premises, they waited for him to come out of the club, and when he did, three guys instigated the beef again, then a scuffle broke out. Naja said she tried to help him, but they beat on her too. Then she heard shots fired, and saw Jakim sprawled out on the concrete.

"I'm sorry, Shana." She apologized, crying uncontrollably when she told me what happened. "I'm sorry... he's gone, he's gone."

When I heard he was dead, I wanted to die to. I contemplated suicide. But luckily for my son, I had the strength to move on.

The thing that made me furious was when I heard that Tyrone wasn't being charge for his murder. The D.A didn't have a stable case against him to charge him with homicide. How could they not? He had motive. Tyrone was manipulative and conniving, he had the gift of gab. He was smart, and smooth. He got others to do his dirty work for him. It was hard to believe that I was once head over heels in love with this man, ready to spend eternity with, now I hated him with a passion. I was so hateful, that I wanted to buy a gun and blow his mutha-fuckin' brains out. I really wanted to, so much for Jakim. He had him killed, and now he was getting away with it.

I managed to build up enough strength to attend Jakim's funeral. Doctors warned me that I shouldn't, but I had to. Naja picked me up from the hospital, and I got dressed over at her house.

"Are you sure that you're up to this?" She asked.

I nodded. I had to be. I had to pay my respects to him.

The funeral was packed; even his mother flew in from California. She was overcome with grief. As soon as I stepped into the building, I too was overcome with grief and sorrow. Naja took notice, and asked if I wanted to go through with this.

I nodded, and we proceeded to the viewing.

She clutched my hand tightly, as we slowly stepped towards his cedar coffin. I had my eyes closed. I started to tremble the closer I came to his lifeless body.

First Terry, and now Jakim, how many boyfriends, and ex's can I lose in my life? I thought. Terry's murder was still unsolved. My suspicion jumped back to Tyrone. He gave me his word, that he didn't do it. But he also gave me his word that he wouldn't do anything to Jakim, obviously his word didn't mean shit!

I stood over his coffin, and slowly open my eyes, and doing so, I saw him, his shell anyway, lying there so peaceful. He had on a gray three-piece suit, his arms were gently folded across each other, and his eyes shut.

As I peered down at him, I suddenly felt this urge of guilt. It was because of me that he was dead. I was the one who messed with his used to be best friend, knowing the type of man he was. I let my sexual feelings get the best of me, and because of it, my true love was killed.

I started to tremble even harder and I felt my knees buckle. I threw all of my support against Naja, who held me up.

"Jakiiiimmm!" I screamed out.

He didn't deserve this.

Naja tried to comfort and hold me, but I was out of control. I felt a few more arms drape around me, pick me up and carry me down the isle.

Then from the corner of my eye, I saw her. She was slowly coming my way. She was dressed in a black blouse and skirt. She'd cut her hair short and her eyes fixated on me the whole time.

"How you holding up, Shana?" Sasha asked, looking concern.

I didn't answer her, just stared at her. She passed me a card and some flowers. I slowly took them from her hands. Why was she here? I thought. It's been months since we'd last seen each other, I haven't seen or heard nothing about her. It was like she just disappeared.

"Shana...look, I'm sorry, you have my condolences. Jakim was a good man. And I'm sorry about us, the way I've been acting. We were foolish, and I just want to put it behind us." She said, not once averting her eyes from me.

Jakim forgave me, took me into his arms after all we done been through. He was ready to have us start up a new life together. He even was willing to raise a child that may not have even been his. Jakim forgave me, so it was up to me to forgive her.

"I'm sorry, Sasha." I also apologized, giving her a hug. It was a long deep hug. Naja even joined in.

I looked around me and said to myself, "I'm ready to start up a new chapter in my life, a better one."

I knew Jakim would have wanted that, after all I had our son to raise and take care of.

The End